CRYPTID

IAN FAULKNER

SEVERED PRESS
HOBART TASMANIA

CRYPTID

ISBN: 978-1-922323-79-8

'He who fights with monsters might take care lest he thereby becomes a monster.
And if you gaze for long into an abyss, the abyss gazes into you.'

Friedrich Nietzsche (1844 - 1900)

CHAPTER ONE

53° 19.44' North Latitude 131° 57.31' West Longitude
Graham Island, British Columbia

July 1996

McKinney wasn't sure how long the two of them had been fighting their way through the island's dense forest wilderness – but it seemed like an eternity. A sharp salty burn around his face told him that there must surely be several deep scratches across the delicate skin of his cheeks and forehead; wounds and contusions caused by the thickly entwined branches they had been forced to fight their way through as they had fled in abject terror.

The man was close to exhaustion. He weaved unsteadily forward, forcing himself onwards, desperately grasping any protruding branch or foliage that was available to aid him - dragging himself up yet another interminable rise on the undulating forest floor - spurred on by a glimpsed promise of a small, rare area of clearing in the trees – a space he had spotted scant minutes earlier when they were higher up a previous slope. He reached it, finally staggered to a stop and held up trembling hands before him - he wanted to know what condition they were in. What McKinney saw made for a grim picture; they were lacerated, raw; fingers and palms had been flayed and were bleeding – the wounds on his hands mute evidence of the herculean effort to tear a path through dense copses and tangled undergrowth on a rough roller coaster terrain. Yet, strangely, despite their appearance, they barely hurt him at all.

His lungs, however, were quite another matter. A pair of shredded, fluttering balloons barely contained within the fiery cavern that was his chest. The clean, fresh smelling shirt he had put on seemingly a lifetime ago, now adhered stickily to his flesh – a stained mangy hide that he had begun to shed – comprised of filthy, ripped wet cotton infused with the pungent stink of acrid sweat and fear.

McKinney desperately needed to rest even if it was for just a few moments. He dazedly looked around at his surroundings, trying to control his ragged breathing and triphammer heart – wait! They were finally in luck! McKinney noted the tree line that bordered the small clearing in front of him. It looked manmade – a firebreak maybe? It didn't matter – all that did matter was it revealed what looked to be a clear path leading down from the tangle. They had miraculously, or so it seemed to him at this moment - stumbled upon - or had been guided to - what must be a well-defined loggers' trail.

His body was trembling with sheer fatigue and adrenal overload, especially the muscles in his calves and thighs. Putting out a hand, he supported himself against the nearest cedar. The bark felt rough to the touch, unyielding; yet somehow it comforted him with its ageless, solid strength. His trembling form oozed copious amounts of sweat from every pore he had, giving any exposed area of the skin an oily, unpleasant sheen. The clouds of midges and other buzzing insects - tiny, hateful denizens of the forest, closed in on him instantly now he was no longer moving, sensing a tasty salt feast.

McKinney was too fatigued to even attempt to bat the miniature whining harpies away. He just let them be. They happily fed off him.

The young girl, Bobbie, who had been several yards behind him in the tree-festooned, nightmarish tangle finally caught up to him. Noisily she staggered up to join him, coming to a swaying stop beside McKinney, and tremulously leaned her tall willowy form against his sodden back; the sounds of her breath were tortured gasps.

He was so exhausted that even this simple act of elicited comfort from the girl was almost enough to push him down to the forest floor. With grunting effort, he straightened, forcing himself away from the cedar tree's welcome respite - in doing so he unceremoniously shoved his female companion back and away from him. With some slight vestige of chivalry, McKinney did manage to turn around in time to support Bobbie's sagging form so she didn't end up falling onto the moist mulch. Going down now would have meant certain death for the young woman. In his present condition, McKinney wouldn't have been physically able to lift the girl onto her feet. Their pursuers, he reasoned, couldn't be far behind. He glanced back and up into the forbidding timberland in the direction they came from. They had to keep moving, McKinney instinctively understood. It was their only real hope of survival.

There had been a total of fourteen people on the university field trip – thirteen men and one woman who had tried to make a stand against the horrors that had relentlessly pursued them. The others were gone now – their efforts to fight back a futility – they had been horribly killed. McKinney and the girl had only survived the massacre because he had grabbed Bobbie's hand and they had fled for their lives.

McKinney believed in God. He did. With every fiber of his being and soul. In the Holy Father and his infinite mercy. So why had He let these appalling things happen to them? Why?

2

He attempted to close his mind off to block the memory of the terrible ways in which he saw and heard his fellow students and their professors die. But he couldn't quite manage it - the grotesque images and sounds he had witnessed would not leave him. They echoed in his mind…ripples on a bottomless blood-red pool of abomination – unspeakable things that no one should ever have to see or hear. It made him glad though in a bizarre kind of way. It was that abhorrence and his utter dread that kept McKinney running on despite his utter exhaustion – desperate to try to escape – so that the others' gruesome fate wouldn't become his or Bobbie's.

The light was fading fast now as it did at this latitude on the Queen Charlotte Islands. Even in the summer months the hours of daylight never overstayed its welcome.

After the daylight, such as it was, there quickly came a barely perceived twilight – then that short-lived dimming was quickly followed by a deep, stygian blackness. And within the dark, deep in the vast forests, McKinney now knew there was contained a dreadfulness – a horror no one could have ever imagined dwelled within. As the night began to swiftly creep and seep through the canopy of dense trees that surrounded them, his hopes began to wane with equal alacrity.

Oh God… he thought…they were going to die here. Screaming out in their death agonies, just like the others. He shook himself mentally to shun the feelings of defeat that threatened to engulf him…no, darn it, no! This wasn't going to happen to them, or at least not to him. He had a home to go back to. Dear close friends in his church - people who truly loved him - mother and father, two younger sisters… he was determined that he was going to see them all again. Whatever he had to do to survive the terror that had been foisted upon them he would do. He was not going to perish here! This was not his time to be called. McKinney willed himself to believe that he was going to live. He was going to live!

As if to purge any last negative thoughts from his mind, he shook Bobbie as hard as his remaining strength would allow. As he did so, the pain finally now registered sharply in his damaged hands, making him wince. The young, tall, wispy girl merely sagged dispiritedly within his arms. The filthy and disheveled woman barely even registered his violent action. McKinney spoke roughly to her, his voice ragged with the effort – an intended shout that emerged as a hoarse whisper from a throat dried out from lack of water and excesses of adrenaline and fear.

"Come on, Bobbie, we have to keep moving! The Dinan Bay logging camp is close - must be. Only a few short miles. We'll be safe. Don't give up. Come on Bobbie, for Jesus Christ's sake, and in His name - we can make it!"

His short tirade ended, and the girl finally tilted her head up, seemingly half acknowledging his presence. Bobbie's once bright green eyes, so alluring to McKinney since their freshman year at SMU, were now dull and dispirited - lifeless in fact. Perhaps a precursor of the fate that she felt certain soon awaited her - them. No real recognition was apparent within their dim depths, only cattle-like resignation of what was to be. The girl slumped even farther forward, becoming a dead weight.

McKinney's weakened muscles couldn't support the woman's burden any longer. Without him propping her up, the haggard girl slowly collapsed to the soft ground in slow-motion; a tall, yet slender young pine that had been felled.

Once there amongst the dead leaves and forest floor detritus, she briefly became animated, curling herself up into a tight fetal ball, angular arms and skinny legs tucked in to wait for what must inevitably follow. McKinney noticed Bobbie was singing in a low, childlike voice. Her mind had retreated into childhood - a place where she obviously had felt the safest, where reassurance had always been within easy reach. It was pitiable and yet terrible. McKinney could hardly bear to listen to her pathetic little voice that had taken on a childlike quality:

"Jesus loves the little children..."

McKinney looked down at her huddled form with a feeling of incredible sadness. Bobbie had given up. Her struggle to stay alive was over. He resigned himself to the grim fact that he'd done everything he could to try to save her. She had given up. However, it certainly wasn't over for him yet. He could still save himself and if God was willing, he would. Maybe if he got help quickly enough, he could still save her too.

With sphincter-loosening suddenness, a soulless inhuman snigger came from somewhere very close, back in the darkening tree line. He could smell the foul rank stink that he now associated with violent death. McKinney's head shot up away from staring at Bobbie's recumbent form - eyes wildly glaring into the gloom, searching in the direction the awful sound emanated from, attempting to visualize the threat that he could only smell and hear. McKinney's weak watery legs suddenly found a new lease of life. Without his conscious volition he took a diffident, foot dragging, backward step. Then another - another. He had covered six hesitant steps in this manner when he suddenly stopped, frozen to the spot.

An obsidian dimness seemed to detach itself from the deeper darks of the trees. An amorphous shadow snaked out towards Bobbie's tucked in feet. A growing, unsubstantial mass encompassed her exposed shins easily. Still feebly singing in that wretched childlike voice, the woman was slowly, almost imperceptibly dragged backward away from the logger's trail and into the impenetrable darkness. All McKinney could do was be a silent, motionless witness to the scene that was unfolding before him. In the last few seconds, before the young woman's face completely disappeared into the blackness, Bobbie seemed to briefly come to herself and comprehend the horror of what was happening to her.

Her eyes were suddenly alive and animate once more. Her gaze locked with his. There was no mistaking the expression. Desperation - pleading with McKinney to help her. Save her from the unspeakable thing that was pulling her away... but even that final, silent plea was lost to him as she slid from his view and into the encompassing dark.

The last thing he saw of poor Bobbie were her starkly white arms and hands semi-bright in the gathering gloom - fingers outstretched, clutching and clawing desperately with an inevitable futility for any anchor they could find within the soft loam of the trail. She was pointlessly casting her hands out, seeking a firm purchase to prevent herself from being dragged away. At this last horrific sight, McKinney was suddenly freed from the invisible force that had rooted him to the spot. He turned jerkily on his heel and staggered down the path for his life.

The well-worn trail turned to the left and headed in a generally downward direction. Away from the overhanging trees, the ambient daylight all around him was fast fading away now as red dusk bled away and gave over to blacking night. McKinney could barely see more than a few feet in front of him as he tore along, but what his human eyes lacked, his ears made up for. They were now pursuing him in earnest, he realized in dread. Yet still content to toy with their prey, they were combining their efforts to bring him down. He could hear their massive scampering forms crashing within the trees in the blackness; their unclean stench gagged him, cloying his nostrils with the foul combined odors of corruption, blood, and musk.

The certain knowledge that they weren't yet in front of him, as far as he could tell, spurred the young student on to redouble his efforts. That logging camp had to be close now. Please God...It had to be! Please let it be!

The path suddenly took an unexpectedly sharp turn to the right, then started up a gentle incline. The trail frustratingly seemed to get steeper with each passing second, considerably slowing McKinney down. The trees on either side of the trail now crowded in, filtering out what little ambient light there had been. Darkness was nearly upon him - metaphorically and literally. The young student knew he was almost at the limits of his endurance. He just couldn't physically go on much farther. His heart was now pounding so hard he thought it might burst from his exertions. The air that McKinney was forcing in and out of his lungs felt like it had a consistency of a molten liquid - heavy and scalding, it tortured the abused tissues within. It was beginning to be an agony to pull it in and out of his wheezing chest. He noticed dully that he could now taste the rusty flavor of his own blood at the back of his throat.

With a suddenness of a switched-on bulb in a dark room he realized he had reached the apex of the path. Through hazy, blurred vision he was looking down into a small but steep valley. There were signs of humanity down there! Bright shining fixed points of light that meant a chance of help – the Dinan logging camp – a sight as beautiful to him as the most majestic stars in the Creator's black velvet heavens! He'd found it, thank the Lord! He could still actually make it!

With only the briefest of hesitations he stumbled forward, willing his leaden legs and numbed body into one final, last ditch effort. He was beyond pain - an automaton - a flawed being of torn muscles and bloodied flesh that could only limp and crab along. McKinney had become a creature with one single abiding thought - just one purpose to his whole existence… to reach the safety of the Dinan Bay camp.

Then suddenly he was on the ground.

He realized he could taste the rich earth of the worn trail in his mouth because he was face down on it. He collapsed when the wrenched muscles and pulled ligaments of his abused body no longer obeyed his insistent brain's instructions to move. McKinney just lay there. The spirit was no longer willing, and the flesh was very, very weak.

He smelt them. He heard them. They were all around him. He closed his eyes in terror of what he knew would come but a part of him was strangely relieved. God would have him soon enough. The growls were soft, almost human. Almost.

He felt an enormous elemental strength lift him up high by just his left arm - the shoulder joint instantly dislocated - McKinney was too much in shock to even scream. He dangled for a few seconds being shaken like a rag doll, then he was on the ground again. His face was planted back firmly in the earth of the trail. Now that soil had a muddy, nauseating consistency. Warm and gluey against his cold skin.

He weakly opened his eyes to look. With horror he understood the reason he now lay in a thick sludge, - even in this light he could see that his own blood had provided the medium to make it that way. His left arm had been torn away, ragged and ripped at the socket and lay just a few feet away from him.

Before he could fully take in that entire gruesome discovery, something was already yanking at his wet denim jeans, moving his torn-away limb from his line of sight, tearing and stripping away the last vestiges of the material from his numb legs. The strength used to achieve that was such that his thick leather belt snapped like rotten twine. He couldn't even resist as his underpants were torn away from him, the force of that cruel action lifted his whole body off the ground for a second and then slammed it back onto the wet trail floor as his drawers were ripped off. Dizzy, sick and unresisting, McKinney dimly accepted that the same something was tugging hard now at his genitals, pulling, twisting at them eagerly with a vicious animal force; their efforts were sliding him bodily along the rough ground. He lifted himself up weakly on his remaining arm just in time to see a huge, misshapen hand reach in, twist and completely tear away his scrotum and penis from his body in a shower of hot, stinking fluids.

Then he did scream. McKinney's high-pitched screech was a signal to the others.

They were upon him at once in a writhing frenzy, greedily tearing out greasy loops of wet intestine and warm succulent organs that they gained access to by simply ripping open his soft belly. They were eating him alive. And he knew it.

And as McKinney slipped into final oblivion; traveling unresistingly to that darkness from which there can be no return - with an odd sense of wonderment he heard an awfully strange last thing....

"Jesus loves the little children..."

CHAPTER TWO

Hendry Media Corp.
California

March 2019

Pete Jervis stuck his head round Bruno Harts' office door.

"Bruno - Have you seen this?"

Harts didn't quite look up, still seated at his desk he managed to show disdain; never taking his eyes from his laptop screen, or his fingers from the keyboard - quite a feat.

"Seen what?" he replied with a studied disinterest. Outwardly the seated man appeared quite disinterested; yet inwardly his guard had instantly gone up.

Bruno Harts knew Jervis – knew him very well – the animus between the two senior executives ran deep - and it was for good reason. Bruno held the not so private and widely shared opinion that Jervis was a slimy sonofabitch, a complete and utter asshole - the embodiment of everything that was wrong with some of today's entertainment industry executives. Jervis was basically a bad human being. Not evil, as such, just a self-serving narcissist who was constantly looking for the main chance – that next opportunistic way to ooze his way up another rung of the corporate ladder.

Whatever he had brought to Harts' office door was not going to be anything good for Bruno. He knew him of old - Jervis was trying to gain some sort of advantage. Everything for the sole benefit of Pete Jervis and his career. That was his MO. Harts regarded him through slightly narrowed eyes. True to form, Jervis was obviously enjoying a private moment – whatever the moment was - and a situation carefully and craftily engineered. There was going to be a problem for someone, Bruno Harts instinctively felt. And he had a shrewd idea whose problem it was going to become.

Inwardly sighing, he repeated the question, as Jervis hadn't deigned to reply immediately.

Obviously savoring the moment, he eased slowly into the office and casually placed a flash drive on the side of Bruno's desk, before pushing it unhurriedly and deliberately with his right index finger along the highly polished wooden surface till it was practically under Harts' nose. The seated man glanced down at it and now looked up, regarding Jervis, finally giving him some actual attention. He looked back to the small thumb drive sitting there.

On it was written, in tiny capital letters in a fine tipped black sharpie: 'Eastman '98'. Bruno looked back up at Jervis, who now had a badly concealed expression of malicious delight.

Sighing out loud now, Bruno Harts finally scooped up the drive, and waved it at the other man, as if he was a bad smell to be wafted away, asking quizzically, *"So, what exactly is this then, eh Pete?"*

"Oh this, Bruno," the other man replied, with a barely hidden sneer…*"is something you will want to see. An awesomely fresh Kimberly Eastman…and what an absolutely hot pleasure she was! Well, at least someone thought she was back in 1998 when they made this."*

Bruno settled back in his chair. *"Kimberly Eastman? What about her?"*

Pete Jervis affected an attitude of obviously feigned surprise, sullen sarcasm dripping from his words.

"You mean you don't know? You went ahead and made the decision to hire her to front the biggest, most expensive show we will be putting out on next year's schedule – and you weren't aware of her true claim to fame?"

Bruno Harts tossed the flash drive back onto his desk with a clatter in irritation before replying. Jervis knew how to push all the right buttons. All his buttons.

"Hold on a minute, Pete. Not that it's in your purview – but I can tell you that no job offer has been extended. Initially she's just coming in informally so we can chat. If I decided she's right for the project, I can then gauge how cheaply she'd be willing to work." He paused for a second, before adding thoughtfully, *"anyhow, my understanding is, she hasn't worked on anything substantive for a while – that means she's probably hungry. Limited exposure will do that – not being in the public eye is never a good thing in our business."* Bruno paused, before adding almost as a private afterthought – *"Anyhow, when all's said and done it's about the money, Pete - the bottom line - no matter how good someone is, or thinks they are. But both myself and Mr. Hendry have reviewed her previous work - she's damned good."*

This last comment was an attempt by Bruno Harts to take the wind out of the other guy's sails - to disarm him. Oddly though, reminding Jervis in a none too subtly fashion that Hendry was onboard with the whole deal didn't elicit the expected response. The smug, self-satisfied look on Pete Jervis' face told Bruno Harts that hurled brickbat had widely missed its mark.

There was something in the asshole's triumphant attitude that his earlier comments were not referencing Kimberly Eastman's past TV or media work. Some insidious personal knowledge was obviously giving the bastard a great deal of confidence.

Jervis turned away and moved towards the open office door, the previous look of barely disguised maliciousness now giving way to one of hateful triumph. He paused, hand on the frame and turned back. Bruno Harts' gambit hadn't fooled him in the slightest.

"Oh, I think you've made the decision to hire her, Bruno. I've already seen the budget sheet for the next fiscal. And I stand by what I said. I seriously doubt that you or Hendry has seen her real work," he said nonchalantly, indicating the thumb drive on the desk. Then he gave another self-satisfied smile adding:

"You know, Bruno, it may be a little nihilist, but I once heard it said that the substance of life is centered in regret. You picked Kimberly Eastman to front the Cryptid project – I keep my ear to the ground - you even went so far as to pitch to the investors that she'd be perfect for it – your recommendation to Hendry to hire her."

Jervis snickered with a hint of satisfaction in his voice.

"Well, after you view that file you may well regret that. There's going to be a lot of explaining to do and there will be a very expensive mess to clean up. Rather you than me, my friend!"

The word 'friend', naturally, had no meaning or substance. There was absolutely no love lost between the two men. Pete Jervis stopped for a second to pick at an imagined piece of lint from his expensive suit jacket, before saying:

"You know, when she gets hired, I'm making a sure bet that this is going to be a PR nightmare for the company. I'm also betting that Mr. Hendry will be regretting things too. Like the fact that he gave you the VP's job over others who were, let's just say, a little better qualified."

At that last comment, Harts shot out a dangerous look just to let the other man know, no matter how senior he thought he was, he wasn't senior to Bruno and he was getting close to crossing a line that he really shouldn't. Pete Jervis either didn't notice the silent threat or pretended that he wasn't cowed by it. He simply let out an affected breathy sigh, before adding:

"Oh well, back to the grind," adding almost as an afterthought, *"friendly piece of advice though, you might want to shut your door before you watch it."*

With this last flash of mock concern, Jervis was gone.

The guy was such an absolute shit, thought Bruno. He couldn't abide the pretentious little fuck. One of these days it was going to come to an inevitable head. An abscess that would need lancing sooner rather than later – and Bruno Harts would be wielding the scalpel on that happy day. Yes - Jervis was going to have to go. Frowning, he plugged the drive into a USB port on his laptop. Then, almost as a reluctant afterthought, petulantly heaved himself up and closed his office door.

It took seconds for the file to upload and his laptop's software to automatically unzip it. Jervis had told a partial truth, at least - it was a video file - although the quality wasn't first rate; the first few seconds saw nothing pictured except a black screen with some poorly edited bright red script reading: 'All In A Day's Work' – that black screen and lettering quickly faded to reveal a tatty brown velour couch.

The shot pulled away to show the rest of a drab room. Jervis had been right about one thing: The decor and furnishings were circa mid to late 90s. The obviously inexperienced cameraman then panned jerkily and unsteadily back to center onto the couch. Nothing for a few seconds then a couple walked into the frame. The guy looked to be about in his mid-thirties – it was hard to tell – but certainly past the first bloom of youth. He was wearing tight dark pants and a hideous lilac golf polo and carrying what appeared to be a bag of tools.

Bruno cringed slightly looking at that polo; he remembered having a remarkably similar shirt back in the day.

The guy was being led into the room by a young girl. Even with the less than perfect quality of the video it was apparent she was extremely attractive - substantially heavy in the chest area and wearing a ruffled mini-skirt. She had great legs, Bruno noticed. A bright, tightly stretched pink cropped t-shirt under a sleeveless denim jacket completed her ensemble. Her age was indeterminate – anywhere from late teens to early twenties. Her blonde hair was loosely permed in the style of the two decades past and she had a complimentary shaggy cut to match.

Bruno looked closely at the girl's face. There was little room for doubt in his mind, this pretty girl was Kimberly Eastman. There was no sound.

Just where the hell had Jervis dug this shit up? Damn him – the fucking weasel!

Bruno concentrated, leaning closer to look at the screen with an unconscious intimacy that the situation seemed somehow to warrant. He had a growing sense – a feeling of disquiet – a vague distaste bubbling up in him – one mixed with an unaccountable hint of morbid arousal.

Kimberly's character was gesticulating at a wall power outlet, obviously conveying to the 'workman' that there was a problem with it. And it didn't really take a great deal of forethought to realize what was probably about to occur; this was the quintessential cheap 90's porn movie.

In an obvious slow manner, she bent down towards the outlet, exposing black tight underwear. At this point the man in the video suddenly pulled her up and guided her to the edge of the seat. He sat heavily down on the left end of the couch and pulled the girl down onto it with him. She ended up on the center cushion, and the male casually draped his arm around Kimberly and looked directly at the lens of the camera. He turned his head and nuzzled into her neck, grinning inanely and whispering something to her. At this, she glanced at the man seated next to her in feigned acquiescence. The man then leaned in towards her, unceremoniously pulling her denim jacket off. The Kimberly Eastman character resisted briefly for a second, trying to put her arms stiffly down by her sides and leaning away with an uneasy, silent giggle; the aging Romeo then said something to his unwilling Juliet. Whatever words he used apparently worked their own insidious magic. The next moment she gave in. Resigned to it all, Kimberly mutely assisted, pulling off the sleeveless denim herself. The acting was truly dreadful.

The guy took it, carelessly dropping it on the floor - then immediately started to yank up her pink cropped top. The camera zoomed in, blurred for a second as the auto focus struggled to catch up - finally focused, the shot framed the top half of both figures just in time to see her tee-shirt come completely up. Now her black under wired bra and rather large expanse of smooth pale cleavage spilling out of it was exposed.

The video camera then panned out again. The next second another 'workman', slightly younger and more heavyset than the one Kimberly had led into the room, now appeared. Beckoned in by the first guy, he sat himself down on the other side of the aspiring actress – for want of a better description. She nervously peered at him, from under her blonde fringe, obviously having been scripted to be surprised with this new turn of events. The first actor then plunged his left hand into Kimberly's left bra cup and slowly levered out the large firm breast contained within …

Bruno found himself somewhat guiltily studying Kimberly Eastman's big breast in detail, from its firm rounded fleshy curves, to the dark brown areola and large erect nipple. Fascinated and yet at the same time honestly quite repelled. Both men had begun to play with her large breasts now in earnest - taking it in turns to forcefully knead the big mounds of fleshy tissue, alternately cruelly twisting the hard nipples, then biting and wetly sucking at them. Kimberly slumped back; eyes dead - face slack. It was obvious what would happen next in the scene and Bruno Harts had no desire to watch more of it – he only felt disgust at how a young aspiring and obviously hungry Kimberly Eastman had most certainly been exploited by others.

He closed the laptop screen and angrily pulled out the thumb drive from the side port. He distantly thought of his own daughter, Sam. She was about the same age that Kimberly had been then. She had never shown any inclination to get into the entertainment industry – but Bruno was certain that he could protect her against the kind of manipulation that Kimberly Eastman had been pulled into – like so many young hopefuls were. There were predatory sharks out there in this industry always looking for opportunity and willing to take advantage - the bastards… the absolute fucking bastards…

Bruno was now filled with a boiling seething rage at what he'd just witnessed. He felt ashamed for just being a member of the male of the species at that moment. His hands were shaking with his barely suppressed fury. He also knew that if Jervis happened to walk through his door at that precise moment, he'd happily contemplate beating the smug asshole to death with the chair he was sitting on. Failing that, he'd certainly shove the flash drive and its filthy contents sideways up his ass, followed by his foot.

What a complete and utter shit. He'd happily used Kimberly Eastman's sordid past to attempt to score points off Bruno Harts with Hendry, the CEO and owner. And it was all because he'd been passed over for the job that Bruno had got instead. It clearly showed him to be the ruthless, heartless bastard that Harts always knew he was. He didn't care who he hurt if it suited his current purpose. The sonofabitch! God, how he fucking despised Jervis.

Bruno sat back in his seat and drew a deep breath. He closed his eyes in cold contemplation, pressing his fingers to his temples, slowing his breathing to gain control of the inner anger and bring his blood pressure down. He was composed a few minutes later when he opened them up again. With the clarity of thought that this calmness brought, he was now certain of two things. Firstly, no matter how senior Jervis was or how well connected he thought he was within the industry, that bastard would be out of this job by the year's end. And secondly, Kimberly Eastman was going to find herself gainfully employed as the host of Hendry Corps Productions' latest big live reality show concept: Cryptid.

Fuck Jervis, thought Bruno Harts. Fuck him to hell and back!

***

Kimberly Eastman's current mood – an unhappily combined mixture of uptight and miserable. Sitting uncomfortably behind the wheel of her car, the cause of the tension was due, not unnaturally to the meeting - or call it what it was – an interview. The misery component - the physical drive to get there. Some days her negative opinion of driving was worse than others. She hated Interstates and freeways with a passion – she found traveling along them frustrating and brain numbing in equal measures. It truly sucked ass.

However, being downbeat or frustrated would not do today, traffic notwithstanding. She particularly needed to be sharp and bright – positively fucking incandescent.

Kimberly sighed inwardly. She couldn't even begin to guess how many hundreds of thousands of miles she had covered on featureless concrete roadways over the years. Kimberly was on her personal autopilot, not really noticing what was going on around her. Without even looking, she knew she was surrounded by other numb individuals – faceless, anonymous men and women hurtling casually down California's linear grey stretches - vehicles that mindlessly hauled them tirelessly with a near perfect symbiosis between the occupant's commute-deadened brains and the insensate cars. Humanity - instinct-animated husks; soulless creatures with blank expressions piloting metal and glass encased private little worlds. Each separately happy from the rest of humanity. Yet all moving together in common purpose - blood corpuscles fiercely pumping along a concrete vein.

The flow of traffic had pulled her to this job interview as unerringly as real blood would have found its way to the heart. Almost unconsciously she had reached her destination. She pulled off the US 101 Ventura Freeway, u-turned under the bridge, and just like her GPS said, she was on North Ventura Road. Following the flat voiced electronic directions, she immediately entered the car park to her right and noted the information board on which, amongst other businesses housed in the tall multi-level, was Hendry Corp Production Offices. That place where she needed to be.

Not actually wanted to be per se, she thought bitterly to herself, *but needed.*

She was almost on the wrong side of forty now - the TV employment opportunities were rapidly drying up - unlike the procession of credit card bills and final demands that seemed to drop in her mailbox with increased regularity these days.

Kimberly Eastman needed this job very badly.

She knew she was desperate, but was absolutely determined that her nervousness wouldn't show to these prospective employers. Anxiety was always a bad strategy and generally the kiss of death in an interview situation.

Turning off the engine, she swiveled the rear-view mirror downwards to check her make-up. Her dyed blonde hair was well kept - the cut expensive and just about the only thing on her that was partially real these days. The startlingly blue eyes that stared back at her were expensive color 20% enhanced contacts. Pursing her full collagen lips, Eastman hurriedly re-applied her shimmering lip-gloss, and then deliberately and humorlessly grinned at herself, exposing two rows of straight, whitened teeth that were veneered to perfection –just to check that no lipstick had inadvertently smeared where it shouldn't have been.

After all, those teeth and the accompanying smile framed by those pouting, plumped lips had cost her thousands over the last few years to cosmetically perfect, she thought ruefully. That financial investment really needed to pay for itself. Oh, along with the nose and the tits, she added to herself. Yeah, let's not forget the tits! Mother Nature had needed that enhanced little lift these days. She made a final manual adjustment to them, careless as to who might be watching. Face north, never south - to quote her expensive boob surgeon.

Kimberly examined her face one final time – she dabbed a finger brushing at her hair realizing, with a small measure of sadness that - all in all - she had certainly come a long way in order to destroy her career and with that destruction any last shreds of journalistic integrity. Not so much in terms of any conventional distance; but in other, subtler ways. She was after all, partially the architect of her own downfall. She couldn't even pretend otherwise these days.

Kimberly got out of the older model Chevy Malibu, pressed the key fob to lock it, straightened her skirt and headed slowly toward the building's entrance so as not to sweat in the warm California sunshine; heels clicking and an interview letter tucked safely in her red leather Fendi tote bag - one of the few remaining possessions of what had been better days.

This city's zoning must be a little out of whack, she decided. The next block down was nestled on the edge of a busy intersection and that area housed what was apparently a large High School. From the amount of kids who were outside and running, it must be morning recess. Kimberly stopped for a second and watched the hordes of children at play. The ones she could easily see were engaged in typical teens' behavior - some were leaning against perimeter fences for that illicit smoke. Another larger group of boys threw a football around in an ecstasy of concentration, while they hurled abuse - some good natured, some not - at each other with equal vigor. Voices loud and distinct and multilayered - she could hear them from where she stood. Groups of girls huddled around each other, moving in a kind of osmosis - the latest smartphones out on display – multitasking - no doubt talking about their newest boyfriends, bands or whatever else was closest to the center of their own particular fickle universe and probably Facebooking it at the same time.

Eastman tried to invoke similar memories of her own high school days - happier times - but couldn't. There had never been any. With cold desolation, she knew that she'd been denied even that by a total asshole. An asshole that was, unfortunately, her father. A father now thankfully long dead. Yep, the drunken, pathetic bastard would have beaten her practically senseless for such frivolous behavior. And enjoyed himself while doing it. Eastman closed her eyes momentarily; she could still hear the hated voice, see that pinched, booze mottled stubbled face and smell the whisky sour breath.

Shit - he'd better not catch her talking to no boys! Boys having their nasty, groping hands pawing at her – dirty hands! Dirty hands! It never stopped him from doing that himself though. She came back to the present in a rush, hurriedly banishing the revolting vision of him away – pushing it back deep inside - unseen and forgotten where it rightfully belonged.

An elderly security guard came upon her unnoticed, moving from a small glass booth strategically placed by the front of the building. He snuffled and shuffled out to her like an old inquisitive dog from a kennel - from the look on his face, he was probably unsure whether to bite her ass or lick her hand.

He actually did neither, and after a cursory look at the letter of interview, he gestured her into the main front entrance door, telling her to use the elevator on her left and to go up to the third floor where she'd find the company's offices - exactly what Kimberly had expected. She'd been in and out of these types of workplaces for most of her working adult life; sadly, recently, more out than in.

The frosted outer glass doors had been neatly etched with the business logo of two concentric circles encompassing a leaping deer or gazelle. Eastman wasn't quite sure which. The very attractive Asian receptionist behind the desk could only kindly be called vacuous in the extreme. The girl was obviously hired as front office eye candy rather than for any admin skills she possessed. In fact, from what Kimberly observed, the girl's talents seemed to primarily consist of simultaneously being able to chat to a girlfriend on her cell, while typing on the online messenger on the office PC, touching up her nails and eyeing Kimberly's patent leather Louboutin shoes, expensive clothes, purse, make-up and boob job with an apparent grudging approval. Thinking about it, Kimberly realized, that was an impressive amount of multi-tasking.

Before Eastman could even have a perfunctory conversation with the receptionist, a door opened on the left side of the reception area. Magically and with obvious long practice, the young girl made nail polish, cell phone and the messenger screen instantly vanish. Framed in the space where a second ago a large door had been, was a guy who nearly filled the whole gap. His sheer size may have been intimidating, but the smile that lit his face was one of friendly welcome.

His clothing, which consisted of an old Caltech sweatshirt and jeans, hardly seemed appropriate for the office, even here in California. He looked to be in his early to mid-thirties. The receptionist got up to perhaps justify her existence but the big guy in the doorway casually waved her back to her seat.

"Kimberly, I presume? Welcome, welcome!" The voice was deep and vibrant, with a strong Southern accent, *"I'm Bruno Harts, Senior Vice President in charge of programming."*

She stood up to meet him, her hand extended in greeting.

"Hello," Kimberly replied. *"Should I call you Mr. Harts?"*

"Or just Bruno, whatever you prefer, Kimberly. I want you to be comfortable, but I personally prefer Bruno. We like to keep thing as informal as we can around here."

Harts realized that this woman was slightly taken aback by his manner and appearance, and as by way of making an apology, he added, putting his big right hand on his wide chest: *"Yes, I know I look like one of the company grips, or the construction gang, but honestly I really am in charge of programming."*

Kimberly laughed for the first time that day. She couldn't help it, but with this gentle giant who emanated such an aura of good fellowship, it seemed the most natural thing to do. He bore more than a passing resemblance to Tom Selleck, too. *Very attractive,* she thought.

"Excuse my manners, Kimberly, won't you please come into my office?"

So they were on a first name basis already. Maybe that was a positive sign, she mused. Following the broad expanse of back, Kimberly went in after him. Harts swept his arm around in a wide circle as he walked – *"Come on, let the Emperor show off his Empire!"* And with a crooked finger, he beckoned her to follow. She trailed behind him automatically and once through the door he took her by the arm and led her back through the maze of open-planned, office-fringed passages that seemed to honeycomb this huge third floor. Everyone she saw and met looked generally relaxed and happy, yet seemingly industrious. That was always a good sign in her experience. The people she observed knew their business. Finally, they reached what Kimberly estimated was the far side of the building. They came upon a large opaque glass door, brightly lit from behind, with the emblazoned words painted or stenciled across its width:

STUDIO AREA: NO UNAUTHORISED ADMITTANCE

The big man seemed genuinely delighted at this part of his tour.

"This is the nerve center Kimberly, where it all happens. We currently produce..." she interrupted him -

"Hendry Corp currently produces fifteen shows, mainly reality TV and live broadcasts. Many shows from the Hendry stable are syndicated nationally - some internationally - including the immensely popular 'Cars of the Stars'."

She glanced up at him guiltily and shut herself off. Gone too far again, Kimberly, fucking motor mouth, she thought, mentally kicking herself. She needn't have worried, Bruno's grin got even wider.

"You've obviously done your homework, Kimberly, but with your track record I wouldn't have expected anything else. Come on, let's adjourn to my office, shall we?"

She followed him in through the switchbacks of twists and turns that led back to his office. As Kimberly walked through the door he held open, she noted that his workspace didn't seem to match his personality any more than his style of dress matched his vocation. With his easy manner and casual attitude, Kimberly half expected the décor to be something like a sorority frat room, replete with pennants and football trophies at every corner; however, this was not the case. Bruno's office showed an ordered mind and a setting of neat professionalism that she could genuinely appreciate.

"Please, sit down, make yourself comfortable," he indicated a chair opposite his own, at either side of the desk which, amongst other things, had a large screened laptop on the top that was beeping fitfully, until Harts' oversized finger punched a random key and put it out of its misery.

"Can I offer you a coffee or a tea, Kimberly? Perhaps you'd like something a little stronger?" He gestured towards a tasteful antique drinks cabinet to his right. Eastman politely refused the offer.

"No, thank you, Mr. Harts...oh, sorry, Bruno," she corrected herself, giving him the benefit of her best and most winning smile. She steeled herself. Come on now Kimberly, don't let him think you're desperate. No niceties, just be professional. Let's get straight to the point. Let's show some of my initiative and assertive qualities.

She leaned forward into the desk, fingers steepled.

"So, Bruno, what exactly does this project involve? And what would be my role in it? I know from the briefing letter I've had, that it's in a reality show format and I do understand that things are kept under tight wraps for obvious reasons. After all, you don't want other production companies stealing your show ideas."

Bruno Harts' eyebrows lifted quizzically, and his big hands came up in resignation. He moved away from her, swiveling in the chair that seemed far too small for him in the first place. Bruno faced Kimberly Eastman at an angle, remarking, *"Goodness... You really are all business, aren't you? I was hoping to chat a little – to get to know you a little first before we discussed that."*

Realizing that she might be overplaying the professional persona just a little, she made a conscious effort and dialed it back, settling into the chair and willing her body to relax. She took a deep breath before replying, *"Sure, Bruno. What do you want to know? I think my resume really has it all covered."="*

The big man turned back to her. He regarded her for a second, drumming his fingers on his desk, playing with the white pages that comprised Kimberly's extensive resume.

"But surely it's what this..." he shook the papers at her, *"...doesn't say though, isn't it? I want to know you. What is it that drives you, what makes you tick, what pushes your buttons? That's what intrigues me."*

This took her aback slightly. For the first time she began to feel uncomfortable under Bruno Harts' stare.

"I don't quite understand," she said hesitantly, her false confidence rapidly draining from her. She was on an unsure footing now. *"What do you want to know, exactly?"*

Harts got up from his chair and walked over to his office window. He stood there for a few seconds, then turned back to face her. He spoke in low tones. Eastman had to lean forward to catch his words.

"OK...I won't bullshit you. I'll be straight with you, Kimberly. To be honest, I don't really care what makes you tick. I also know that you've been out of the game for a little longer than can be considered healthy in this business. Even that isn't important to me though. And that's because I have no qualms that you are the person I want for the project. Yep, no doubt. You have all the qualities that we need in order to pull this new production off. You have the looks, the personality; in fact, the whole serious quality and genuine on-screen authority that we're sure is going to make this thing fly higher than a migrating swallow's fart. We're projecting that this show will be syndicated in record time."

He paused for breath. Kimberly was getting her hopes up again. Shit, it sounded like they wanted her! Be calm. Be calm, she chided herself.

Then Bruno Harts continued, and with his words, Kimberly knew that her hopes were about to be dashed hard. His next remark came like a glass of iced water poured over her head. Her stomach sank.

"...But we might have, let's say, a little concern regarding..."

She instinctively realized what was coming. She'd heard this from different studio or network execs on different interviews during the last couple of years. She didn't have the money or clout to sue and get the damn thing taken off the net, even if it was possible. Yes, he knew about that fucking porn video; that disgusting, shitty incident from her past had followed her around in one way or another from one place of work to the next. Like the proverbial pariah.

She dimly realized that Bruno Harts was still talking: *".... I cannot obviously guarantee that the video won't become an issue later with the suits upstairs. But I can promise that if it comes to that, I'll do my best to soften the blow. I'm counting on you, Kimberly, to make yourself irreplaceable from the get-go."*

Oh God, he was going to offer her the job after all! And as she was listening to his words, she felt the blood return to her cheeks, and her fingertips regain their warmth.

He was continuing, *".... that's the way to make yourself secure. Make it so they can't can your ass. If the viewers like you, then it always follows that the advertisers will too. It isn't about integrity or anything else. It's all about the bottom line, Kimberly - it's all about the money and the ratings, it always was and it always is."*

She stared at him, almost afraid to speak; but she couldn't help herself, she had to ask. It was the cynic in her - she'd been hurt too many times not to be wary, if something was too good to be true, in her experience, it generally was.

"And what is it you'll want from me in return for your support?"

She had half suspected a catch – one that might put her in a bad position; a kind of a sexual favor quid pro quo deal – this had happened twice before and her refusal of an 'arrangement', although morally correct for her, had cost Kimberly a great deal financially. But she need not have worried. Bruno Harts was one of those rare individuals, all the more surprising in this business of fake smiles, double deals and backstabbing. He really was exactly what he seemed to be.

He looked at her and flashed his infectious broad grin, replying: *"In return for me having your back? I'll tell you exactly what I want from you, Kimberly. I want you to make Cryptid the best damn reality show there is on affiliated primetime American TV! Then my stock options go up, I'll get richer than I already am and my wife will get the new beachfront property she has her mercenary little eye on!"*

By pure instinct Kimberly put her hand out, placed it on Bruno's thick wrist and smiled. It felt like the right thing to do. It was. She had found a friend.

CHAPTER THREE

Graham Island, British Columbia

July 1996

Bobbie was a happy little girl.

She sat tight up on Mimi's lap and could smell the wonderfully familiar sweet scent of lavender and fresh crisp laundry that was always to be found there. She looked smilingly around. The inside of the church was washed with the clean light that streamed in from Sunday summer morning windows. Dust motes danced like tiny golden angels caught in the warm shafts of light. Music filled her ears and lifted her heart.

Mimi always said to her, *"Jesus is everywhere, child. But he's especially found in the gift and pleasure we take in the good Lord's music."*

Bobbie loved her Mimi. The little girl also loved the Sunday morning walks with her to the big old church with its fresh white siding walls and tall sharp steeple that pointed straight up, showing the way to God's kingdom. She always held on tight to Mimi's hand as they walked slowly up that long, warm, dusty road on their way to church.

This was the place where Bobbie was happiest. This was where she wanted to be forever - listening to the church people singing, joining along where she could, and cuddled up with her Mimi. She opened her mouth and sang along to this one, it was her favorite:

"Jesus loves the little children..."

And Jesus loves me, thought Bobbie. She knew it was true, 'cus Mimi had told her and Mimi always told the truth, telling lies was a sin! That's what she said to Bobbie. Telling lies was a sin.

She looked up to her Mimi's beautiful crabapple sun worn face to see if she was singing along. But she wasn't. She was staring down at her as if she didn't know her. That frightened Bobbie terribly. She was eight years old and her Mimi was everything to her. A graveside - Bobbie was dropping a single red rose into....

No! No, no, NO!

She was with Mimi... Mimi was there, she was! She willed herself to .be back in Mimi's lap. She was there with her in the church. She could hear the music and was singing along with the others:

"...children of the world.
Red or yellow, black or white,
All are precious in His sight,

Jesus loves the little children of the world."

Bobbie looked up for some fresh reassurance at Mimi again but she wasn't there anymore. Mimi was gone. But of course, she was gone, she reminded herself. Silly, silly Bobbie! How could she possibly be here with her now? Her grandmother had passed. Mimi was in God's heaven now and had been for years - reality washed back to her, a creeping flood of misery. She was laying on rough ground in the encroaching dark. Everything stank - blood, rot, dankness – terror. The others, she recalled - oh my Lord, the others! She put her hands to her ears to block out their agony – terrible sounds that had long since ceased – but nevertheless those shrieks of death echoed in her head, still fresh and terrible. She was beginning to remember it all now. The mental blocks and barriers her mind had quickly thrown up to preserve her sanity were now crumbling away - the true horror registering.

Bobbie dimly felt a sudden pressure tighten across her ankles - a band of gripping iron that constricted more tightly with each passing second. She looked up, more aware of her horrible surroundings with each moment. A scarecrow figure, ragged and bloodied, stared at her from the approaching gloom - the face starkly white against the darkness; the expression it held was pure fear.

Bobbie knew that face - McKinney…it was George McKinney. He was slowly moving away from her, but somehow motionless - frozen to the spot - fear transforming his features. George wasn't backing away from Bobbie - she was inexorably being dragged from the clearing by some terrible thing that was back there in the dark.

She tried to scream out at the young man… to help… to save her - but the yell was trapped inside - a fly in amber - frozen, powerless, and mute. All she could do was pitifully try to grip hard with clawed hands into soft and yielding earth - a vain attempt to help herself - to anchor her fingers in the soil as deep as she could - to halt the relentless backwards motion. The inhuman power of whatever was dragging her away was elemental. Her efforts were less than futile - a feather pitted against a storm wind. Bobbie's fingers gouged out eight perfectly formed furrows in the ground - shallow rifts that reached back into the safety of the clearing - her mind howled as she was drawn away deeper into the darkness.

The last sight she had of her friend George McKinney was of his unsteady legs and leaden feet running away with a milling, terrified gait. The blackness of the night swallowed him up almost instantly, like the dark, deep waters of a lake.

The irresistible force drew her away in the opposite direction into that same dimness. With a horrified fascination she finally summoned up the courage to peer into the abyss - to fearfully try to see what was dragging her away. Bobbie was fully into the tree line, the thick leafy canopy above her blocked the remaining light; she could see almost nothing. She was enveloped into a void that deprived her of sight, but this deprivation seemed to exponentially sharpen her other senses. Flesh exposed through torn clothing could sense every twig and dried leaf - each small, hard object on the forest floor. Oddly though there was no pain despite the skin being already cruelly abraded in many spots from their headlong dash for survival. Bobbie could hear the heavy breathing of whatever had her in its grip… at least she thought she could until she realized, with fresh shock, the labored breathing was her own.

Her ears might have betrayed her momentarily, but her nose had not. The stink of whatever had her in its steely grip was appalling - rank, rotten, and yet incongruously musky and sweet in the same measure. Overwhelmingly, it had the reek of death about it. It was a stench of an old, long buried kill that had been inadvertently disturbed. Yet at the same time it had a fresh, flesh-rending quality to it - stinking of prey newly slaughtered. It made her want to vomit, and if she had any food in her stomach she may well have done - her retching just brought up thin traces of harsh bile to the back of her throat, which in turn started the cycle of dry heaving once more. Bobbie fought to control it - tried to breathe primarily through her mouth, which helped her discomfort a little.

The grip that held her legs together was as an iron band. She could not have freed herself from that incredible strength even if she'd tried. The whole lower portion of her body was twisted at an odd angle and lifted off the floor. Bobbie's left side was the only part of her still in contact with the ground. As she was unceremoniously towed slowly along, soil, mulch, and general debris was pilling up inside her torn t-shirt as it was dredged up by the erratic path her torso made along the forest floor.

There was a dim glow in the far distance she dully noticed when she turned her head to the right. A question formed coldly in her mind. Was she being pulled along the periphery of the forest, adjacent to the track? It was hard for the exhausted young girl to judge. She just wanted the nightmare to end, wanted it all to stop. Then suddenly, it did, but not in the way she had ever expected. Whatever held her, simply let go. One moment she was being dragged, the next she was motionless again - lying flat on her back on the forest floor.

Bobbie found herself alone. From the sounds that rebounded through the dense undergrowth, whatever it was, was moving quickly away from her. Whatever allure was previously held, other matters were now engaging the vile creature's immediate interest. Something or someone was drawing its attention away with a fresh urgency. More faint crashing movement from further away - multiple sounds; there must be several of them - their fearsome presence contained in the dark all around her.

She had no care for that right now – wherever they were, they weren't here. Sobbing quietly to herself in grateful relief, Bobbie muttered a quick word of thanks to God under her breath. She lay there and listened to the darkness as hard as she could – but could now hear nothing. All was silence. No, that was not quite true… there were the general sounds of normal nocturnal forest life. But the important thing to Bobbie was that the creatures had become still and silent. They might have moved on! This was her chance! Perhaps her only one if she wanted to survive.

Rolling painfully onto her side, she struggled shakily to her feet. As she did, the accumulated debris from the forest floor suddenly spilled out from the bottom of her shirt and scattered to the ground around her feet. Her muscles hurt everywhere - so much so that when she straightened up, she had to clench her teeth hard together to stop herself from crying out in pain – but it also stopped them from chattering together in fear. Her ragged jeans were wet and filthy. Her hands traveled quickly across her torso, feeling the torn tattered cotton hanging in shreds. She had lost her left tennis shoe, pulled off as she was dragged - her wet and mud encrusted sock was all that covered that foot.

But there was no more time for self-examination. God had given her a blessed opportunity – one she had to take right now. *Go, Bobbie*, she thought fiercely, *go, go, go!* The silent thought became instant action. She stumbled away into the dark, in what she sincerely hoped was the opposite direction from those nightmarish monsters of the forest.

Bobbie fell heavily within a few scant feet, tripping over an exposed tree root. Fortunately, the fall left her unhurt. She wearily picked herself up and started off again with a kind of ungainly, short-stepping trot. Within a few hurried paces she collided hard with the invisible trunk of a large tree, even with groping hands outstretched in front of her – the terrified girl careening off it, her shoulder taking the main brunt of the impact - this time it did hurt. Bobbie bounced off the solid rough obstruction and dropped down again. This time she lay there amongst the damp earth and dead leaves and silently sobbed in frustration.

It was impossible over this rough uneven ground! She couldn't move safely, not in this nightmare festoon of unseen trees, rocks and bushes - at least not with any appreciable speed. Nothing could. She may just as well be blind! A chilling thought came to her; no, that wasn't quite true, was it? Because those monsters could - with apparent absolute ease.

Bobbie was more scared than she'd ever been in her nineteen years. Somewhere deep inside, a calm and as yet untapped part of her instinctively knew that running around in unreasoning panic was a sure way for her to end up dead. After all, that strategy hadn't helped the others she had been with, had it?

When the first of the group had been dragged undetectably away and then horribly killed, ripped apart just within earshot, they'd all taken off in panicked mass. They went from being a group of educated, rational people to nothing better than a terrified herd tearing through the forest and thick undergrowth in a crazed fright. The only tangible result of that mad flight was that four more had died very quickly, easily picked off by their monstrous pursuers. Then they had regrouped finally - tried to make a stand - hurriedly gathering up anything that could be used or improvised as a weapon to make a fight of it with whatever it was that was out here. An even bigger, more terrible mistake. Five had died even faster as a result of that ill-conceived plan. More flesh shredded apart - bones audibly and horribly splintered by the huge creatures that moved amongst them with superhuman speed. Victims silently snatched away with blurred movement, thrown back into the trees, and the horrific sounds as they were literally torn to pieces.

The only two to escape the massacre had been her and George. Where was he now? Was he even still alive?

There were twelve of them just thirty-six hours ago.

Likely, Bobbie thought coldly, she was probably the only one left alive from the entire group. She began to shake again. Bobbie suddenly needed to pee very badly. She put her hands between her thighs and squeezed back, killing her urge to urinate. Get a grip, Bobbie. Get a grip.

She hunched down, bathed in pain - dripping sweat into the darkness, desperately trying to think herself out of her predicament. Come on, Bobbie...concentrate! Looking around, the girl thought that she could maybe still see the edge of the forest which surely must border the track she had been on before her capture. The monstrous apparition that seized her had been hauling her along in that general direction.

There was the faintest ghostly hue to the perceived horizon in that direction. If she could make her way there, she might be able to stay close to the tree line, hidden from the creatures. Then she could work her way along the track and hopefully find some help. On balance, it seemed to be the best chance to get to safety – probably her only chance.

Gritting her teeth again, this time more with solid determination than fear, she set off as quickly and quietly as she knew, picking and feeling her way along, praying that she could reach her first objective without further mishap. She was terrified, but her luck held. Within a couple of minutes that seemed to Bobbie like an age, and with a few occasional missteps with one or two heart faltering stumbles, she gropingly arrived at the edge of the forest. Through the tree canopy a little light now sluggishly spilled from a dull pre-dawn sky - she could dimly just make out the logging track once again.

Praise to God and all His Blessed Saints, she thought. She crouched down, just within the limit of the barrier of trees, shaking, breathing hard, sweating profusely and trying to bring her racing, pounding heart under manageable control. She stared hard into the gloomy half-light which discernibly revealed the uneven track, determining to study both directions - left and right - and considered which way offered her the best chance for escape.

To the left, as far as Bobbie could make out, the rough track was rising up unevenly and then twisted off to the right till it vanished. She couldn't see where it was leading, but reason dictated that it must surely be almost at the crest of the western valley wall. That was where the Dinan Bay logging camp lay nestled below in the valley. Or at least that's what George said, she recalled, and that he'd also said it wasn't too far away. Bobbie prayed that he had made it to safety. She wiped the dripping sweat from her forehead with a filthy forearm - salty fluid was painfully stinging her eyes. To the right, the track dropped into the darkness in a steady gradient. Bobbie shuddered despite the held promise of a warm dawn light and her overheated drenched body. That was surely the way to Satan's kingdom. The place where the demons first fell upon them - rending soft flesh and tearing fragile bodies apart - the silent, near invisible bringers of frenzied horror. She shut her eyes for a second. She would not willingly go that way. That was where hell held dominion on Earth.

Bobbie opened her eyes again to shut out the terrible visions in her mind. She would - could - think about it no longer; she pushed the self-defeating thoughts out - to do anything else would let loose the fear that was welling up within – a paralysis that would bring total inaction.

Taking deep silent breaths, she started to cautiously follow the path to the left. She crept along shadowy contours of the edging trees as quietly as she could, keeping to the darkest shadows. The terrified girl stopped every few steps to listen - ready to drop instantly to the ground and hide herself away at a split second's notice. The progress up the track was necessarily slow – however she was making a noticeable advancement. Bobbie stealthily followed the rutted track steadily upwards as it wound its uneven course to the outer valley western wall.

At last! She could make out the summit of the path, the change from the darkness of the track to the brighter horizon that could be viewed from the top lifted her spirits considerably. Hardly still daring to hope, she inched forward, making full use of the sheltering cover from tree to tree. The girl was just a few yards away, almost at the apex, when she saw it.

Her blood turned instantly to a sluggish frozen slush in her veins and she couldn't force air in or out of her paralyzed lungs.

A monstrous, formless shape had suddenly appeared at the top of the path in front of her, it seemed to stretch upwards to an impossible height. Bobbie judged that it must be at least eight feet tall. Then, from both sides of the path less than twenty-five feet away, other similar dark and indistinct shapes slunk into view - some upright, some ambling on all fours almost like bears but far more massive and graceful than any ursine creature could ever be.

They must have been around her all the time and she hadn't heard a thing.

Her chest was aching with the effort of unconsciously not taking in any oxygen; suddenly Bobbie remembered she had to breathe again. She let out the stale contents from her chest as quietly as she could. Her grateful lungs pulled in welcome fresh air.

As she watched in horrified enthrallment, the shadows started to shrink. Bobbie realized that the creatures were moving away from her, down the path. Dare she move? Should she creep in their wake and follow them on down the path? Surely, they couldn't have noticed her. If they had she'd already have been recaptured or, more likely, dead. With infinite care, she forced her trembling and unwilling legs to carry her forward, to silently trail these formidable slinking brutes over the rise. She reached the top, still embracing the deepest shadows that the tree line could provide her with.

What the heck was going on? she wondered. Bobbie could now see the lights of the logging camp down in the valley, but they might as well have been on another planet for all the good they did her at the moment. As for the hulking forest dwellers - she could just discern that they seemed to be silently grouped around something. She couldn't accurately say how many of these immense things there were, their positions and shapes seemed to flux and change on the darkened path.

There must have been ten of them, maybe more. The stink that wafted from them in the light breeze that blew up from the valley was an abomination. She felt the gorge rise in her throat and had to work hard not to heave again. What were they doing? One was considerably bigger than the rest. She realized that this assumption was incorrect. The others in the group, she now noted, were hunkered down, seemingly waiting for something that the single upright one was about to do.

Bobbie's hand flew to her mouth to stifle the scream that almost erupted from it, unbidden. Oh, sweet Jesus, no!!

She bit down on the flesh till she could taste blood. The silhouette was now unmistakable. The terrified young girl hadn't fully comprehended how truly enormous these things were. Dangling from the creature's lifted thick arm was a human figure looking pathetically small compared to the creature that hoisted it. It had to be George...Oh God, please help him! Bobbie bit deeper into her hand. She wanted to look away from the terrible scene that was playing out, but like a startled rabbit caught in the headlights of an oncoming speeding car, she was transfixed by what was unfolding before her. It was all too much for Bobbie. She could hold off the inescapable need no longer and ceased to care. She peed.

George McKinney she knew was six feet one. Hanging limply down in this fashion, he looked like an insignificant under-stuffed doll being held aloft by an overgrown child. She began to pray for him under her breath. As if to counterpoint her prayer, the fearsome creatures began a low keening growl that had an eerily human quality to it. The sound they made was unholy - vile and unclean.

The huge being began to shake George McKinney like a terrier dog with its jaws deeply fixed into a rat's throat. Bobbie watched in dread as the inevitable happened - George's arm ripped and separated away from his shoulder - the rest of him fell wetly in a twitching heap to the track. It was terrible to see – aghast, Bobbie wasn't sure, but in the darkness, it seemed that the giant form was carefully examining the torn away limb. The rest of the squatting group now became motionless - enthralled by the spectacle, the growls ceased - and they fell into a hushed, expectant silence.

The upright creature casually tossed the mangled arm close by where poor George lay - quickly bored by his gruesome acquisition. A spoiled kid, weary of tormenting a fly whose wings had just been pulled off. Was George already dead? Bobbie asked herself. She thought he must be, as he'd made no sound whilst he was being mutilated.

She was wrong again. The colossal hairy beast stepped over the poor man, straddling him and obscenely began tearing at him again. The sight was thankfully obscured from the girl by the absence of good light. A distinctive ripping of cloth...something flew up into the air. Bobbie thought that it must be George's ... why was it tearing his clothing off? The creature bent forward, reaching down - horrific high-pitched squeals of agony were wrenched from what was left of the man. The death shrieks broke the spell that had transfixed the rest. A mountain of stinking vileness flowed over the writhing McKinney. They began to tear him apart. They began to noisily feed.

Bobbie's fragile mind could cope no longer, this fresh horror was one sight too many and she promptly withdrew into herself once more:

"Jesus loves the little children..."

The creatures ignored her while they greedily fed.

After they had finished their gruesome feast, they sought her out from the side of the track… The now uncaring woman was lightly scooped up by her original captor. Then the gigantic shapes silently melted back into the stygian depths of the forest, leaving absolutely no discernible trace they had ever been on the track.

They carried the softly singing, mindless Bobbie away with them.

CHAPTER FOUR

California

April 2019

It was an incessant banging on her apartment door that finally pierced the grey oblivion of Kimberly Eastman's sleep and forced her awake. A groan accompanied a half-muttered curse as she kicked off the light comforter and wearily sat up, perched on the edge of her bed with her legs hanging down. Tilting her head, through sleep blurred eyes, she squinted at the alarm clock on the bedside table.

The bright red digits read 03:14. Sighing, Kimberly reluctantly turned on the lamp that stood by the side of it.

Who the hell was it at this time in the morning? A redundant question – she already knew the answer. If the building wasn't burning down, there was only one person would have the brass cohunes to come hammering on her door at this unholy hour.

Putting her feet down on the bedroom carpet, she stood in her tee-shirt and panties, still half asleep - body swaying slightly. She snagged a crumpled sweat top from the bedroom floor then pulled it on, not caring or even noticing it was inside out. Kimberly then stumbled to the apartment door, bare feet slapping on the hallway floor tiles. Glancing through the peephole to confirm what she already knew, the door chain was slid off, and she opened it. Without looking back, the woman headed for the apartment's small kitchen to put on a pot of coffee, flicking on the living room lights as she passed by them.

Kimberly Eastman's early morning caller let himself in, closed the door loudly behind him before unceremoniously flopping himself heavily onto her lounge couch with an explosive grunt.

"Hey, Kim, how's it going?"

She didn't answer him straight away. She busied herself with making coffee, then returned to the lounge, thrusting a steaming mug under the guy's nose that he took with a nodded grunt.

"So, what happened this time, Rankin?" she asked quizzically. *"Maria kicked you out again?"*

Leaning against the kitchen doorframe, sipping at her own coffee, she studied the disreputable looking man sprawled on her couch. Wrinkled blue cotton shirt that went untucked into his faded jeans. He was overweight – and presently soused.

His name was Scott Rankin and he was a Texas boy transplanted to California years back. They'd known each other for over ten years, and he was the closest thing Kimberly Eastman had to a friend. This corpulent drunk was a cameraman and videographer by trade; one of the best cameramen on the West Coast. Technically brilliant and possessed of a rare and uncanny knack - frequently obtaining an elusive perfect shot – a skill that transformed the mundane into the extraordinary. Scott Rankin could be relied upon to do that consistently - when he was sober. However, the sober times were sadly now few and far between. The man was his own worst enemy.

His drink problem had slowly escalated over the time she'd known him. Well-known and respected in the industry but his boozing had cost him several well-paying jobs making him practically unemployable of late. Rankin's alcohol abuse was beginning to take a toll on his personal life as well as his professional career, from what Kimberly had been hearing.

Rankin's head lolled back into the cushions; the harsh stink of sour bourbon seemed to have permeated the whole room since he had staggered in.

"She hates me, Kim... fuckin' bitch hates me...." he mumbled, the alcohol slurring his words.

Eastman walked over and plonked herself next to him on the couch. She put a gentle hand on Scott Rankin's meaty thigh, before replying, *"No – you're wrong. She doesn't hate you, Scotty; she just can't cope with the drinking. Maria's watching you destroy yourself slowly by inches, and she can't bear to see it. She can't stand for Abby to have to watch it either. How old is the kid now...six?"*

A melancholy smile played out on Rankin's chubby face at these words. He lifted himself to one side, extracting a wallet from his back pocket. Opening out the stained leather folder, he pulled out a small two-inch square glossy photo and held it out so they could both see.

The picture was of a handsome Hispanic woman, Maria, Rankin's long-suffering wife of several years. She had the most wonderful lush, long tresses of thick black hair, a strong chin and deep dark eyes - beautiful if in a slightly severe way. On the woman's lap she was holding a cheekily grinning dark-haired little girl, a young, softer version of the mother, with the notable exception that her lighter colored eyes that stared back were clearly those of her father.

Rankin studied the picture intently for a few seconds, before slipping it almost reverently back inside the slotted worn leather. He then closed the wallet carefully together again, holding it tightly in his hand, close to his chest. Kimberly watched him with genuine sadness as he put his head back once more, staring off into space for a few seconds; finally, he slowly closed his eyes, before speaking in gentle, soft tones.

"Abby'll be seven in two months' time. Where will her dad be then, I wonder? The way it's headin', certainly not with her or her mother..." A maudlin tear leaked out and rolled down his stubbled cheek. He was getting mawkish again. Kimberly knew Scott well enough to recognize the signs. Once he became entrenched in this kind of depressive mood the drinking really took a hold of him, and he'd be unhappily off on another prolonged bender.

She'd seen him do it many times in the past, and never with a good result. She quietly asked him: *"C'mon, seriously Scotty; what happened this time?"*

"Same as what always happens," he replied, with a non-committal half shrug.

He sat forward and rested his arms on his knees; the wallet Rankin had held so carefully was now forgotten - it slipped carelessly onto the floor. He hung his head down in his despair. Silence for a second, then the man finally mumbled again, shaking his head.

"Yep...same old reliable Scotty...I can always be counted on to come home late, loaded, and a dollar short."

He lifted his head and turned to face Kimberly with a forced grin wrinkling his round features.

"Y'know Kim, I don't know if I've ever told you this, I have a little problem with alcoholic constipation."

She looked at him enquiringly, knowing what was coming. She'd heard the line from him before many times, but decided it was safer to play along as if it were new and fresh.

"Oh, really, and what's that?" she asked.

He grinned in stupid triumph, before replying, *"I just can't pass a bar!"*

Then Rankin happily chuckled drunkenly to himself over the inane, pedantic joke. A joke that had lost its comedic value long ago. Kimberly patted him on his knee again and told him to drink his coffee.

He took a tentative sip from the ceramic mug, intently studying the wooden flooring at his feet in contemplative silence for a minute before looking up at her again. When he finally spoke, it was in a tone that elicited a substantive measure of pity from her. Kimberly knew feeling that for him was a mistake, but she couldn't help herself. She'd known him too long.

Scott Rankin, she knew, had many character flaws. She had no illusions. He was a drunk; ridiculously stupid at times - infuriatingly so in fact; he also possessed the tact and manners of an ape on occasion.

However, in times past, when Kimberly Eastman had been at her lowest, nastiest, absolute bitchiest, and had really needed a friend, he'd been there. No questions asked - he hadn't deserted her, and he'd never turned his back, like so many others had around her. You don't forget things like that - or at least she didn't.

"Kim, I really think Maria meant it this time, she was deadly serious. She says she wants me out of her life and out of Abby's. She ain't never said that before. What the hell am I going to do?" He was tearing up again. *"I love 'em more than I can say, I really do. If...."*

Kimberly interrupted him, hoping the moment was right for stark unvarnished truth. It was needed.

"Yeah, you love them more than you can say, Scotty; just not enough to say 'no' to a drink."

His silent expression radiated a sense of helplessness which spoke louder, and said more, than any words ever could. Eastman stood up. Her tone was now harsh, quite deliberately so.

"You've got to face facts, Scotty. You need to quit the booze. If you don't, it'll cost you everything. Or at least everything that means anything to you."

Rankin looked down again in shame, unable at that moment to look at the face of his old friend; he merely nodded at the lounge floor in quiescence and agreement.

Kimberly took a breath, and a little more gently this time, she added: *"Have you thought about checking into a rehab,"* she asked, *"have you got any health insurance that might pay for it?"*

Rankin shook his head. *"I had it when I was working over at Eddington's Studio...even had good dental...but not since I got my fat ass canned from there...that was three months back."*

They were both silent again. Kimberly sighed, got up from the couch and sat down close by his feet, cross legged, reached up, putting her hands up onto the baggy jeans' knees.

Looking up at him, she saw that Scott Rankin's face was a study in absolute wretchedness. Kimberly Eastman had already come to a quick decision on how she thought she might help her friend out. Damn it, she might well regret doing this later, but that would be then - and this was now. And now was when he needed her help and support, such as it was.

"How about this, Scotty," she said, a little hesitantly, choosing her words carefully, *"I might - and I do stress might - be able to swing it, to get you a job over at Hendry Corp Studios. We'd be working together, just like old times, eh buddy. You keep me honest, and more importantly beautiful on camera - I'll keep you sober and firmly on the rails."*

Rankin looked at her, his mood perceptibly lightening fractionally. Before he could say anything, she quickly added a codicil.

"But Scotty, you've gotta understand this. It's going to be your last chance to straighten up and fly right. Maybe if you can tell Maria you have a regular job again and convince her that you are honestly trying to quit the booze; well, you'd have a real shot at getting your family back...but I absolutely mean what I say. I'll vouch for you – I'll help you - just remember it's my professional ass on the line. You have got to stop drinking. That means being totally sober, 24/7. If I catch you drinking even one time, or if you let me down in any other way - then that will be all she wrote. I mean it, Scotty. There'll be no 'give me a second chance, Kim', or 'it was just this once'...'cus it won't fly with me... I won't speak to you again. You'll be dead to me. If I see you in the street, I'll spit in your shadow and cross over the road. Is it a deal?"

She now held his watery eyes with her gaze. Kimberly was deadly serious - hoped he could see and sense the hard determination within her. Kimberly was willing to help but only if Rankin was inclined to help himself. This was what tough love meant.

He put his own big hands on top of hers.

"I will, Kimberly. Swear it."

The look of sincerity in his watery eyes was genuine, for that moment at least. Time would tell. She stood up again.

"OK, just stay here then till you're straight," she said. *"And if you ever call me Kimberly again...well - just don't! With us, it's always been Kim!"* Warm, comfortable smiles were exchanged – the sort that only old friends share and can never be faked.

Scott Rankin nodded his thanks, settled back down into the couch - rolled onto his side - facing away from the room and was almost instantly snoring. Kimberly got up and pulled his shoes off, then took a spare blanket from a closet and draped it over him – then - almost as an afterthought - she kissed him lightly on his head and smoothed his hair down gently. She turned in herself, but between listening to Rankin's heavy snores and worrying what she had let herself in for, sleep was a long time in coming.

***

Kimberly's bedside alarm tone was harsh and discordant. She pulled the comforter over her head - an ineffective barrier against its insistent, annoyingly shrill bleeps. Shit, she didn't want to get up, but had no option. She hoisted herself miserably out of the warm refuge that was her bed.

The hateful tones from the alarm continued unabated, seemingly now doing it just out of pure spite. *All right,* she thought savagely, *I'm up…. I'm fucking up, damn it!*

Eastman had a sudden compulsion to viciously hit the alarm. She yielded to the impulse. A hard and well-placed blow was delivered to the top of it. At that, the machine agreeably stopped its annoyingly penetrating sounds. She rubbed her tired face. It was 07:30 in the morning and she had a meeting in a little over two hours with Bruno Harts and some 'experts' he'd coopted onto the production team; namely two writers that would be part of the creative crew for the pilot program. Apparently one of them, it had been mentioned, was the originator of the whole 'Cryptid' show concept.

She really needed to be alert again today, but thanks to Scott Rankin she'd had less than four hours of sleep; Kimberly probably looked as frightful as she felt. The apartment's bathroom was connected conveniently to the bedroom. And as she walked in, the wall mirror over the sink told its own honest, if somewhat unwelcome tale. Kimberly wearily looked into it. Her weary reflection stared back. She not only felt like crap, she looked like crap personified.

With a tired sigh, Kimberly shrugged off the sweat top, dropped it carelessly to the floor, pulled down her underwear, stepped deftly out of them, and got straight into an invigoratingly hot shower. Ten minutes of steaming water coupled with a further twenty minutes of strategic and expert makeup application – coupled with a good business suit didn't exactly fix the problem of having far less sleep than she'd needed. But it certainly helped her appearance along.

Kimberly Eastman didn't feel like death warmed over when she came out of her bedroom and into the lounge, merely elderly.

Rankin was already up and pacing about – a little disheveled but lively. He handed her a cup of coffee with one hand…in the other he was holding a couple of sheets of paper. She recognized them as her brief for the 'Cryptid' show that she'd dropped on the kitchen counter the evening before. Scotty had obviously been reading it. His hands were still shaking slightly she noticed from his previous night's excesses - Eastman diplomatically said nothing.

He crossed over to the kitchen's small breakfast island counter and leaned against it. He certainly appeared like he'd gotten himself together - but still. She looked at his mug and then back at him questioningly. He guessed her inquiry straight away. Quickly and with insistence he said: *"Nah…just coffee Kim…not a drop, I swear it. Taste for yourself, if you don't believe me."*

She relaxed a little and smiled at him before saying, *"Glad to hear it, Scotty. We'll beat this thing together."*

Rankin returned her smile, if only briefly, then turned his attention to the papers that he still held in his hand. His face said it all; she knew him so well she could read him like a book. Something was obviously bothering him.

"This is the new show they pitched to you then?"

She replied evenly, *"Yep, this is what we'll be working on..."*

He stared at her for a second, turning things over in his mind. He then put the papers up to his nose, sniffing at them like an inquisitive puppy.

"What the hell are you doing?" Kimberly asked, raising her eyebrows quizzically. She couldn't keep the amusement spilling out in her tone; Rankin really looked so silly sniffing delicately away at the sheets he held.

He brought them down from his nose, his face almost cherubic in its innocence. Then:

"What am I doin'...? Well I'll tell ya what I'm doing. I've read the 'Cryptid' show brief. I really wanted to see if it smells as shitty as it sounds. Even the detail is a bit thin, isn't it? Where are they taking you to? British Columbia is a big place, damned huge in fact...it all sounds totally half-assed if you ask me."

Eastman stepped over to him and snatched them back, cradling the papers in a protective manner to her substantial chest - as if Scott Rankin's ridicule could somehow physically harm the printed notes.

"I wasn't asking you," she chided. *"And yes, the details are a bit thin. Bruno Harts at Hendry Corp is keeping a tight lid on the whole thing. It's strictly 'need to know' for now. I think they're scared that some other company will try to get the jump on them. You know how that song goes."*

She paused for a second, before adding pointedly: *"Anyhow, don't knock it, Scotty...this,"* she said, waving the papers at him, *"is going to be my ticket to the big time - and yours as well if you have brains enough to fucking see it."* Kimberly then added in a slightly mocking tone – *"Anyhow - There's something wrong with your nose, Rankin. This isn't poop you can smell – it's that rich odor of money, success and primetime exposure!"*

Rankin scoffed loudly, replying in a voice that fairly dripped with incredulity: *"So, let me get this straight, Kim. Your 'big break' will involve you probably dressing up like a blond version of Lara Croft – your big boobs hanging out - running round in the middle of a forest somewhere in the wilds of British Columbia, riding herd on a collection of science geeks - while trying to look good for the camera and not step in the bear shit. And y'all are looking out for what now? Bigfoot? Fucking Bigfoot!"*

The cameraman couldn't contain himself. The laughter exploded out of him, loud and raucous. It was completely infectious - initially Kimberly had been annoyed at him for deriding her. But nobody could stay mad at Scott Rankin for long. She just went with it and laughed right along with him, realizing that she'd probably have to redo her mascara as a result of the tears that were running down her face. After their shared laughter had subsided, Rankin got serious again.

He walked over to her, and placed a hesitant hand on her shoulder, before saying with a genuine concern: *"In all seriousness, do you really think doing this thing is a good career move? You're a damned good journalist - one of the best I've worked with in this business, and I've worked with them all. You really are worth so much more than this junk science hypothetical 'Cryptid' crap. Honestly Kim - you need to think it through."*

Eastman put a smaller hand up and patted his arm with affection, before saying, *"You're the one who's not thought this through, Scott, but I have. Cast your mind back - way back to '86. Recall a certain syndicated hosted by Geraldo Rivera? 'The Mystery of Al Capone's Vault'?"*

A slow smile spread on Scott Rankin's chubby face.

"Oh, yeah...I remember that," he chuckled at the memory. *"A damned fiasco – total clusterfuck. I was only a little kid then, I watched it live. They spent friggin' hours digging around in the dirt with a bunch of so called 'specialists'. There was even an actual City of Chicago medical examiner on hand, just in case any bodies of some Capone gang murder victims were unearthed. All the regular programming was interrupted; and for what in the end? What did they uncover? The anticipation was high – edge of the seat stuff - was it gonna be Capone's secret stash of loot? Or perhaps the horrific site of some terrible 1920's gangland massacre?"*

Rankin laughed again before saying, *"Nope...We both know what they found,"* he added in triumph," *a stinking pile of trash, a few broken bottles, and some very, very red faces..."*

Rankin snorted again. *"Oh, I remember it, alright,"* Rankin continued, he was on a roll now, *"there was Geraldo Rivera, proudly holding up a bottle for the camera, and announcing that it had once probably held bootleg gin. Man, that guy was trying so fucking desperately to salvage some little nugget of credibility, anything at all, from the steaming pile of crap that the show was...the whole thing was a farce, Kim...a big pile of steaming horseshit."*

His mood suddenly sobered. *"Kim - this is exactly what 'Cryptid' is going to be. It's just a crazy hunt in the woods for something that doesn't exist! Ah shoot - come on girl! What you thinking? Your reputation will be permanently shot if you're involved with this sack of shit!"*

Eastman interrupted him, shaking her head: *"No. You're still missing the point, Scotty. Firstly, and importantly, it's a job... I haven't had one of those for a few months now if you hadn't noticed and I'm pretty much flat broke, same as your ass is. Secondly, they're paying me a fair amount of cash to run around the forest with, as you so indelicately put it, my 'big boobs hanging out'."*

She paused and took a swallow of her coffee – before saying, *"Besides that, far more importantly to me, this 1986 Rivera 'clusterfuck' as you called it had a massive viewing audience of over 30,000,000 people nationwide. 30,000,000! It generated millions in advertising revenue for Chicago's WGN television station - as for Geraldo Rivera, remember what happened to him? 'Cus, if you've forgotten, then I'll remind you...his career skyrocketed after the exposure from that one awful TV special. He got his own chat show that was syndicated. He personally made millions as a result! That, my friend, is precisely what I hope 'Cryptid' is going to do for me and my career. I'm meeting with some people this morning at Hendry Corp. Apparently one of them is the guy that thought the whole concept up. He's going to 'bring me up to speed' as the cliché goes."*

She looked at Rankin, and then said with more enthusiasm than he'd seen from her in a long time; *"I have a really good feeling about this, Scotty; and if you have any sense, then you'll stick around for the ride."*

Those last comments from his friend shut Rankin up. Thoughtfully, he walked back to Kimberly, extracted the 'Cryptid' brief from her hands, took it back to the couch, and began seriously studying the limited information once more with a serious eye. Smiling at her little victory, Kimberly Eastman went to the bathroom to fix her laughter tear stained make-up. She needed to get her ass moving – she had that meeting in less than an hour.

***

Bruno Harts broke off the conversation he was having upon hearing the polite tap and got up from his chair and opened the conference room door.

"Hey Kimberly, come right on in, you're nicely on time. Let me introduce you to a couple of faces you'll get to know exceedingly well over the next few weeks." With his big broad back turned to the room, he shot her a surreptitious look that she was experienced enough to instantly interpret as 'we might have problems'.

Looking quickly away from his face, Eastman walked in through the door that Bruno held open for her, giving out one of her best and most radiant smiles that was partly for Bruno Harts' benefit, but more particularly for the two men seated at the large centrally placed table.

The first thing she noted was that there was a distinct probability that these two people may not possibly be on the best of terms. If they could have sat any farther apart, they'd have been in separate rooms. Bruno came to her side and made the introductions.

"Gentlemen, please let me introduce you to 'Cryptid's' host, Ms. Kimberly Eastman. Kimberly, can I introduce you firstly to Mr. Edward Benson, Author and...what would I best describe your specialty as, Ed...Folklorist? Mythologist?"

Benson spoke, leaning forward to take Kimberly's hand, shaking it in friendly greeting, saying; *"Either really, Bruno. But if you're giving me a choice, I prefer Folkologist. It's that kind of word that conjures up visions of the settlers coming to the new world; of campfires and trekking and that genuine old pioneer spirit that we're going to channel when we are miles from any real civilization."*

Benson smiled at Kimberly, and winked. *"I'm just kidding. I made the word up. Don't give a good goddamn what you call me, to be honest. You can call me Whistler's Mother if you like guys, as long as I'm getting paid!"*

Kimberly instinctively liked Ed Benson straight away, even if his gaze had seemed to settle a foot below her eyes. He was in his early thirties, tall, almost gangly, but quite handsome with hawk-like sharp features; but it was his eyes that struck her. They were a warm deep hazel color; twin limpid pools that somehow twinkled and flashed with inner warmth and genuine humor. The same eyes she noted, with some mild irritation, that hadn't really moved away from her breasts.

"Err. Yes, quite," interjected Bruno Harts. *"And this is..."*

The other man stood up. He was short, stocky - pudgy faced but probably still just on the right side of forty. The Armani suit he wore was at least $6,000 and the hand that was proffered to shake hers had a Rolex Yacht Master wrapped around the wrist. The man brusquely cut Bruno Harts off and introduced himself.

"Good morning, Ms. Eastman. My name is Norton Bailey."

That name rang a bell dimly in her mind. Where had she heard of him before? she mused. Bailey must have seen the flash of recognition in her eyes. He said - *"You may have heard of me. I'm the author of, amongst other things, 'Myth and Super-Myth: Racial Memory Explored'. I'm also the person, who originated the 'Cryptid' show concept, and today, I can divulge more information to you; you must be very curious."*

That's who he was. She was extremely curious but decided not to let it show. She'd certainly heard of Bailey and of his book - although she'd never read it herself. Kimberly recalled vaguely it was something about how myths and legends are part of our collective race memory - or something to that effect. She also remembered that it had been on the New York Times best seller list for several months. No wonder he could afford to dress the way he did.

However, even with the expensive clothes and watch - or maybe because of them - Kimberly took an instant dislike to Bailey. He seemed polite and gracious enough – however, there was something about him that she felt just wasn't quite right. There was something off - although she couldn't put her finger on any precise reason, the guy made her uneasy, but she was professional enough to hide it.

"I'm certainly looking forward to you filling me in, Mr. Bailey. Bruno has been a little, shall we say, 'mysterious' on the subject; but obviously I comprehend the basic premise of the show."

Norton Bailey smiled and said, *"Yes, Ms. Eastman...but the reasons for Mr. Harts' unwillingness to impart too much information at this early stage are fairly obvious I would have thought? If another production company can steal the idea..."*

God, this man made her feel like she was a kid being told off by the fucking principal. Kimberly's dislike grew. She changed the subject completely, saying - *"Oh, yes Mr. Bailey, I do have to say that I've certainly heard of your book...sold well, didn't it?"* she politely asked.

He smiled at her, but the smile she noted didn't extend to his eyes which were icy blue yet quite dull. They strangely reminded her of a shark.

"Quite well, over a million and a half in the first year actually."

Harts, who was watching the exchange, began to sense that Kimberly was perhaps uncomfortable, and he broke in; *"OK, guys, intros are over, let's get down to business, please. We have a lot of ground to cover, so let's begin."* He ushered everyone into a chair.

After they were all seated, Bruno kicked the session off.

"OK folks, if I can just explain for Kimberly's benefit, this whole 'Cryptid' project was devised by Norton here as a direct result of certain research that he did for his 'Myth and Super-Myth' book. With that, I'll turn things over to him... Norton?"

Bailey cleared his throat. *"Thank you, Bruno."* He sat back and steepled his fingers, looking up at the ceiling, trying evidently to produce some sort of lame dramatic effect.

God, thought Kimberly, *this guy is so full of himself.* She glanced over at Ed Benson, who sat just a few seats away. From the expression on his face, it was obvious that he thought Bailey was full of something too.

Kimberly quickly looked away from him, suppressing a giggle, and concentrated hard on Bailey. She hoped that the embryonic smile beginning to appear on her face had been wiped away quickly enough. Thankfully it had been, and no one had noticed.

Bailey began to talk once more, and it was obvious he liked the sound of his own voice. Pompous ass, thought Eastman. Still staring at the ceiling, Bailey began to speak in the crisp clear tones of some lecturing professor.

"If you could all please take a look at the briefing notes that I have provided."

There were manila folders on the conference table. Kimberly had to admit Bailey might be an ass of the first order, but he was a thoroughly prepared one. She opened the file that was nearest to her and glanced quickly at the contents. It appeared to contain several pages of detailed notes on someplace she thought she might have heard of in British Columbia called 'The Queen Charlotte Islands' and more particularly 'Graham Island'. Kimberly didn't have much time to have more than a perfunctory glance. Bailey was forging on - she needed to concentrate on what he was saying.

"In 1996, fourteen people; to be precise, ten students and four professors from the Texas SMU...that is, of course, the Southern Methodist University...traveled to Graham Island, one of the two largest islands in the one hundred and fifty Charlotte Island archipelago. They were there essentially for a nine-week comparative religion course - studying the Haidan Indians customs and religious practices, which, as you might be aware, are native only to that part of the world."

Kimberly could feel a spark of interest beginning despite her personal misgivings about the man relating the information to them.

Bailey continued: *"On 23rd of July, they set out from the Dinan Bay logging camp for a three-day hike into the island's interior to view various Haidan religious sites that were located to the west in that general locale. The terrain, you will appreciate, in that part of the world is obviously rugged virgin forest, and the island's square acreage is quite vast... erm, it's the twenty-second largest in Canada, so I'm led to believe. However, the party was well equipped and several of them were experienced hikers. When the party did not return by the pre-arranged time on the 26th, search and rescue parties were immediately dispatched."*

Bailey paused again for dramatic effect. The theatrics were getting a little wearing, Kimberly thought. However, her curiosity was now fully aroused - she leaned in towards Bailey, asking somewhat impatiently, *"Well? What happened to them?"*

Bailey smiled infuriatingly, saying, *"I was just coming to that, Ms. Eastman. Basically, they were never found. Not a trace, not a sight; nothing at all, in fact. Not even their camping equipment was ever discovered despite an intensive month-long search of the whole area. They walked into those forests – and never came out."*

Ed Benson barked a short derisive laugh from his side of the table, drawing attention away from Norton Bailey. *"Oh, come on, man,"* he protested vehemently, *"this story is old...old news! This is like the 'Marie Celeste' or the 'Roanoke colony' of the Pacific North West backwoods world."* Benson batted a dismissive hand at Bailey. *"You see, folks, what Bailey doesn't tell you was that there was and is no evidence that anything 'mysterious' happened to them. There are any given number of explanations as to what occurred."*

Benson started ticking off points on his fingers to demonstrate and seemingly keep score at the same time. *"The area is well known for geologic instability; a fissure could have opened up. There are extensive cave systems they could have been trapped in. They could have pushed on to the other side of the island, smoked a little pot then decided to go skinny dipping and the Pacific Ocean could have claimed them..."*

Kimberly settled back in her seat and observed the interaction; this was getting very interesting and opened some genuine artistic possibilities...if she could use the combative energy of these two guys, it would make for some great TV.

"Benson, we have debated this subject at length," Bailey broke in, *"the explanations you postulate have, admittedly, some merit; but you have to accept that what the old..."* Benson suddenly stood up, placed his palms on the table and leaned in. As a defensive measure, Bailey did the same a fraction of a second later. *Jesus,* thought Kimberly, *these guys are going to start fighting in a minute!*

"Bailey," yelled Benson, *"you're a goddamned hack...the research you did on this was entirely questionable and completely subjective at best...and do you honestly have the temerity to think you're the only person who has studied this phenomenon and written a book on the subject, in this room?!"*

Bailey shouted back: *"I'm the only one who sold more than 137 copies, sir!"* They seemed to be getting dangerously nearer each other.

Kimberly thought it was time to try and defuse the situation a little. Bruno Harts, she realized, had just sat there during all this, merely observing the exchange, making no move to referee. She thought she had to do something; this was a test by him to see how she'd resolve conflict. Well, she thought, he won't be disappointed.

In placating tones, she said: *"Guys! Some rationality please. You're two intelligent men – experts in your fields – as a lay person I'm assuming you don't tend to bust each other's teeth in during a debate?"*

This comment seemed to work well and quickly took the heat out of the rapidly escalating situation. Both men looked at each other with angry glares but sat back down. Benson put out his hand towards Bailey, obviously in a gesture of supplication and an offer to continue.

Bailey took a deep breath to calm himself, and continued: *"Ms. Eastman, there is an ancient legend among the Haidan people of the 'Gogit'...the Wildman of the woods, if you like. It is widely held belief by these native peoples that this creature inhabits the forests. They also believe that this creature is responsible not only for this particular group's disappearance in 1996, but for several other well documented disappearances over the years."*

Bruno Harts cut in at this point.

"What Norton is saying Kimberly, is that in his opinion, there may be a possibility of something - some cryptozoological creature unknown to science - ranging about on Graham Island. It also may have been responsible for several unexplained disappearances over many years."

Bailey nodded in earnest agreement. Then said gleefully: *"It will be a great adventure, Ms. Eastman. A classic true-life mystery! Think what will happen if we discover what happened to those poor people in 1996. This is the plan, the concept of the whole show. We will retrace their steps to see if we can discover what happened to them, to throw some light onto their fate. And think, what about if we find evidence of this creature? What about if we even manage to capture one's image on video?"*

Ed Benson chimed in.

"Oh please! And what if we find Jimmy Hoffa living out there too? Hey Bailey, that's it! Everybody's there! The twelve-missing people, Amelia Earhart, Elvis, and they're all sharing a big warm cave with the Swiss Family Sasquatch."

If Norton Bailey's look that he shot across the table could have killed, Ed Benson would surely have been struck dead on the spot.

Kimberly decided it was time to ask a few things herself.

"So, who would be coming on this little trip? Myself obviously; Mr. Bailey & Mr. Benson, I take it?"

She looked at Bruno Harts and he nodded in agreement. Then he said: *"I have a list of the people that Mr. Bailey has requested. Other than the crew, it numbers just three more people."*

He flipped open a legal pad in front of him.

"Let's see. We have Dr. David Sterling - he's a forensic pathologist that works up in Orange County. Then there's a Dr. Olivia R. Hanna,

apparently she's taught in various universities across the States and is a renowned cryptozoologist. And finally, we have one Mr. Franklin Barr, he's a local hunter who lives on Graham Island; knows the country like the back of his hand. He'll be your insurance against the local wildlife."

Benson sniggered again. *"You mean he's our Bigfoot protection?"*

Harts lifted an eyebrow, before saying mildly: *"I was thinking in terms of the bears..."*

Ed Benson was a little subdued at that remark. *"Oh...I guess so, yeah,"* he said. *"I hadn't thought of that."*

Kimberly held up one finger, saying. *"A small request, if I may...have you allocated a cameraman for 'Cryptid' yet, Bruno?"*

Bruno Harts shook his head. *"No but we have plenty on staff. Why, you got somebody special in mind?"*

Kimberly swallowed and mentally crossed herself. Nothing ventured, nothing gained. *"Well, I was thinking about Scott Rankin."*

Bruno Harts stared at her in disbelief, before he said, *"You can't be serious? Rankin?! Sorry but absolutely not. He's a drunk and been fired from more places than..."*

Kimberly cut in, *"I know that, Bruno. But he's quit the booze. He's straight now, I know he is and he's the best video cameraman I've ever worked with..."*

She looked at Bruno Harts to measure his reaction, to see if he was wavering. She sensed that he was, slightly. *"Pretty please, Bruno? I'd feel very happy with him there...he really is the best."*

Harts sighed. *"If you're personally vouching for him and I can see him sober in my office tomorrow morning, 9am sharp, I'll talk to him. But no promises, mind! Best I can do...OK?"*

She grinned at Bruno.

"You won't regret it, you'll see."

Bruno stood up and looked down at the three people still seated in the conference room, before saying quietly to himself, *"I think I already do."*

CHAPTER FIVE

Graham Island, British Columbia

July 1996

For Bobbie, existence had become as a shattered crystal.

New nightmarish memories reflecting at her - a myriad of broken shards. Every facet contained fresh and subtle horror to be reviewed and re-experienced. Her terrified mind could make no sense out of what was happening - her world comprised of abstract terrors; times in her life, recent and long gone. Events her brain could not rationally connect.

Past and present intertwined in a symbiotic and parasitic relationship where both lived and thrived - each fed from the energy of the other. She relived the dread of being dragged backward by a stinking, faceless horror that lurked in the darkest shadows. She could feel the powerful grip around her ankles, the forest floor debris digging into raw flesh. In her tortured mind the vista changed yet again...she was suddenly fifteen at Lake Whitney, swimming in the water on a school field trip - happily splashing about - laughing and fooling around with friends. Bobbie had surface-dived – kicked hard once submerged - gone far deeper underwater than she had intended. The pleasant sun-warmed surface of the lake suddenly became a murky icy swirl that sucked her further down in an unseen powerful current. She began to panic. In the freezing water, arms and legs quickly cramped - became unresponsive - lead weighted and numb. She fought to hold her breath; struggling to swim to the light-dappled surface with limbs that no longer seemed to belong to her - actually managing to hold on for a few seconds before her oxygen starved lungs desperate to reflexively breathe sucked in the cold, dirty, green-tinged lake water. The traumatic shock of the liquid entering her lungs was so severe the teenage girl tried to cough, vomit and urinate simultaneously.

Bobbie was drowning and it was an agony. Someone swam down to her - grabbed the dying teen by the hair and pulled her back up to the light...her face broke the surface – change –

A new scene opened out in her jumbled memory. She listened once more to the terrible squeals and screams as George McKinney was torn apart. The vile scents of fresh blood - pungent sweat - foul excreta that leaked from bodily orifices at the moment of death - change –

Now she was a petrified young kid in North Texas years past – it was deepest night and her head was buried into her pillow to lessen the roaring sound of the thunder and howling roar of the wind - the pounding rain joined in, a screaming fugue, sound layered upon sound - noise that deafened the young Bobbie to the rest of the world. Then her white-faced mother was yanking the child out of bed, bellowing at her to 'c'mon baby', and that 'it was on the ground'…pulled into the closet with a comforter wrapped around her - a pathetic shield of feathers against the storm's fury as the immensely powerful twister brushed so close to the house the walls had literally bowed and breathed in and out - change –

Bobbie was deep in a thick tangle of trees again as she ran and struggled for her life through an impossible snarl of branches and brambles that tore at clothes and delicate skin with equal impunity - change -

She was now in the blackness of the forest, cowed and dazed, too terrified to protest what was happening. Feeling utterly helpless she was lifted; hoisted up by an unimagined and irresistible brutish force and carried swiftly away with effortless ease.

It felt that the madness would never end. Was she alive or dead? Was this hell truly hell or was she merely insane?

Bobbie unhappily knew that she was neither dead nor mad; at least not yet. Instinctively the girl understood that if no effort was made on her part to grasp reality, forcibly dragging her mind out of this fractured purgatory that her consciousness was manufacturing, then madness would certainly follow for real. With a supreme effort of will, Bobbie started with the little things.

Small thoughts and sensations that could anchor her ripped and wandering mind to the present - the here and now - perhaps then she could use that knowledge; to discover something of the true nature of her present situation…

Taste - she could taste her own blood and traces of sour vomit in her mouth; it was unpleasant, acrid and foul.

Touch - she could feel greasy, matted coarse hair, hard solid bone, and just a hint of the incredibly powerful muscles and thick sinew that pulsed and writhed under her trembling, questing fingers.

Smell - whatever was carrying her had a repulsive stench – a stink of death. There was also the sweet hint of vibrant animal musk in almost equal measures.

Hearing – Bobbie concentrated hard - all around her, she discovered, was a cacophony of sound; the crisp noise of foliage being forced aside as the unnamable things pushed through it. Low harsh grunts and obscene growls - laced into it all were odd snatches of other more familiar nighttime forest noises.

Sight - this was the one sense she feared the most. The girl, up till this moment, had kept her eyes tightly closed. Bobbie was too afraid to directly look upon the features of the creature that had taken her.

But she knew it was time to confront the nightmare; to stare it in the face and be strong in the Lord's gaze.

That was her intention as she opened her eyes wide and forced herself to look around…and was instantly frustrated by an absence of any useful light. Bobbie could barely see anything. Even the immediate surroundings were lost to her within the deep forest canopy. The foliage was so thick that light couldn't penetrate.

So, all she knew for certain was that she had been slung over a huge shoulder - and was now being carried away deeper into the interior of the forest in the company of nightmarish gigantic beings.

They truly were otherworldly monsters in every true meaning of the word, she thought coldly. Inhuman brutes devoid of any pity or soul – things that had savagely butchered eleven people in cold blood. What was their design for her? The only possibility that readily occurred to her was she was being hauled away to God-knows-where as a sack of groceries. She was fresh food; a warm meal to be consumed when the need arose.

Bobbie was exhausted - emotionally burnt out with panic and fear from the last several hours to even bother crying or screaming at this horrific revelation. The best she could hope for was that they'd kill her quickly – not toying with her as they had with poor George.

Time passed. She may have dozed off intermittently with fatigue - she couldn't be certain. The only certainty was that there was no hope or prospect of escape; the young girl just prayed to Jesus that she wouldn't suffer too much before she was eaten. Before her despair could get too great a grip upon her, Bobbie forced herself to try to consider other things. To take her mind off her impending slaughter; to think instead of feel.

She was in considerable physical discomfort. Her fear had mercifully blocked many things from her consciousness. Perhaps it was part of a body's survival mechanism. The girl tried to rationalize her predicament; long delayed sensations of pain were unwelcomely pushing into her brain.

The position that she was being carried in meant her midsection was compressed uncomfortably – her whole upper torso was confined against a solid mass of bone and muscle - the impossibly large span of her captor's huge shoulder.

Bobbie's legs hung down - her knees were exposed through torn, filthy jeans. They had been rubbed raw by friction against the creature's coarse hair-covered hide. Her head and arms meanwhile, dangled down on the other side. Any exposed skin that had come into prolonged contact with the wiry hair was likewise chaffed and abraded. These things' tough hair-covered hides were perfectly adapted for moving through this kind of environment. But holy God, the smell from it! It was almost beyond description. The foul stink was unbearable. One further thing she noticed. It was beginning to get lighter. The creatures must have been traveling for quite a while she reasoned, because dawn was now long past, and the sun was higher on the horizon.

Looking directly down, the girl could now dimly pick out the forest floor. Even with the slow swaying motion of the thing that carried her, Bobbie estimated her head must be at least seven feet up in the air. Sweet Jesus, how big were these things?

Then all motion suddenly ceased as if by an unspoken agreement amongst them. The group of what were essentially unseen creatures – otherworldly beings which traveled practically noiselessly around her in the shadowy dark of the heavily forested island began to make a weird collective noise. Sounds she had not heard from them before. It was a low noise - barely audible - high pitched – it undulated in tone so it would carry for a considerable distance within the trees. An eerie sound - keening and disturbing.

Bobbie found that despite her already terrified condition, it still had the effect of making the short hairs on the back of her neck stand up.

Then the resonance was answered in kind from an indeterminate distance away in the gloom. The same uncanny, rising and falling high pitched hooting wail that chilled and frightened her.

What did it mean? Bobbie wasn't sure, but one thing she was sure of - there were several of these terrible creatures out there, concealed in the deep woods. Was she being hauled back as a feast for those others?

She was resigned to her fate now - beyond caring…the Lord in his infinite wisdom had decided what was to happen. What would be would be, according to His will and design. As the last strange sounds echoed into silence there was an unspoken communal understanding. As one, the creatures began to move forward once more. With the ambient light increasing, Bobbie's curiosity wasn't replacing her fear – but it was not to be denied either. She was now able to discern odd glimpses of the creatures.

The girl had caught the occasional stolen sight of them as they glided with a silent effortless ease through the thick canopy of trees.

Of the one that carried her, she could make out nothing.

Hefted around like a carcass of beef didn't lend itself to view anything - other than the creature's shaggy, stinking pelt - little else could be seen of it. The others, though: Bobbie caught tantalizing fearful peeks as she craned and twisted her neck up to wonder at them as they flitted through odd pools of early morning mist and the grey light that spilled through gaps in the green leafy canopy that stretched above.

They moved with a serpentine boneless grace for such huge creatures, effortlessly going from space to space - yet taking complete advantage of any cover that the environment provided them.

They seemed to do it all totally without thought, as easily and naturally as breathing. On occasion, for a reason only known to them, one of their number would drop down on all fours and suddenly surge ahead of the rest of the hulking, slinking shadows with a blurring speed. When they did this, they were almost completely silent in their movement and fearsome in their grace and agility. Bobbie realized that creatures possessed of these kinds of uncanny abilities would be practically invisible in the nighttime of the deep woods – or even the daylight.

It was little wonder that these shadowy wraiths of the forest, whatever they were, had remained undiscovered. God had apparently endowed them with an almost supernatural ability to remain undetected. The light had now improved to the point that she could get a good look at them, to properly distinguish their features. And what she saw and observed frightened her even more than she had already been. Bobbie had thought of these monsters as just further examples of God's diverse creations - animals; bizarre perhaps, but as yet still unidentified. However, she now came to the horrifying conclusion that whatever these things were, they were not animals - at least not as she understood the definition of the word. Daylight was properly established upon the island now and Bobbie could discern the creatures quite clearly. They seemed to have an established behavior or perhaps a preference to keep to the darker places; areas that were still bathed in shadow. They were quite magnificent in a terrifyingly odd way.

The average height of them, she estimated, was at least nine feet tall when upright. Some were just a little smaller - a couple of them were considerably larger, she noted. Their bulky appearance was probably more to do with the fact that they were covered in a thick pelt of greasy and unkempt, wiry hair which varied only slightly from a dark brown to shades of charcoal, blended in from top to bottom – excellent natural camouflage. Their arms were totally out of proportion to the rest of their bodies - far longer than any human's could have been. Their huge leathery hands had opposable thumbs - and were almost level with their knees. They walked hunched forward slightly and tended to 'plod' along whilst in this attitude. They had a rolling, swaying gait whilst moving upright on their legs - awkward and shambling; much like a huge ape would be although their legs were not bowed out as a primate would have been. But when utilizing their abnormally long arms to accelerate away, those abnormally long arms became a second pair of legs, their speed and grace were incredible to witness. Akin to the difference between a seal's clumsiness on land compared with their speed and maneuverability in water. But it was their heads that captivated Bobbie's attention - an elongated tall dome shape becoming a blunt point at the apex - completely hair covered. So much so, that their ears were fully concealed, and whatever auditory organs they had were not apparent. But it was their faces that enthralled and frightened the young woman the most. Bobbie had half expected them to have the flattened facial featuring of a gorilla or other large ape, judging by the rest of their bodies.

But when one came close to her, so near that it had stared at her for a few long seconds, she felt her stomach drop and her bowels turn loose and watery. One of the larger creatures within the group had noticed that she had her head up and was looking curiously around. It suddenly decided to do some observations of its own.

One moment it was at the limit of the periphery of her vision several yards away, adjacent to her position slung across her captor's shoulder. With an incredible turn of speed, utilizing all fours, it covered the distance that separated them in scant seconds. Its face was suddenly less than a foot from Bobbie's, its breath was rancid and foul, so bad she could almost taste its filthiness. She wanted to gag with the stench but suppressed the reflex with a supreme effort.

Petrified and unable to meet its eyes directly, she instead looked at the lower half of its face. The lower jaw protruded pugnaciously out - as it opened its mouth slightly she was proffered a glance of the terrible teeth that were contained inside the gaping wet, red maw. They were vicious, wickedly pointed. Some were fang-like, designed to puncture, while others were serrated or so it looked like. They were a carnivore's teeth – primarily evolved for cutting, rending and tearing away flesh from bone. They looked like they belonged to a shark rather than to any omnivorous mammalian ape.

But Bobbie hadn't needed to look inside one of the monster's mouths to understand what their dietary requirements were. She'd already horrifyingly seen the evidence of that firsthand. She closed her eyes tight in terror, unable to look further. However, what happened next gave her no choice.

An immense hand, rough and callused, cupped the lower portion of her face and effortlessly lifted her head and shoulders up. The stunned girl's hands instantly rested on the ridge of the creature's shoulder that was carrying her, as she had to try to brace and support her neck the best way she could. The monstrous figure that was carrying her had slowed down and now stopped moving, apparently somehow sensing its larger fellow's presence behind it. This is it, thought Bobbie dully - my last mortal seconds on this Earth. She began to pray; under her breath she mouthed an entreaty that begged her Lord God to have mercy and please take her soul swiftly. She hurriedly tried to prepare herself for the terrible agony that was certain to come. Unbelievably though, absolutely nothing happened to her. The huge hand kept a grip on her face. It was as if time had suddenly stopped its ceaseless motion and the world had become paused and still. She opened her eyes again. Her breath caught, and then stopped in her chest in wonderment and shock. The eyes that stared back at her were enormous. The pupils were enlarged beyond the point of reason. But that wasn't what was so shocking to her. It was that the orbs that stared deeply and inquisitively back at her - they were a clear and shocking cornflower blue. The eyes that thoughtfully regarded her were not like any other animal's on the face of the planet. Even with the anatomical differences, those eyes were at the very least almost human-like - and they clearly possessed what must be approaching human intelligence. Bobbie suddenly remembered to breathe again. And with that, the being - for with this new perspective she was now having difficulty in thinking of these forest dwellers as merely creatures - released her face and bounded silently away.

She didn't know what to think now…were they just animals or something else entirely? Could they maybe understand her or be reasoned with? Was there any hope of her salvation and survival if they possibly could? She hardly dared think it, but the smallest, faintest ember of hope began to glow deep inside her. With a newfound energy and concentration, Bobbie now studied them even more intently and closely; looking carefully for true signs of intelligence as they moved forward.

Indeed, there was nothing random or instinctual about their progress. Each movement appeared to be precise – exactly planned out.

After all, a herd of animals would amble along in a given direction, some parts of the group inevitably straying from the path inquisitively with an innate stupidity, dimly exploring the new surroundings before rejoining the group. A mindless meandering process that would repeat itself over and over again until the eventual destination was reached.

These beings, however, showed no sign of a slow-witted bovine mentality.

There was some silent communication going on between them, the method and process yet unfathomable to Bobbie. From observing them only for a short time it was abundantly clear that every move was planned. Not one member of the group strayed from the route that was pre-determined by some means she could not work out. Every individual seemed to have a function in the journey. Watching them move along reminded her of something she couldn't quite place. It was a few minutes till it suddenly occurred to her - old newsreels she had watched as a kid. The ones from America's involvement in Vietnam; of the way that army patrols moved cautiously and smoothly through hostile jungle territory - that's what their movements put her in mind of. Not exactly, of course. It lacked any tight discipline or formation. But unmistakably that was what was occurring.

Then things changed. Bobbie could almost feel a tremor of anticipation that was running through the group. They were arriving at their ultimate destination, she instinctively felt it. The majority of them suddenly sped off, streaking past her field of vision towards something. The topography was steeply uphill now and the vegetation was getting sparse and the ground slightly rocky. Her captor's own plodding pace suddenly increased exponentially, desperately hurrying to get out of this new open terrain.

With a movement that knocked the breath from her, making Bobbie gasp in shock and fright, it suddenly dropped forward but without relinquishing its grip on her and sped away. It used its free arm to assist itself in an uneven but extremely rapid gait up the steep slope towards she knew not what. One of the others she saw in her bouncing vision – possibly the one that had looked at her earlier - remained a few yards behind, scanning all around it as it moved slightly more slowly upwards, acting as a lookout for the rest.

Then instantly, all around her grew dark.

The terrified young woman was now in a low dank passage or tunnel that went steeply downwards, leading seemingly into the very bowels of the Earth. The only light was the cave entrance, and like any hope she had previously gained, it was rapidly receding from her.

And as the huge bulk of the last of the group entered the passage, even that precious light was all but gone.

And the softly sobbing Bobbie was carried relentlessly down into hell.

CHAPTER SIX

California

June 2019

Bailey turned his head and watched through half-closed lids as the young and deliciously lithe Asian girl - still clothed for the moment - moved across the room to the large hotel bed. She then slid herself with slow, seductive movements along its surface to get next to him. The attractive youth that was with her had already removed his own shirt and had begun to seductively fondle the front of his tight jeans, squeezing at his genitals in self-stimulation as he watched. Of course, it was all part of the act; the performance Norton Bailey wanted and had paid top dollar for - and as such, should be savored by him.

Norton ignored the youth, at least for the present. His time would assuredly come later. At the thought, he licked his already wet slack lips in anticipation of the young man and what he would have him do.

But pleasure postponed is pleasure prolonged, he thought languidly. He forced his musings away from him and back to her. She now lay on her side, close to him, without coming into full contact - per his precise instructions.

The young slut really was quite beautiful, he thought; her hair a shining, cascading silky waterfall of obsidian strands that flowed past her shoulders and over an expensive white blouse. Her face a pale oval and the almond shaped eyes were warm dark pits of sensuousness. She really was perfect, flawless, and so was her handsome young partner; neither of them looking much older than fifteen as he had specified; but there again, Bailey mused with a trace of irony, they should be all that he wanted, and more, for two-thousand-eight-hundred fucking dollars an hour.

The older man lay on his back in just his jockey shorts, hands behind his head, while the girl traced a long delicate finger in a languorous figure of eight around both of his already erect nipples.

Her body had the deliciously sweet yet subtle odor of jasmine.

Now he took his hands from behind his head and roughly pulled open her blouse; time to see those tiny boobs, he thought.

She had no bra on, again as specified, and her own nipples were dark, large and hard, however her actual breast tissue was almost non-existent. Perfect!

Bailey pulled her small body down to his face and flicked his tongue on one of the hard nubs of flesh, before biting down hard, savoring the feeling of it, the power he had over her. The girl tensed at the sudden pain, but wisely made no sound. She'd better not, the bitch, he thought. He was paying a lot for this! In response to her obvious discomfort, Bailey felt a stir in his penis; his scrotum tightened up and he breathed a little heavier…but it was all too soon, he scolded himself. Norton mentally forced his erection to subside by thinking of other thoughts that did not involve the Asian whore with the perfect tits; his mind shifting to other matters that weighed on him - like the soon to be success of his latest venture.

Bailey knew that things were falling into place now. Both Hannah and Sterling had agreed to be part of the 'Cryptid' program and Franklin Barr, the hunter who actually lived on the island was a sure thing. The only encouragement any of them had properly needed was payment. He smiled to himself. Prosperity truly was the great seducer.

Norton rolled over, ignoring the girl again for now, and instead studied the young, handsome male. He clicked his fingers and motioned him to come closer; the youth instantly obeyed Bailey's imperious summons. This was real power…the greatest aphrodisiac, and his flaccid penis grew instantly hard again at the thought. Norton Bailey had come to the inevitable conclusion quite early on in his life - that money could get the things someone truly wanted. Everything had a price, and anything could be purchased. It wasn't the good-looking people or the lucky people, or the intelligent people, or even the survivor types that did really well in life.

It was the rich.

If you had money, then practically anything was possible. No experience could be denied or indeed ever should be denied to oneself. And all it ever took was money. All things and anyone had a price ticket attached; people could be readily controlled with the power that pure wealth brought with it. These two youngsters that Bailey held captive to his wealth were a prime example of that truism. In a few days, he mused, once ensconced on Graham Island along with his troupe of assembled marionettes, Bailey would deftly pull the strings, and consequently would significantly add to his already considerable fortune and fame. How was this possible? Well that was simplicity in itself, really.

It was because he knew things; dangerous secrets that most of the others involved in this little undertaking could never suspect.

And, as Norton Bailey fondly accepted - the knowledge he possessed, once seeded on that fertile soil, would bring forth a rich crop indeed.

He sighed inwardly. It was a pity though; that this crop must be watered and nurtured with human blood…but such was the way of the world.

After all, no achievement of any greatness or consequence was ever forthcoming without a little sacrifice from someone. And naturally, that someone wouldn't be him.

Happily, his own personal risk in this venture would be minimal; he'd already made quite sure of that. Bailey had every step of this titanic chess game properly planed; every move plotted with precision.

Grabbing the girl, he easily lifted her across himself, so she ended up on the same side of the bed as the boy. He ordered her what to do with the youth. Hurriedly, sliding off the mattress and dropping quickly on her knees, she obeyed his command. Yes, Bailey reflected smugly as he watched her bobbing head; life is good. And such is power.

***

Ed Benson was perched on his ass in his garage and was smoking a cigarette. He balanced his tall frame on an old discarded stool, carelessly flicking ash to the floor and was mournfully regarding several stacks of books that stood mutely in one corner - neglected piles that had slowly gathered dust for almost two years now - silent reminders - tangible testaments to a dream that had only ever been half realized.

Ostensibly he had wandered into the space to dig out his old hiking boots and jacket; not that he'd need them, though. Hendry Corp had generously promised a complete wilderness ensemble to everyone as part of his or her participation in the show. What that meant exactly, he wasn't quite sure - but he had a good, if somewhat cynical idea on that particular subject.

Probably some leftover shit from a late-night tacky infomercial they'd run sometime in the past…he could picture it clearly now in his mind's eye:

'This handcrafted, superb, rugged outdoor jacket is comprised of a special secret blend of fibers and plastics; materials known only to our top researchers…and is guaranteed not to let in water, cold, or wind…and all this is yours for an amazingly low one-off special TV order price of…wait for it… only $39.99…yes, you heard it right! And if you order within the next three hours, we'll include this amazing pair of socks constructed of…'

Yeah, thought Benson with a chuckle, *guaranteed my ass.* The only thing that probably was really assured was that it would shrink; the colors would run and the whole thing would almost certainly fall apart at the seams after the first heavy rain shower.

He'd appeared on several programs for various TV companies over the years in his capacity as a credited anthropologist and erstwhile folklorist; they were cheap-assed bastards to a man, in his experience.

On reflection, he decided, it wouldn't be such a bad idea to really find his old hiking stuff out, after all - he might well need it.

Grinding the butt of his cigarette under his heel, he eased himself up and nonchalantly sauntered over to one of the book piles and scooped one up off the top. He first brushed the thin layer of dust from the face of it with his palm, blew on it, and then studied the title:

'Mythology and Myth: A modern perspective' by Dr. Edward Benson.

He flipped it over and there was his own face mockingly smiling back at him from the rear of the shiny dust jacket. Without giving it further thought, he petulantly tossed it back onto the stack – perhaps a little harder than he had intended to. It slid straight off the top and fell noisily to the concrete floor. He left it where it lay. There it was, on the ground, just like all his other dreams and ambitions. Ed Benson was forty-two now, well out of the last flush of youth and fast entering dreaded middle-age.

He was beginning to reach a certain time in life, a realization that there might be fewer years ahead for him than he'd already had. That sobering thought didn't particularly frighten Benson as such; but it did sadden him a little. He'd never married, had no kids and had been quite happy in his chosen role as one of life's perpetual wanderers. His specialist bent, academically speaking, was anthropology, and that was his doctorate.

With his enthusiasm and extensive knowledge of the subject, he'd drifted from one place to another around the States; taught a little, lectured some…hell, he'd even managed to put enough by to purchase a small house and fund a run of his own book, when no educational publisher had had the good sense or foresight to pick it up.

And what had happened to most of the results of that print run?

Well, they were to be seen here stacked up right in front of him. Benson had sold twenty some-odd copies of his Opus Magnus to his friends. The other one hundred and ten had gone to members of various audiences over the last two years, when he had been a guest speaker on various field related subjects in the winter months on the college and university circuit in California. That's where he knew Bailey from. He despised him so much…illiterate goddamn moron! They'd butted heads as guests several times on various panels over the years. Shit, cursed Benson to himself, the guy was nothing - a conceited, pompous, complete and utter fucking asshole with delusions of grandeur. The ideas and theories that he pontificated on were reactionary, un-provable and mainly populist's bullshit!

But his brand of fantastical 'creature' crap oddly appealed to the masses, - he'd tapped into a vein - captured their limited imagination and did actually sell books, Benson had to admit; copious amounts, in fact…but that didn't make him friggin' right! Hell - it didn't even make him a passable scholar!

Upper echelons of academia both despised and envied him; they shunned Norton Bailey for his views and bizarre unscientific hidden 'creature' theories, and yet at the same time courted him for his fame and wealth…the essential dichotomy of being. Yes, his books had certainly made the sonofabitch rich, Benson conceded dourly to himself. He looked at his own stacks of dust gathering failure that were piled up in front of him.

And the more he looked at them, the greater the resentment for Norton Bailey.

He reluctantly tore himself away from glaring at them and pushed away his dark thoughts before beginning a proper hunt for his old jacket and boots.

This gig might not be a total loss, he reasoned. If nothing else, this trip to Graham Island was certainly going to leave that smug bastard Bailey with egg on his fat face! Benson chuckled to himself as he imagined what lame ass excuse the pompous dickwad would come up with, as to why no creatures, not even any small evidence of their existence, were discovered by them. Despite all the hi-tech equipment they'd be taking along and with a team of so-called experts. Yep…this was going to be funny, smiled Benson to himself. He was really going to enjoy watching the high and mighty Norton Bailey squirm in abject failure. Hell, there were plenty of positives to this 'Cryptid' business now that he was thinking about it!

Like the money these TV dumbass fools were paying him personally was good - Olivia Hannah was going along. He didn't know her extremely well, but at least he liked her. Dr. Hanna's interests ran to the bizarre and esoteric - she'd been a fellow guest panelist on the same circuit on several occasions over the last five years.

Her actual doctorate was in - of all things - theology; but her passion for cryptozoology had blossomed if the rumors were anything to go by. She'd recently lost a tenure as theology professor; he'd heard on the grapevine, as a direct result of those other interests. In fact, Benson had heard her new affectionate nickname around her campus was now 'The Monster Mamma'. However, Olivia Hannah was a good egg. From listening to her over the years she obviously thoroughly knew her subject - even if that subject was all a bit 'off the wall' at times.

Then he cheered himself up a little, with another doubly happy thought that suddenly occurred to him. Damn, he really was getting older! How the hell could he have overlooked those? The truth was, he hadn't for one moment.

In just one month, Kimberly Eastman's amazing tits were going along for the ride too.

***

Scott Rankin turned back to the house that was bathed in bright yellow morning California sun and waved goodbye.

Abby was still at the downstairs window, her fat little face pressed hard against the glass, her breath making a slight film against the clear barrier, her chubby arm waving back frantically. Maria though, he noted sadly, was already gone out of sight. He couldn't really blame her. She'd been dragged down this rough road before with him many, many times; a rocky journey replete with pleas and promises, of threats and tears.

But this time he actually meant it; he really was determined to change. He wanted to be the man he was when she had first met him. No damn it - he didn't. His true heart's desire was to be a person he'd never been before; well, at least not since he was a kid. A sober standup guy whose life didn't revolve around where his next drink was coming from.

He waved one final time to his baby girl, then opened the car door, got into his vehicle, squeezed himself behind the wheel, started up and pulled away without looking back. He determined that the next time he laid eyes on them he'd be a very different Scott Rankin. Kim had somehow talked her boss at Hendry Corp into taking him on as cameraman for the 'Cryptid' program, bless her. Although he'd done his part convincing Bruno Harts that he was clean and sober - he didn't forget that she'd really gone to bat for him on this one, and that opportunity had now given Rankin a chance. By all that was holy he wasn't going to let anyone down. Not her, not Maria, not himself; but more importantly, not Abby.

He turned on the radio. The song playing on KIFM was Bill Withers 'Lovely Day'…and if that wasn't a good omen, then Rankin didn't know what the fuck was! Yep, it was a lovely day, all things considered. He hadn't had a drink for a while now, and he had a job that paid well above scale. True, he was going to be away on location in the wilds for ten days or so - but that was ten more precious days to add on to the several weeks he already had away from the bars, booze and temptation.

Singing loudly and outrageously off-key, Scott Rankin happily negotiated the Freeway on-ramp and merged with the heavy commute traffic on his way to pick up Kimberly Eastman…

"...and I know it's gonna be, da ta da dah, a lovely day...."

***

Bruno Harts gave the appearance of a very happy man when he entered the room – he had every reason to be. They were already three months into it. 'Cryptid' promotional teasers had been airing over the networks for the past 3 weeks. Kimberly Eastman looked great in them - she had gotten a very positive sample audience reaction. People were intrigued by the mysterious vibe of it - the whole idea had obviously tapped into a rich vein - press inquiries and magazine articles about the show were generating even further interest. It was snowballing. Advertisers were clamoring for a piece of it and Bruno was increasingly aware that this show was going to be a massive hit even before it aired. As he made his entrance, the already muted muttering conversations tailed off into an expectant silence.

With a quick sweeping glance - huge hands clasped in front of him - he quickly took in the normally spacious conference room which now had become full with the addition of seven people - including himself - and their accompanying luggage. Added to that were various items of camping gear and other specialized technical equipment needed for the show - most of it electronic in nature. It made for a crowded space.

The big man grinned at them broadly - opening his arms out, he exuded a genuine bonhomie.

With tones of genuine enthusiasm he said: *"Well, good morning to you all! Great to see everyone together at last...and raring to go! You haven't had the opportunity to do more than meet and greet each other - but I'd like to personally thank all of you for being onboard with the 'Cryptid' project, which is essentially a real first for us here at Hendry Corp Productions. Don't be too intimidated by the mountain of equipment and things you see around us. You won't be lugging it yourselves, at least not yet. You'll only be carrying the traveling essentials for now."* Harts noted the relief on at least three people's faces at that last snippet. He continued, *"The majority of the gear and everything else that will be needed will be awaiting you at the departure point; and of course, as you know, that's the Dinan Bay logging camp. The logistics are all in place. The gear is being transported to the island separately by carrier. When you arrive, you'll have five days there to check out all the equipment again, familiarize yourself with the route - get to know each other a little better; and then you'll be on your way."*

Bruno paused, smiling beatifically at the assembled group.

"I'll now hand you over to Norton, who's made this all possible. I'm sure he has a few words to say to you all...Norton?"

At that invitation, Bailey quickly trotted his way to the front of the room to join Bruno Harts, obviously trying to appear self-important; but standing next to the impressive bigger man he looked like a small, ridiculously fat puppy – a little dog about to chase his own tail in excitement.

Several of the people assembled politely stifled giggles at the absurd sight - with the notable exception of Ed Benson. He just laughed out loud. Bailey huffily chose to ignore him; almost that is. To his credit he deflected with, *"Thank you all again for agreeing to be here; even you, Dr. Benson."*

Ed bowed low in mock salutary acknowledgment at the comment.

Everyone laughed at this, with Bailey rather than at him. Sensing a small victory, Norton pressed on with renewed vigor, rubbing his hands together in a contained enthusiasm.

"This is going to be a wonderful, exciting voyage of discovery for us. For me personally, I genuinely feel there will be a validation of my much-maligned theory that a colony of as yet unclassified creatures is thriving in British Columbia - as I believe they are in many other parts of the planet's wilderness regions - but more especially in the dense forests of Graham Island!"

In the meantime, Kimberly Eastman was doing her job – she wasn't observing Norton Bailey as he spoke – a deliberate act on her part. She had moved forward unnoticed by the rest and was casting a critical eye around the others - gauging their reaction to what Bailey was saying. First impressions of them as individuals were what she had expected.

Benson had a sneer of condescension on his face - she had privately been made aware by Bruno Harts that there was no love lost between the folklorist and Bailey.

David Sterling, the medical examiner and pathologist, who she hadn't really had chance to converse with, had a look of complete bored indifference. She had no illusions about his involvement. It was financial - pure and simple. He had already been categorized by her as a 'hard science' guy. That was good though - Kimberly could use that objectively to balance some of the other more fervent views; a strategy was already forming loosely in her brain.

Scott Rankin wasn't really listening, she noted with no surprise. He was in full tech mode now and was seated at the back of the room, meticulously examining some electronic component or other that was necessary to his trade - he looked every inch the professional - he really was one of the best at what he did.

However, it was Dr. Olivia Hannah she couldn't get a handle on.

When working on any kind of ensemble project like this it was necessary for the presenter to orchestrate the team; to know who'd say what - but more importantly to know just when to let them say it. That's what made for great TV – and to achieve that, any good producer or director had to have an instinct for it - the innate ability to quickly sum up people and predict who'd be the right person for the right moment. Everything had to balance – that's what made some TV moments rise above the mundane, propelling them into a whole new level of excellence.

Kimberly was convinced with this explosive mix of characters, the untamed location and the outlandish subject matter coupled with a genuine, honest to God mystery, she couldn't fail. Hannah bothered Kimberly. Her bio said the Dr. was forty-one – a year older than Eastman; however, she appeared at least ten years older – a tall grey-haired woman, severe in her features, cropped hair - wearing little or no make-up. Olivia Hannah had sat silently and politely listened intently to Bailey's speech; but her expression or body language gave nothing away - absolutely no hint of her internal thinking. She was unquantifiable – almost flat - and those reserved characteristics wouldn't make for good screen time. Boring, not to put a finer point on it.

Still, Kimberly decided, there was plenty of time to work it all out. If necessary, she could subtly arrange it with Scotty to sideline the woman altogether. Let's just wait and see how it works out, she thought.

But with what transpired next, things took an unexpected turn for the better. Ed Benson sidled up to Eastman as she was contemplating the group dynamics and tried one of the lamest pick-up lines she'd heard for years:

"Well, here I am, Kimberly. What were your other two wishes?"

Oh, Jesus, how cheesy! Before Kimberly could respond with two of her own favorite words, Olivia Hannah came to the rescue. She maneuvered her tall frame between them.

"Oh, I'm heartbroken! And here I was, Edward, thinking that I was your dream date!" Benson smiled with more than a little chagrin – nevertheless, he took the less than subtle hint. As this avenue was firmly closed off by the intervention of Olivia Hannah, Ed Benson sloped off to busy himself in what was obviously his second favorite pastime - annoying the shit out of Norton Bailey.

Dr. Olivia R. Hannah was nothing like the severe persona that she projected, Kimberly Eastman soon realized. As the tall woman unexpectedly put her arm around her shoulders protectively, guiding her to another part of the room, it felt quite motherly, even though Kimberly was older than she was.

"I can see we're going to have to be friends on this excursion," said Hannah. *"Please don't mind Edward. He's a sleaze on occasion and can be a complete rascal, but his heart really is in the right place. He's actually quite a nice fellow when you get to know him."*

Kimberly laughed - she was warming to this tall, austere looking woman..

"We're just two women together, eh Dr. Hannah? Fighting off the wolves...or should I say the wolf?"

"Well," returned Hannah dryly, patting Kimberly's wrist, *"three women in fact...I really think we should count Norton."*

Kimberly laughed out loud again, that was too funny! Olivia Hannah was quite wonderful! They were going to become fast friends; Eastman could instinctively feel it even after this short time.

"Let's sit down over here and get to know each other, Kimberly; is it OK to call you Kimberly?"

Eastman nodded. *"Sure - Kimberly's fine, what do I call you?"*

Hannah answered, *"Olivia or Hannah - either one works for me."* Then she added in a quiet, conspiratorial tone, *"And when I know you better, Kimberly, you can call me something else."* And with that odd remark from Dr Olivia Hannah, the two women left the room.

CHAPTER SEVEN

Graham Island, British Columbia

July 1996

Bobbie didn't want to die like this - not alone in the dark - away from God's sight and mercy. Bobbie carried a secret dread inside her, a fear held over from when she had almost drowned in that murky lake water in Texas a few years past. She had honestly believed that if the Lord couldn't see her when she passed from this earthly realm - if He didn't witness her death - then she'd be lost to him for eternity.

She'd be an everlasting pariah, one cursed through no fault of her own to wander for a troubled eternity. A miserable wretched spirit. Forever barred from entering the kingdom of heaven. The young girl had prayed hard as she was carried away from the light into the blackness by these denizens of hell.

Praise be to the Lord God; He must have heard her entreaty and taken pity on her poor soul. Unbelievably to her at least, she was still very much alive. Being alive, however, was subjective at the moment. She hadn't eaten, or far more importantly, drank now for several hours. She was starting to feel woozy – partly because of the mental privations she suffered and the exhaustion she felt. Bobbie had been existing on a diet of adrenaline for almost a day and a night. Her body was beginning to reach the end of its endurance. It had been a while – and still Bobbie was carried on – ever further down into the realm of these terrible beings.

The girl had sobbed but it brought her little comfort, so she had quit doing it. She was so tired and thirsty now - dehydrated to the point that no real tears would come anyway. Still Bobbie doggedly continued to fight the fatigue she felt; battling the blackness of sleep that threatened to engulf her. She went in trepidation of it - fearing that if she slept she would never awaken again. She needed to concentrate on something, anything to keep her from drifting into sleep. Bobbie had hoped that her eyes might adjust to the darkness, but the reality was that there was nothing for them to work with, a total absence of any light. Not being able to see, she strained to listen instead. From the echoes as they moved ever downwards, she realized that the passage they were traveling along had now widened out to become spacious…also quite wet. She could smell the dampness in the rocky tunnel; sense the moist surroundings and slick floor without having to see it.

And this reinforced how dry she was. She'd even be willing to lick the moisture off the walls right about now to help her raging thirst.

She tried to push this fresh torment back inside herself with distracting thoughts. The creatures' sense of balance, she reasoned, was uncanny. There was total blackness around them – the floor of the passage must be slickly smooth – glass like. Yet her monstrous captor had not slipped – there was no hesitation or faltering.

Just a single-minded, steady and paced descent downwards with its burden on the treacherous surface underfoot. And as far as she could tell - by hearing alone - none of the others had slipped either.

Another thing Bobbie couldn't believe was the absolute silence in which they traveled. Whatever form of communication that they used between each other to coordinate their actions, eluded her. Perhaps some audible communication that went beyond the range of human hearing? And still downward they went…her heart quickened…it may have been wishful thinking on the young girl's part, or possibly just her imagination, but was it actually getting lighter? Wait! There was no doubt of it! Strange patches of suffused green radiance began to appear on the tunnel walls; a weird glow that gradually permeated the wide passageway with an ambient otherworldly light.

As the minutes went by, the clumps of luminescence were more frequently dotted about and were starting to join up to form swathes of glowing green phosphorescence that cast out a dim, low light.

The being that was carrying her paused for a moment for some unknown reason, and it gave her the briefest of opportunities to study a large patch of this bizarre otherworldly green light. She couldn't believe what was creating it - some type of mushroom anchored on the damp wall mere inches from her lifted face, a genus of fungi that was giving off this green glow.

She dimly remembered in a high school biology class some teacher or other once talking about something called bioluminescence; and that some organisms - plants and animals – that gave off a cold chemical light in certain conditions. Didn't some fungi use something called luciferin to make it? That sounded right to her, but she wasn't sure.

All Bobbie knew was that the strange lime-tinted light that was scattered around the passage walls and high roof made her feel better.

The girl tried to greedily reach out to collect a few drops of moisture she could see glistening on the tunnel wall surface. But it was too late; they had started moving again and to her dismay the chance was missed. The girl's throat felt like it was stuffed with dry cotton. She couldn't even summon up a groan. The slick passage leveled out finally, even rising slightly. Suddenly they were out of the tunnel and Bobbie found herself suddenly and shockingly dumped unceremoniously to the floor. Despite landing on something that was soft and yielding as she fell onto it, the length of the unexpected drop knocked the breath out of her. It left the already battered girl dazed and winded. She lay there gasping spasmodically for a few moments - like a fish out of water – realizing with horror that her lower body had no feeling - legs numb and unresponsive - she couldn't move them at all – not even her toes. Was her back broken? Oh God, please no! Not that!! But even as she considered it as a horrible possibility, a welcome prickling agony of returning circulation informed her that her spine and legs were OK. Bobbie took a few minutes to recover slowly – keeping her eyes shut - dreading what was to come.

The minutes stretched on – she waited with a sick anticipation in the pit of her stomach– but still nothing happened. Bobbie finally opened her sticky eyes and gazed around her - running a rough dry tongue over painfully cracked lips. A burning curiosity temporarily overcame fear, exhaustion, and thirst. Of the creatures, she could see or hear nothing of them at present. They had seemed to vanish; it was as if they had never been.

Bobbie stared directly upwards – she gasped in wonderment at the astonishing sight she beheld. She had arrived in an alien world; a place that she assumed must be the gigantic beings' cavernous lair. It was a huge empty cavern that had a domed rock sky that arched above her at a great height. The girl had no substantive point of reference. Distances were impossible to judge with any accuracy.

Far above her, a naturally formed roof was dotted throughout by the same fungi patches she'd seen earlier on the tunnel wall - a glowing luminescent witch-fire that looked to her like an immense star field or nebula when viewed from afar. The cave had a unique unearthly beauty in the true sense of the word; Bobbie had never seen anything that even approached the bizarre magnificence of these creatures' underground habitat. She explored with her eyes further - although entranced by the cavern she was still too frightened to move, and far too weak. The rocky cavern walls surrounding her were embedded with a patchwork of huge patches that gave off the same odd glow. Although they didn't exactly illuminate the immeasurable darkness to any real extent, it did make it possible to see a little of these things' realm. The cave was truly vast; it must have covered an area of several thousand square feet - to look at it was breathtaking; however, the overpowering stench was equally breathtaking…but not to be embraced with the same delight. The stink was appalling, considering the voluminous space she was in.

It smelled of ancient rot, the putrescence of old kills - stale acrid ammonia, animal feces – a disgusting mix of musk and death. Trying to breathe shallowly through her mouth to minimize the nauseating effect the smell was having on her already ravaged stomach, Bobbie began to explore a little nearer to home now.

She felt around herself, curious to see what had broken her fall, cautiously moving her hands gently about her. The young girl had been thrown onto a thick pile of dried out vegetation. It had the feel and smell of the forest about it - a combination of roots, leaves, small twigs and dried out grasses. She wriggled down into it a little, releasing its fresh earthy odors that were quite wonderful compared to the foul stink of the cave. It could only have gotten in here if the creatures had brought it in themselves - it was all fresh, so this suggested that it had been placed here recently. For them, or for her? She wasn't sure she wanted to know the answer to that question.

Bobbie's heart sank, sphincter tightening. Something had gently brushed against her leg. The touch came again. This time it stayed where it had made contact. The girl's body stiffened and started to tremble, but with a supreme effort she forced herself from crying out. She turned her head slowly. In the strange green-tinged gloom, she could make out the hulking shape of one of the creatures that was hunched down by her. She had never even heard it approach. It might have been there the whole time for all she knew - watching her. Observing…waiting.

Bobbie used every shred of willpower she possessed to remain absolutely still and silent. A single huge hair-covered paw - or was it a hand - ran up and down her legs from her feet to the top of her thighs. It poked and prodded at them with gigantically thick fingers. It then lifted her left leg up effortlessly and touched and twisted gently; examining her limb thoroughly with what could only be an intelligent curiosity. The probing was not hard or forceful despite the thing's obvious incredible strength - but the examination had a deliberate inquisitiveness to it. Above all, the titanic being seemed inordinately fascinated with her jeans. The thick denim material obviously intrigued it; the terrifying being brought its odd shaped head down, and sniffed at the sodden, filthy cotton a few times.

Apparently not satisfied with what had been found up till now, the questing being's fingers explored where the jeans were ripped at the knee.

She felt its coarse skin rub up against her flesh that was exposed through the tear. It was all Bobbie could do to stop herself from screaming out loud.

The hair rose on the back of her neck and gooseflesh ran in waves across her at the monster's touch - far worse ordeals were yet to come.

The terrifying thing's investigation now switched to her upper body.

The enormous stinking hair-covered entity moved itself slowly but fluidly around from her legs until it was kneeling in the dried-out bed of foliage that Bobbie lay on. It was now almost level with her face. Time had slowed…events was now an oddly perceived slow motion, robbing her of the ability to act or react.

Monstrously huge hands – reminding her of misshapen gigantic prying spiders - began to crawl over her chest, delicately feeling into the folds of her filthy tee-shirt - groping around the material in a slow languorous deliberate pattern that encompassed the entire front of her torso. Bobbie's breasts seemed to mystify and captivate it. The being spent a long time squeezing and poking at them on top of her clothing. Thankfully, the creature was very gentle in its examinations. The girl had seen what these incredible things were capable of. She lay there too scared to hardly breathe, let alone move. She was aware that if it had wanted to, it could have quite easily torn the fleshy mounds from off her ribcage with those huge powerful hands.

What happened next was almost enough to stop her pounding heart. The great hairy dome shaped head of the huge hominid jerked back - jaw jutting forward - maw open wide. The monstrous titan's colossal hands lay flatly upon her chest. From its mouth a high-pitched hooting tone emitted – an unearthly wailing sound that chilled the blood in her veins.

It was an unnatural noise – one designed to reach into the furthest confines of the darkened labyrinths that surrounded them. There was the faintest rustling that echoed from all around accompanied by a frenzy of scampering. The air around Bobbie seemed to grow even thicker and cloying than it already was. Within seconds the terrified girl was surrounded by several of the grotesque creatures. They were milling around in proximity; a foul group comprised of hair, teeth and foul breath - they reminded her of a pack of hyenas circling around a wounded prey, eager for the kill.

This is it, thought Bobbie. This really is the end.

She tensed, waiting to feel the creatures' tearing teeth rip off her flesh; huge hands yanking out vital organs from her exposed body cavities. Once again, she was wrong. She was too frightened to even close her eyes – and what she saw totally astonished her.

The one that had been examining her was clearly signaling to the others with elaborate hand motions. They were talking to each other! She couldn't believe it. That cinched it for her. These things - whatever they were - were not animals. No other living thing on the face of God's Earth communicated in this kind of fashion – with the possible exception of humanity's ancestors of the ancient past. Bobbie turned her head fully to the left to watch the complex hand gestures that were being returned by the others.

She had absolutely no real idea what was being silently communicated between them but whatever the conversation - it was central to her.

All movement had now ceased from the assembled group; all attention was fixed on the creature that was gesticulating quickly to them.

One hand motion was repeated several times. A downward motion with the palm facing up, fingers curled in a half fist. But each time it was made, the girl had the distinct impression that this sign referred to her specifically.

One of these fearsome beings - the largest Bobbie had yet seen - seemed to have been drawn into the conversation. The first creature that had howled out to initiate the gathering - the one that had taken such an interest in her - now stopped the fluttering hand signals and was patiently and intently watching while the bigger one gestured back. Bobbie - her other ills and fears forgotten temporarily - watched in fascination as the conversations continued in the same vein...alternating backwards and forwards primarily now between the two of them - but on occasion another gigantic pair of hands from one of the group would make some sort of quickly signaled contribution to the proceedings.

What exactly was being discussed, she had no idea. Bobbie was certain that the conversation was regarding her fate in some way.

With a grand gesture from the largest of the colossal creatures - possibly the leader - the smaller one who had not moved from its kneeling vigil at her side closed one hand onto the material of her ragged tee-shirt and with one swift effortless motion tore it off her body.

Bobbie, naked now from the waist up, instinctively brought her arms up to cover her exposed breasts.

The creature took exception to the young girl's modesty and leaned over her - its face literally only inches from hers - the remnants of her torn clothing still in its hand.

Bobbie's bowels felt loose as the being pulled back its lips and bared its awful jagged teeth and fangs in a soft, vicious growl - she interpreted this immediately to mean 'put your arms down'. Bobbie obeyed instantly. First the largest one moved close in to apparently stare at her semi-nakedness. After a few short seconds in deference, the others crowded into her, to likewise gaze at her breasts.

Some reached down in curiosity, prodding tentatively at her small fleshy mounds with their huge fingers - poking repeatedly until it began to get painful. Why were they doing this to her - had they never seen a human's breasts before? The blindingly obvious occurred to her.

Of the fourteen students and professors in her group she had been the only female. Was that the reason for their behavior?

However, this question was pushed away because having these things so close was almost more than she could bear. Bobbie wanted to hide away from their bizarre, human-like hair-covered faces. From gigantic eyes and wet gaping maws that contained formidable, serrated, shark-like razor teeth.

The fear that they would attack her was great - but the revulsion at the stench from them was almost as bad. The girl hadn't smelled anything so fetid in her life. She knew if she wasn't so exhausted and if her stomach wasn't so completely empty, she would have vomited. Eventually they seemed to tire of this examination of her and began to drift away singly to disappear silently once more back into the shadows of the cavern. Much to Bobbie's relief there was only two of them left with her - the largest creature that she thought might be the leader and the smaller one that had taken such an interest in her.

What followed was quite unnerving - one simply kneeled at her side - the other stood motionless, silently observing her. This fraught situation continued for what seemed an eternity - probably only a few minutes in actuality. Finally, she could stand this silent torture no longer. Her thirst was so bad that death would be preferable than suffering with it any longer. Desperation spurred her on to take some action. Very slowly she pushed herself upright into a sitting position - the effort of that simple action nearly made Bobbie pass out. She was at the point of losing consciousness – however, she closed her eyes for a moment or two, steadying herself down - concentrating fully on keeping herself from fainting. After a few moments when her head had finally stopped swimming and spinning around, she forced her sticky gritty eyes open.

Neither of the hair-covered titans had changed their position in the slightest. They were as statues - frightening grotesque sentinels that watched over her every move with huge unblinking eyes. Bobbie decided it was time for an experiment. She pointed to her mouth and made drinking motions. If they understood her desperate need they made no sign. She tried again making her actions slower, more deliberate and exaggerated. She repeated them again. Finally, after the fourth time, there was a reaction from the pair.

The smaller creature, who still had not moved from by her side, and still clutched the ragged shirt that it had torn off her, made a brief pattern of hand signals to the larger one. Its huge companion made a single gesture back.

At once the lesser being was twisting away and with a blinding speed was lost into the darkness. The gargantuan thing that was left there still gazing at her suddenly dropped to all fours, and in a blur of motion, departed swiftly away into the blackness of the cavern as well. Before Bobbie knew what was occurring, the first wraith was back at her side. She was sincerely hoping that it would have the intelligence to understand her need to bring water back with it. And it had, but just not in the manner she was expecting.

With a gentle push of its massive forearm, the girl found herself supine once more. A huge calloused finger that spanned the length of her lower face deftly rested briefly on her cracked lips, and then gently prized open her mouth. Its vast head then leaned down, and its horrible face was pressed almost against her own. She closed her eyes instinctively. It was just as well, for the next second she received a torrent of saliva laden foul water directly from the creature's mouth into hers. She could taste the filthiness of it - knew that same mouth had wolfed down human flesh. She gagged – trying to vomit out what had been poured into her - her dehydrated body knew better however and had no such niceties. Before she could act on an impulse to regurgitate the tainted water, she mercifully slipped into unconsciousness.

There must have been some infection in her weakened body. For some immeasurable period, Bobbie was delirious. There were vague snatches of half-lucid memories - fragments too outlandish, too vile for her mind to fully accept. More than once she knew that the same creature had brought her water as she had needed it. She was just too weak to fight its ministrations, so she succumbed to the inevitable.

Why it had succored her she didn't know - but for some reason known only to these hellish things - they had decided to keep her alive.

The aid didn't stop with the water. She had misty memories that the colossal hominid had brought her other things too - food. Things salty and rich, yet gamey enough to make her heave. Things that wriggled at times…possibly maggots…and it was food delivered in the same way that the liquids were…horribly the stuff had already been partially chewed - just enough for her to swallow it down without choking. Bobbie was too ill to protest. In her weakened state her body merely accepted what was, leaving the fragile mind behind. Her physical self did what it needed to survive. This pattern went on for an indeterminate time - until Bobbie suddenly came to herself. One day she awoke, and the fever had left her. Everything was clear and lucid once more. The fatigue and horrendous thirst were gone - although she was weak, she didn't feel anything like as unwell as she had.

She hadn't been moved from the nest of rough foliage. Wriggling her legs and butt, she came to a nasty and mortifying conclusion. She had been soiling herself - laying in her own filth for what may have been quite some time. Bobbie forced herself gingerly upright as she had before - this time, though she felt dizzy, there was no real danger of losing consciousness.

In the diffused green gloom of the enormous cavern she could neither see nor hear her captors – however she was also aware that she couldn't really trust her senses. Just because she didn't think that they were around didn't mean anything. Bobbie was well aware that they could be less than fifteen feet from her, and she wouldn't even know it. Still, if nothing else, she didn't want the awful indignity of having to lie in her own excreta anymore.

And if they were going to kill her as they had all the others, she'd probably be dead already. So, she slowly stood up anxiously, her head buried submissively in her shoulders, waiting for the dreadful advent of any of the giants; yet none appeared.

With tiny tremulous steps she began to move away from the dried-out foliage that had been her home and started to attempt to explore the rest of the cavern - she might even find a way out.

As time passed, she concluded that she was alone for the time being. She had listened hard for any noise, however small, that her captors might be making; a tell-tale indication that would give warning so she would be able to scurry unnoticed back to her 'nest'- but could discern nothing.

However, Bobbie had a distinct impression that she could hear a faint echo of running water from somewhere within the cavern. Where did that creature get the water from that it had given her? The girl followed the sound that appeared to be leading her into the heart of the grotto. The rock floor was not as slick as the passage that led into it had been - the footing was good. The only difficulty was the further she moved into the center, the darker it got. The faint green luminescence thrown out by the fungi got weaker until she was almost in total blackness.

Bobbie nearly fell into a sunken pool of sluggishly moving water that blended into the inky blackness of the floor - only luck prevented her from tipping headfirst into it. Dropping quickly to her knees she dipped her hand into the surface. Bobbie could feel a powerful current dragging her hand in the cold water just below the surface. On all fours she made a quick scampering circuit of the pool's edge to determine its size. It wasn't particularly big, perhaps only a few feet in diameter – possibly an underground stream of some kind that had been uncovered by erosion. Or maybe the creatures themselves had exposed it to obtain a fresh water supply for themselves. From what she had seen of them - their intelligence and organization - it seemed entirely possible.

Bobbie's eyes had begun to adjust to the lack of light - she noticed the occasional bright flash of scales in the water. There were fish swimming in it. Taking advantage of the moment, the girl touched her lips to the surface and had her fill of the invigorating ice-cold liquid. She then listened and looked carefully around – realizing she had no precise idea where the entrance was to the outside - except that it was somewhere close to where she had been dropped – maybe it wasn't a good plan to try to get out that way…she might meet some of those things in the blackness of the tunnel whilst trying to escape.

She shuddered at the thought. The Lord only knew what would happen to her then. She thought for a few seconds - her head far clearer than it had been in a while. First things first - she pulled the tattered filthy remains of her jeans and encrusted socks off. Her only remaining training shoe had long since vanished.

Then she peeled of her disgustingly soiled undies. With some shame, she washed her filthy body with the freezing water from the pool. The flowing water was so cold it burned her skin before leaving it numb - but she managed to scrub off the worst of the filth that encrusted it. Next she attempted to wash out her panties, socks and jeans. As soon as she started to bundle up the denim and scrub at it in the water, they promptly fell apart. Seeing that it was useless she gave up and let the current carry the shredded blue cotton away. The socks were heavy hiking ones and fared much better than the slacks, as did her underwear. She wrung the three articles out by hand as best as she could and put them back on again. Bobbie then took a little time to explore around the pool.

Upon careful examination of the rocky verge that surrounded it, it was clear that her thought that these creatures had opened it up for themselves to gain access to the water and food was correct.

Marks around the edge clearly showed a tool of some kind had been used to either open the pool completely - or at least make a pre-existing opening bigger. She was still looking around the pool when a startling noise from somewhere back in the cave made her jump. Bobbie's senses were beginning to get sharpened by her ordeal. As quickly and as silently as she could, Bobbie made her way back across the cavern and onto her bedding of dried out grasses and twigs and settled herself on it.

The creatures had evidently returned from wherever it was they had been.

***

Her captivity went on for several indeterminate days, or so she estimated.

She was fed by the same creature once a day - twice a day she was given water. The original method of mouth to mouth food transfer had been abandoned - her monstrous captors understood that she was no longer in need of care. The food was usually raw fish that she assumed had been caught in the pool. On occasion, Bobbie was given chunks of a raw gamey meat. Both were brought and tossed at her - as someone would feed a caged animal. The girl was not neglected exactly – but she got the impression she was being tended to more out of necessity. Water was delivered in a huge crude bowl made from a hollowed-out piece of wood - further proof of their rudimentary use of tools.

The 'tribe' as she had begun to think of them, more or less ignored her most of the time, which suited Bobbie the novelty of her sharing their lair was apparently wearing off; although one smaller and she thought younger creature - perhaps only a mere seven feet in height - had taken to sniffing around her on occasion. And she meant that literally. It would slink over to her 'nest' and sniff her all over. Terrified, she just lay perfectly still and let it. Disconcertingly, it would pay close attention to her crotch area.

She began to realize this one was a male of the species. The girl came to understand that these titanic beings had a distinct social order and sense of community. They were organized, intelligent, and certainly creatures of habit. When they went out, they generally did so as a group - and would be gone for several hours.

During this period, Bobbie hunted round her prison for a way out – however as yet she had been unsuccessful in finding one. As far as she could gather from her observations of their coming and going, there was only one way in and out. The girl was just too terrified to go into the tunnel that the creatures themselves used. The horrifying thought of running into one of them in the absolute pitch dark of the passage was beyond contemplation. She had spent her time exploring the cave, whilst the 'tribe' had been out on one of their frequent foraging trips. Bobbie now knew the confines of the cavern quite well- she could easily find her way around, even in the dim light.

The girl had also discovered that she wasn't the only one to sleep on a mat of foliage. Huge sleeping 'nests' of forest material were scattered far and wide against the cavern walls. The creatures seemed to have their own either assigned or designated spots. When the gigantic beings came back, they would on occasion tote armfuls of new flora to replenish the stocks within the cave. The older sleeping material was disposed of in a way that eluded her at present - she had assumed that it was carried out and simply dumped.

From careful observation, Bobbie could more or less time it to make certain that she was back upon her own sleeping corner before they slunk back. Laying on her sleeping material after another unsuccessful search for a fresh exit, she had started to drift off to sleep when her titanic keeper appeared and tossed her a chunk of something that landed wetly at the girl's side. The creature was already bounding away before the food had landed. Bobbie picked it up and brushed away a layer of dirt that had adhered to its wet surface – long since abandoning any pretense of the niceties or conventions against eating raw flesh. She just imagined that it was steak tartare and bit deeply into it. It had the same gamey taste as all the other meat she had been given and Bobbie chewed at it - although the taste was revolting as usual, this piece had a different texture - she couldn't understand why. It prompted her to study it carefully.

A scream burst out from the girl that she couldn't suppress – in horror she threw the meat from herself.

She screamed again. The flesh had stubble on it. Ginger stubble. George McKinney had red hair. This meat was his cheek. She'd been eating human flesh. She staggered up - caution thrown to the winds – running blindly into the center of the cave. She got almost as far as the pool - and that was where the smaller creature that had been sniffing at her bounded up and in an instant, she was knocked to the grotto floor, her head almost in the dark swirling water.

Dazed, her mouth bleeding, she couldn't even begin to contemplate the vileness that was going to happen next. Bobbie was pulled up by her waist and forced onto her knees...then pushed forward. She was on all fours like a dog.

A crowd of the creatures gathered in a rough semi-circle; the only opening being the pool itself. The extraordinarily strong hand of the seven-foot male clumsily tore off her underwear - in the next instant she felt herself agonizingly violated from behind - white hot searing pain tore into her and seemed to exit through the top of her head, she felt internal delicate skin rip. Her ears were assaulted by the sound of screams - screams that were coming from everywhere...it took her a while to realize they were her own.

The brute pumped into her with bestial grunts - each plunge an outrage that caused fresh damage to her mind, spirit and body. Everything became crystal clear to Bobbie. She could feel every agonizing thrust; hear the inhuman grunting from the creature as it ploughed into her. The girl could hear the approving low sniggers from the assembled others as they were clearly enjoying the spectacle. With a jerking shudder, the being spilled his seed deep into her. With a grunt it pulled out, leaving Bobbie a broken bleeding doll lying on the rocky floor. Whatever mystique she had held for them in the past was now swept way with the brutal rape. She could sense that they were closing in. They had finally decided to butcher and eat her.

Putting her head up she saw that she had one slim chance of life left to her - or rather a death she might prefer. She scrabbled forward and slid into the pool before any of them could reach her - the rough-hewed rocky edge gouging her. Then she was in the icy water and the powerful current carried her under, instantly pulling Bobbie away into tumbling, raging blackness.

***

The young man stood at the riverbank and smiled with true contentment, taking in the beauty of the wilderness around him - a beautiful late summer morning that promised to only get better as the day went on. He looked casually down into the gently flowing water below him that reflected the bright sun in a million diffused sparkles and shifted the weight of his heavy 30.06 Remington to his other shoulder. Taking a deep breath, he reveled in the silence and solitude that he truly loved. He sighed, and knew it was time to be moving on; he had plenty of things that needed doing today. He turned to head back up the trail and away from the river when he stopped and gave a double take. What in the hell was that?

Carefully placing his rifle to the floor, he scrambled quickly down the slippery bank and waded into the slow moving current where he reached out, dragging a pathetic bleeding figure of a naked girl from the water – not sure if she was dead or alive.

She was pitifully emaciated - chalky white skin a mass of bruises, cuts and contusions that stood out starkly against the pale hue. The girl's lank hair was a tousled mess of greasy sodden rat tails, and she had on only a pair of socks. Her eyelids fluttered - she was alive. He laid her down on the muddy bank and draped his jacket over her shivering body. Despite asking her several questions he could get no response from her. Her wide eyes held no recognition or understanding. She was catatonic.

He reclaimed his rifle from the floor and slung it over his shoulder before hefting the girl up to carry her to his waiting truck a few hundred yards away. As he struggled with his burden down the rough track, having to rest occasionally - he had the troubling and uncomfortable feeling that his progress was being watched from the deep forest by unseen eyes.

CHAPTER EIGHT

'You can't stay in your corner of the Forest waiting for others to come to you. You have to go to them sometimes.'
A.A. Milne (1882-1956)

Graham Island, British Columbia

July 21st, 2019

The journey over to Graham Island had been a long and tiring one - yet uneventful. From LAX to Canada's Vancouver International - then a quick 30-minute trip to the Harbor Flight Centre. A bumpy flight by a hellishly noisy twin-engine Dornier Seastar followed. That took them the remaining 770 odd km to the tiny town of Masset on the north shore of Graham Island.

Finally, from there, they boarded an aging Super Puma L2 sixteen-seater helicopter that headed south across the isle. The chopper drifted lazily along in the warm summer air like some monstrously outsized metallic insect; a course that carried them over huge areas of thickly packed coniferous trees, and barely skirted the western edge of Naikoon Provincial Park. Finally, after circling a small group of rough looking buildings, it touched lightly down, bringing the weary group to the old Dinan Bay logging camp.

The 'Cryptid' TV team had finally arrived.

Before the whirling blur of the main rotor had even begun to slow, two men were already striding out from one of the buildings - coming out to greet the arriving passengers. Norton Bailey was the first one out of the helicopter, hefting a large and heavy bright orange rucksack. The rest clambered out, staying low from the still rotating overhead blades - helping each other with their packs. Bailey, moving away from the others, held his hand out to greet the smaller of the two men that had formed the two-man welcome committee. The smaller of these two guys pushed himself forward, taking Norton Bailey's proffered hand.

"Mr. Bailey, isn't it? We haven't officially met, but I'm Lou Gharr, the local site transport manager for La Ree Logging Corporation. We still operate several sites here on Graham and Moresby Islands. Hendry Corp arranged the transportation of your equipment through our company offices in Vancouver."

Bailey shook Gharr's hand warmly. The man was in his early fifties, lean as a whipcord with dark skin that gave the appearance of old cured leather.

He'd obviously spent a great deal of his life outdoors. Bailey nodded at Gharr's quiet companion in acknowledgment, and with more than a statement than an enquiry said: *"Franklin Barr?"*

The man gave a single nod back in agreement. Lou Gharr's silent partner was cut of the same basic cloth - obviously used to being in this wild outdoor environment – there, however, the similarity between the two men ended. His age seemed indeterminate. The man's handsome features with the raven black hair, high cheek bones and bronzed skin marked him strikingly as an obvious Haidan Indian native. He didn't just look like he was used to being outdoors in the forest…he seemed to be an immutable part of it.

The rest had hung back while these introductions were going on - Kimberly amiably chatting to Olivia Hannah - Sterling helping the cursing Ed Benson drag a large hold-all from the Puma's cramped cabin. But even while performing these mundane activities, none of them could help but notice the patched-up buildings and general air of neglect in their surroundings. The place really was an obvious shadow of its former self. A couple of open-framed rusting Grader Trucks once used for hauling away the huge cut trees were scattered around the site - along with a mixture of other discarded vehicles - including three fuel trucks that were abandoned when the logging operation had pulled out.

Scott Rankin, the consummate professional, was already wandering between the huge metal hulks, peering here and there, and sizing up some good angles for setting up shots.

Norton continued speaking: *"I'm glad you could be here to meet us, Mr. Gharr. Let me introd…"*

The other man butted in.

"Please Mr. Bailey; shall we have the introductions inside? The weather can change here quite quickly…there will be rain later, and I think we'll be far more comfortable in there."

Lou Gharr jerked his thumb over his shoulder and indicated the larger building behind him that they had emerged from. It had a strange shape, like the bow of a gigantic rowboat had been sliced precisely in half, and then planted firmly into the ground.

Gharr continued with an explanation of the building's original purpose.

"That was the old office and bunkhouse back in the day, there's still a kitchen of sorts and we've prepared some food for you and your party…it's simple stuff but I guarantee it's good and hot!"

Rankin joined them… *"Hey, did I just hear someone mention food?"* With that he was already heading towards the structure.

That was the signal for the others, and collectively they moved in that general direction. Franklin Barr politely held the door open for the group as they trooped in. He turned his head and gave Olivia Hannah a thoughtful look as she filed past him. Norton Bailey had held back and was the last person in. As he squeezed past the other man through the partly opened door, a surreptitious but imperceptible nod that he gave Barr spoke volumes.

It was one of those comfortable gestures; one that is often shared between two old acquaintances.

***

Lou Gharr, the La Ree Logging employee, had been right on the money.

The food had been hot and was good. Between the culinary efforts of himself and Barr, the meal had been wonderful with the wilderness setting making it even more palatable. The light was fast fading in the forests outside and a hint of rain blew in from the west. As the precipitation began to softly cover the bunkhouse windows with a fine wet sheen, and a good meal inside them, the people began to relax. The eight of them sat closely around a large trestle table set squarely in the center of the room. The food comfortably digesting, the after-dinner banter was light and amusing.

Ed Benson was dominating the conversation. His wit was sharp and acerbic, and Kimberly Eastman was certainly beginning to warm to him. There were a few bottles of wine open on the table, along with a couple of six-packs of beer and Kimberly had glanced surreptitiously at Scott Rankin opposite her at the table. He had not indulged in the alcohol - good to his word – and was nursing along a bottle of Evian water. Eastman tapped his foot with hers under the table and grinned at him. Rankin looked up at her, startled for a split second, then relaxed, lifted the half empty plastic bottle up to her in a mock toast and smiled knowingly back.

Eastman realized that David Sterling, the forensic pathologist, was now talking quite loudly. He'd been a little standoffish with the rest of them up till now – apparently though, half a bottle of chardonnay was all it took to loosen the good doctor up a little. He was now heatedly debating with Norton Bailey on some point that had been momentarily lost to her.

Kimberly turned her full attention away from Scott Rankin to listen to what Sterling was saying: *"…not very likely, is it, Mr. Bailey? I mean essentially, you're talking about a very large creature, some type of giant primate that science has never categorized, let alone seen?"*

Eastman looked at Bailey as he settled back in his chair and steepled his fingers together. *Oh God,* she thought, *he's going to start lecturing again.* She was right. The stocky author comfortably leaning back in his seat – nose superciliously in the air - began speaking.

"Essentially, Dr. Sterling that is exactly what I think is living on this island, and on several other secluded locations throughout the world. My research on this particular subject has been thorough, extensive and most importantly, objective."

A derisive snort from Ed Benson at the far end of the table, at this last assertion, was deliberately ignored by Bailey…unaffected by it he blithely continued in the same vein.

"Dr. Sterling there are a plethora of references and myths to this elusive creature from all around the world. In places as far apart as Tibet to Australia. From diverse and geographically separated cultures such as the Native American Indians, the peoples of East Asia or the Aboriginal tribes of Western Australia. It is known by several cultures by different names: Sasquatch, Yeti, Yowie, and Bigfoot. And on the Queen Charlotte Islands, particularly on Graham Island, the Native Haidan peoples call it Gogit…different names for what I firmly believe is essentially the same creature."

Ed Benson couldn't help himself. Leaning forward from his end of the table, he interjected: *"OK, Bailey…I'll grant you that many cultures do have very similar takes on the same type of creature. Much folklore has almost identical morphologies about giant ape-like creatures - but there is absolutely no evidence that this animal exists. Even if it did exist at some point in the far past, Bailey, where's your proof that it did? Where's the hard evidence that it still exists now?"*

Eastman decided to join in the conversation.

"Ed does have a point, Norton. Where is the evidence? If something like this was running around, then someone would have inevitably seen it. There would be a photograph - a video - some tracks - …surely some proof of its existence would have been presented by someone, somewhere."

At Kimberly's question, everyone around the table now fixed their attention onto Norton Bailey, interested to hear what his answer would be.

He stood up and crossed to the windows that were behind him, as if considering his answer. With his back still turned he quietly said one word: *"Specialization."*

Sterling, the pathologist, was the first to speak.

"Pardon me, Mr. Bailey? Did you say, 'specialization'?"

The thickset author turned from the rain painted windows and back to the seated group - his short heavy arms now folded in front of him.

"I did, sir. I did. You heard me correctly. Let me try and answer your question in this way, if I may." He unfolded his arms, moving back to the table, placing his hands on the back of his chair, he continued.

"Look at the koala and the panda for a moment. These creatures are often cited as prime examples of species that have become victims to 'extreme food specialization'. It may surprise all of you to learn that the koala's physiology is now so integrally adapted to the consumption of Eucalyptus leaves that it could not readily adapt to another food source. Essentially - if it couldn't obtain a ready supply of that particular vegetation it would rapidly starve to death."

Bailey had an engaged audience now and knew it. He pulled the chair out from the table and dramatically planted one foot on it, leaning against his raised knee with folded arms, he continued.

"However, the panda is a slightly different case. Biologists assumed this creature had become specialized in digesting bamboo as it lived primarily on this vegetation – and if one considers the evidence, it wasn't an unreasonable assumption to have - that is until quite recently. Biologists, it seems discovered that they got it the wrong way around. The reason that pandas eat bamboo isn't because they have become specialized in digesting it and thus dependent on it, as in the koala's case - but because there is a lack of alternate food supplies in the panda's habitat, especially in the winter months. It became clear from extensive field study and research that these large creatures not only eat at least twenty-five other varieties of plant life - but they prefer to eat meat whenever possible. The fundamental reason that meat does not form a bigger percentage of their dietary intake in the wild has more to do with opportunity to obtain it, rather than any conscious choice on their part. So, you see, giant panda because of their forced dietary requirements spend 40% of their time at rest…and with the high bulk and low nutritional content of the bamboo, you'll never see one running." Bailey paused for a moment to see if his audience was understanding the implication of what he was alluding to. Uncertain if they were or not, he pressed on regardless.

"I believe that in the rain forests of this island there has evolved a creature that has become adapted and highly specialized for this one particular environment. They probably exist in small numbers, are elusive in the extreme and very probably nocturnal."

Norton Bailey finally finished this interesting if overly long diatribe. There was silence for a few moments as the group digested his words.

Ed Benson stood up. Out of apparent sheer devilry and evident dislike of the pompous Norton Bailey, he pulled out his own chair and mockingly mirrored the stocky writer's exact posture; one leg on the chair and arms folded across his knee. If this less than subtle condescension was lost on

Norton Bailey, it certainly wasn't lost on the others. Scott Rankin actually had to bite down hard on his lip to stop himself laughing.

In half serious tones, Ed Benson said: *"So, Norton, would it be fair to say that what is hiding out on this island is a type of giant panda? One that is very shy - only comes out at night - and chows down on cedar tree leaves and hapless parties of Texas theology students? Now that's what I call specialized diet! No wonder there aren't many of them around. Hey, maybe they should think about expanding the menu - how about some tasty TV people?"*

Ed got off the stool and came around to the rear of Rankin, putting his hands on the cameraman's meaty shoulders, jiggling them vigorously.

"Scott looks to me like he could provide at least a cou…"

The hefty guy laughed good naturedly at Benson's remark, and shrugged his hands off. The two of them were rapidly becoming like a double act, turning his head around to him, Rankin quipped: *"Less of the 'fat' jokes, Benson; I'll have you know that there are some purty big muscles underneath all this, hoss. Some people got cursed with a six-pack…I got blessed with the whole goddamn keg."*

Everyone was laughing now at Rankin's self-deprecating ridicule. Even Norton Bailey cracked out a slight smile. One of them did not join in the general gaiety. Franklin Barr had silently got up from the table and had moved away from the group. He crossed to the other side of the old bunkhouse and was leant casually against one of the supporting floor-to-ceiling posts. He deftly rolled a cigarette one-handed, using the rough tobacco and papers he kept in ample supply in a worn leather pouch that he had around his neck - his back was to them. He was staring out into the darkness listening to the steadily rising wind and the now heavier rain that was held at bay by the glass windows on the far wall.

Olivia Hannah had said nothing to anyone for a while. For some unaccountable reason she was uneasy and unsettled - both with the talk and the place in general. She stood too. Something about all this just didn't feel right. Perhaps because of her odd disquiet, Olivia had noticed that the quiet Haidan Indian had moved away from the group to be on his own. She did likewise and moved away from the rest. She quietly observed them collectively picking over and discussing the relative merits of some of the camping equipment that had arrived with Lou Gharr and had been neatly stacked in several piles not far from the table where they had eaten.

Making a decision, Olivia Hannah sidled up to the tall Indian, nudging him in a friendly fashion with her shoulder.

"Hey there," she said. Barr nodded in acknowledgment, never taking his eyes from the blackened wet windows and continued rolling his cigarette.

"Barr isn't your real name, is it?" Hannah asked, but it was less of a question than a statement. He finished rolling his smoke, and then pulled a match out of the right-hand pocket of the long drover's coat he had on and deftly struck it with his thumbnail. It flared up, and he lit the slim roll-up before answering.

"No ma'am. Given name's Yahgulanaas. Like my father, and his father and probably his father too, I guess. We're an old people and tradition means something to us here." Barr finally deigned to finally look at her. He continued:

"You know these islands in our language are called 'Haida Gwaii'? It means 'land of the people'."

Hannah nodded, *"Yes, I did know that."*

The tall Haidan nodded to himself, as if this admission satisfied him in some odd way. Looking away again and studying the window once again, he said: *"We've had linguists coming here now for three generations, and they still haven't been able to classify our ancestral language. There have been some very learned professors up here on the islands, trying to figure out our speech. Last one I talked to said it had 'uniqueness'. No other languages like it on the planet, or so he reckoned."*

Olivia Hannah moved from his side to face him. The laconic man was beginning to irritate her more than a little, and she had absolutely no idea why he was telling her this. She asked him outright:

"I'm sorry, Mr. Barr, or Mr. Yahgulanaas, or whatever it is you like to be called...why are you telling me this? Is there a point?"

Barr took a last pull of his smoke, then with a dark thumb and forefinger removed a shred of the tobacco that had adhered to his bottom lip. Then he answered her.

"Barr'll do; the point I'm making, if there is one, is everything ain't always cut and dried. Had university folks coming here for years trying to figure things out about these islands. Shit, they can't even find out where our language comes from. Our elders tried to tell them it was Raven, but they didn't believe them."

Hannah was intrigued now. *"Raven?"* she asked quizzically.

"Hmm hm... Raven," answered Barr. *"Raven - or Hoya as we call him - brought us everything. Y'see it's like this...he's a trickster is old Raven, and he never actually creates anything. In the first days, Hoya made the world by stealing things, redistributing, exchanging and generally moving things around. Raven brought us our islands from someplace; he found fresh water, the salmon, deer and the bear...even the first people were brought here. He found them under a cockleshell on the beach. Even our language was brought to us by him, stolen from somewhere else."*

Barr started to roll himself another cigarette. Hannah turned for a few seconds to observe the rest of them were now pulling items from the pile of camping equipment and oblivious to her conversation with the Haidan. All except Norton Bailey. She got the idea that although he was ostensibly involved in the examination of the camping gear, he was still managing to observe the two of them in a clandestine way.

"I don't understand, Barr," she said, turning back to him. *"What's all this got to do with...?"*

Franklin Barr cut her off in mid-sentence. He said: *"That is the point, Ma'am. Raven. He brings things to the Haida Gwaii. He borrows things, moves them around, like I'm telling you."*

She began to get a glimmer of what he was driving at.

"I see. So, in your mythology he brought this creature, what do you call it, 'Gogit', to the island...the one we are looking for?"

Barr shook his head, looking at her long and hard before replying.

"You still don't get it, do you? Gogit was already part of the forest. If I was you folks, whilst you're here on the island at least, I'd be real cautious and careful. Y'see, the way I'm looking at it, the thing that Raven brought here was you folks."

Hannah laughed at this. Then she said: *"Well, Barr...I'll certainly bear that in mind if we come across any of your 'Gogits' out in the forest."* She chuckled to herself and was turning away to rejoin the others but Franklin Barr's incredibly strong hand pulled her back round to face him once more. The look on his lean, weathered face was deadly serious.

In low tones, he said: *"Ma'am...you can laugh if you want. That's OK with me - I was hired to guide you people and keep the bears away, and I'll do that. I'm fifty-one years old and I've made my living hunting and as a guide around this part of the world for most of my life - I'm telling you - and you do have to believe me - that something is here. We know. It's something that's never seen, not as such. But I'm saying to you here and now it is out there."*

There was a tangible and convincing fear in his eyes; Hannah could almost feel it oozing from him. But something else too...was it concern? Then suddenly that feeling vanished and Barr became far less intense. The brief storm within him had passed as quickly as it had come. He released her shoulder and straightened himself, stepping back almost apologetically. He seemed to lighten up considerably - and in a poor attempt at levity, with a broad smile that showed two rows of perfect, if somewhat tobacco stained teeth:

"Anyhow, the money's real good this time out...better than the last job I had taking those American fishing fellahs to the other side of Awun Lake last month."

Hannah moved quickly back towards the others, putting a more comfortable distance between the two of them, saying; *"I'm sure it is, Barr."*

She then turned away and joined Eastman who was still dubiously picking through the Hendry Corp supplied camping equipment.

But even as Kimberly was asking Olivia Hannah if she had any damned idea of just how the hell to put up a dome tent, the strangest feeling that she had seen Barr before wouldn't leave Olivia's thoughts.

***

It was the early hours now – the table had been put away and cot beds had been dragged into the bunkhouse from another storage.

The only dim light came from a single propane lantern that had been suspended from a ceiling beam in the center of the room.

Kimberly Eastman lay tightly curled up in her sleeping bag, listening to the heavy rain that was lashing the outside of the building.

From somewhere in the darkness there was a perceptible drip-drip from the leaking roof as the wetness had found a way inside.

She couldn't sleep and found herself going over tomorrow's schedule in her head. There were equipment checks - the route that the missing party had taken back in 1996 needed to be looked at once more; a course that they would faithfully follow. There were at least a dozen nagging worries plaguing her. Would the satellite uplink work? Were Rankin's video cameras going to operate normally with this kind of humidity? How to stop Ed Benson and Norton Bailey killing each other on or even off camera? In the end these irksome problems faded away - she finally drifted into a tired and much needed sleep. They all slept.

And far outside, in the dripping tangle of wet pitch-black forest, several huge eyes observed them from a distance - and patiently waited.

CHAPTER NINE

Graham Island, British Columbia

22nd July 2017

Everyone was awake early that morning to be greeted by a bright and intense blue sky that the fierce overnight rain appeared to have scrubbed clean just for their benefit. They had, for all intents and purposes, 24 hours left before they would start the trek into the forest interior and begin the filming schedule. Scott Rankin, unnoticed by most of the others, had skillfully been employing one of his smaller video cameras. He had already started to surreptitiously film their preparations – catching some candid footage onto its digital hard drive early that morning with the intention of being able to assist the editing process on their return.

After a quick breakfast prepared in the bunkhouses' small kitchen by Gharr, which was accompanied by a very large pot of coffee, Kimberly Eastman started to get things organized. Division of labor had already been agreed weeks before they'd arrived.

Overall coordination of the group's activities whilst on the island was Norton Bailey's responsibility. He insisted on that role as the originator and creator of the 'Cryptid' project – he'd had it put into his contract. The directorial and technical side of operations was to be jointly Eastman and Rankin's purview. The logistics of moving everyone and their equipment from point to point in the footsteps of the 1996 ill-fated Texas University people was Franklin Barr's, as indeed were all matters regarding safety whilst they were in the forests.

Dr. Sterling was on hand if anything untoward or of interest were discovered during their three-day trip into the wilderness regarding the long missing Texas party. He had brought with him various pieces of medical equipment he thought might be needed in the unlikely event his services were called upon. Olivia Hannah was there jointly with Norton Bailey to comment on matters touching on anything that had to do with the crypto-biological aspect of the program; Ed Benson would proffer an overall opinion from a purely anthropological perspective. The plan was well thought out. Everything was now moving along reasonably smoothly and more-or-less as anticipated.

There had been of course a few predictable issues with communication - the main one being technical in nature - cell phone reception here on Graham Island was non-existent. However, the satellite phones provided by Hendry Corp worked fine. Kimberly Eastman had used it several times during the last couple of days to contact Bruno Harts back in LA, giving out regular updates as to their preparations and progress. It took Scott and Kimberly most of that day to check out the AV equipment and perform the time consuming but necessary tests of the satellite uplink that would beam their signals from the forest back to the studio. This was the normal process for a 'live to tape' program. It allowed studio time to edit out the extraneous, the superfluous, and keep that edgy 'live' feel.

At the end of an exhaustive several hours of checking and rechecking, both Kimberly and Rankin were confident that everything regarding the technical side of the project would work as expected – and hopefully would keep working flawlessly once they were out in the field.

Norton Bailey had requested that everyone meet up in the old bunkhouse at 4:00 p.m. so he could give people a little further background – and Kimberly Eastman could refresh everyone on what was to be expected of them regarding the making of the show during the next few days. At the appointed time it was a weary Eastman and Rankin that slouched in chairs drinking old warmed-over coffee - while the rest sat with them not having a great deal to do during the day other than hang around.

Barr leaned against the bunkhouse's roughly planked wooden walls, rolling yet another of his interminable cigarettes. The general chatter in the room tapered off as Norton Bailey stood up, coffee mug in hand, and began to address them. Rankin had a feeling this might be interesting, so he quietly took out the small camcorder and moved away from the rest… unnoticed, he began to film the proceedings.

"Let me just start by thanking Ms. Eastman and Mr. Rankin for today's hard efforts…it is very much appreciated by both me and I'm sure by Hendry Corp back in LA."

The author walked slowly back to the table, obvious collecting his thoughts and placed his mug down on the table in front of him before continuing.

"I'd like to take just a few moments, if I may, to discuss with you some of the current theories regarding what it is thought these elusive creatures actually are. A mysterious and yet uncategorized species that I, amongst several others in the field of cryptozoology, am firmly convinced inhabit the Queen Charlotte Islands. I think that this will be of some use to you when you are framing your answers on camera during the next few days."

Uncharacteristically for him, Bailey, who was the archetypal showman, pulled out a seat - instead of a normal grandstanding posture that he readily adopted, he merely sat down. At this atypical action, the others in the group regarded him with a mixture of curiosity and anticipation. Picking up the mug he sipped at his coffee, holding it with both hands clasped around it, staring vacantly inside the cup for a few seconds as if inspiration could be discovered in the steaming contents. He continued with a wry but obviously forced smile.

"I'm quite aware that many of you here think I'm a joke, a deluded idealist. Like Arthur Conan Doyle searching vainly for fairies at the bottom of the garden. Or perhaps the more jaded of you", at this point he looked directly at Ed Benson, *"may even believe I'm here on Graham Island, purely for financial gain. That I'm cashing in - using this whole TV program as a good way to publicize my next book."*

Ed Benson looked at Norton squarely in the face, and said in a deadpan voice: *"What you, Bailey? Out to make even more money than you already have and getting a shit load of free publicity for yet another new book? Oh, surely not."*

There was a muffled subdued laughter from around the room at this acidic comment from Benson. Bailey, however, didn't go for the bait. He merely shook his head sadly as if he pitied the other man before replying.

"You're quite wrong about me you know Dr Benson and being unfair. Have the courtesy to hear me out while I explain why I'm convinced that I'm correct on this matter- and that you - amongst many other skeptics are not."

Norton Bailey paused for the briefest of seconds; then spoke again quickly before Ed Benson could interject with more of his acerbic wit. *"This is my line of reasoning. Science quite naturally accepts the existence of chimpanzee and gorilla. The reason is understandable, because the type can be observed. We see them; therefore, we know that they exist. But it may surprise you to learn that there is absolutely no fossil record of either species. So, the lack of fossil evidence doesn't necessarily constitute proof of something's non-existence. After all, nothing unreal exists."*

Benson glanced sideways with narrowed suspicious eyes at Rankin, and under his breath he muttered in a de sotto voce: *"This is such bullshit, even from him! Didn't Mr. Spock say that in 'The Voyage Home'?"*

Rankin shook his head imperceptibly, before quietly murmuring back from the corner of his mouth, *"Nope, 'Wrath of Khan'."*

Before Benson could take issue, the pathologist, David Sterling spoke out: *"What's the point you're trying to make, Norton - if there is one? Are you saying that because there is no fossil evidence then these creatures might exist? That's preposterous, really quite absurd!"*

Norton Bailey answered in reasonable and measured tones: *"No, Dr Sterling, that's not what I'm saying at all. I'm merely pointing out that there are many preconceptions science has had to reassess as fresh* evidence and new discoveries come to light. The natural world is replete with such examples. Creatures scientists adamantly proclaimed extinct or could not exist. The giant pandas that we were discussing yesterday, for example. They were first reported here in the west in 1869 - then were lost for a further 50 years. The first living specimen obtained here as late as 1936. The discovery of the Komodo dragon was in 1912 – a giant man-eating lizard that was thought to be an entirely mythical creature. In 1939 the Coelacanth was hauled up by fishermen off the east coast of South Africa - a fish thought extinct for almost 70 million years…recently in this last year a species of large deep sea eel, never before Catalogued or observed was discovered in the Atlantic Ocean at the depth of over 16,000 feet. Need I go on?"

Sterling held up his hands, saying "OK Mr. Bailey, your point is taken. But you do have to admit that what we are talking about isn't a fish or an eel, is it? Perhaps I might be laboring the point, but how could something as large as this creature have not been seen or even photographed?"

Norton Bailey inclined his head in a perceptible nod, replying, "You're making good and valid points, Dr. But the assumption that they haven't. It is my contention that they have."

Ed Benson couldn't now resist from chiming in.

"Come on, Bailey…for God's sake, how can 'eye-witness' reports ever be corroborated? We've all seen the grainy photos and blurry video footage. The plaster casts of the footprints of the supposed Bigfoot over the years. It's faked or highly suspect to say the least. Look at the fiasco a few years back – that stunt two guys pulled out in Georgia. It was a rubber goddamned suit – a mask sewn onto a moth-eaten bear hide."

Kimberly Eastman was puzzled by this reference. She spoke up, asking, "What's that, Ed? Can you explain to those amongst us who don't know what you're referring to?"

Before Benson could enlighten the others, Olivia Hannah broke in, beating him to the punch: "It was just a silly hoax Kimberly. A few years ago, two young men in Georgia called a press conference and announced they had the proof that cryptozoologists had been waiting for. They said that they had the decomposing corpse of a Sasquatch. That they had found it in North Georgia. They dragged the remains out of the backwoods and froze it in a chest freezer. Of course, it turned out to be utter garbage; like Ed said it was a fake constructed of rubber, bear hide and a latex mask."

"Oh," said Eastman simply, through pursed lips.

Benson cut in again. "You see Kimberly, Bailey has the same problem that all these cryptozoologists have - no offence to Olivia of course," he turned to Hannah as if in apology. She simply waved a magnanimous gesture of dismissal at his inferred slight. He picked his point up: *"...but the thing is, they have all these amazing and sometimes even plausible theories on how these creatures came to exist - where they fit into the evolutionary order - what they eat, drink, their preferred habitat. It makes for some very profitable books that fire up the public's imagination. It's good for the tourist trade - and scary movies that fill the theaters - even some atmospheric campfire stories while you're out in the woods. Sadly, as much as we'd all like to believe in these gigantic creatures, it's still just a fiction. They simply don't exist. There's no empirical evidence that they do. No tangible proof to back up the assertion that they are living here or anywhere else for that matter."*

He stopped, perhaps realizing that he was being a little too intense and tried to lighten the mood, saying: *"Hey - look on the bright side! We're getting paid lots of money to get 'Joe Public' to sit on their behinds at home for hours - happily watching a bunch of us tear up the woods looking for a no-show Sasquatch - while the advertisers equally happily try to sell them everything from car insurance to hemorrhoid suppositories."*

Laughter rang out around the room at Benson's flippancy; laughter that is from everyone except Norton Bailey and Franklin Barr.

The tall Haidan took offence to the conversation. He got up, noisily pushing his chair back, and glared at the faces around the room. Barr then simply walked to the door. There was silence. All eyes followed him. At the door he stopped and then turned back saying: *"You know, there are some things in this world that really shouldn't be mocked at, people...it just ain't right."*

Then without another word he turned sharply round and yanked the door open and stepped through into the bright sunlight and was gone. Lou Gharr coughed nervously, saying; *"Hey folks, don't mind Barr. I've known him for years; a good man but he isn't what you'd particularly call a humorous one. These Haidan native's kind of take these legends of the Gogit very seriously."*

An embarrassed silence continued in the room, broken after a few seconds by Norton Bailey, who said, *"If you'd be so kind, Mr. Gharr can you please assure Barr that no offence was meant by any of us. It's just that some people in western culture find it difficult to believe in something if it isn't first gift-wrapped and then handed to them with a certificate of authenticity. Please convey to him that no one meant any disrespect to either him, his beliefs, or his culture."* There was a general murmured consent from everyone.

Lou Gharr nodded that he would do as Bailey requested and left the room in search of the disgruntled Barr. Bailey continued the discussion.

"As I was saying, Dr. Sterling, to get back on topic - you made a good point earlier. Despite what Mr. Benson was saying there are several instances of sightings, photographic and other physical evidence that cannot easily be dismissed. Let me give you just one. Dr. John Bindernagel, a renowned Bigfoot researcher and former wildlife advisor to the United Nations, personally took a cast of a footprint measuring some 15.5 inches in length on Vancouver Island in 1998. This was not some hoax or publicity stunt. This was a serious scientist presenting the scientific community at large with examinable, measurable physical evidence of a huge hominid that is or was living within the forest confines of Vancouver Island."

Kimberly Eastman had sat back taking mental notes - watching the interaction. Olivia Hannah had said little during the discussion, she realized. Like Eastman herself, Hannah had for the most part quietly observed the proceedings without really investing in it. Rankin, at the back of the room, was getting it all on camera. Good man, she thought. There was some excellent footage in all of this that they would certainly be able to use later.

Ed Benson was talking again, she realized, addressing the room at large - but Bailey in particular.

"C'mon Bailey – please! Any evidence is open to interpretation, examination and extrapolation. As you pointed out yourself, nothing is sacred or sacrosanct when it comes to science. Even you with your sloppy research methods should know…"

Kimberly's attention shot back to Norton Bailey. The stocky author had now jumped up - pushing his chair backwards with enough force that it wobbled precariously and almost toppled. He was dangerously red in the face - obviously close to being provoked enough into explosively losing his cool with the abrasive Ed Benson. She jumped in to defuse the heated situation. Now wasn't the time for fireworks between those two. That time would certainly come, she realized. But when she was ready for it and not until; their showdown would have to wait until she decided it was going to make for good viewing. That was her job.

Kimberly stood up herself, saying: *"Well thank you, Norton; that was certainly very useful for us and has given plenty of food for thought. However, can I possibly have everyone's attention at this point? We'll be setting off into the wilds soon now, so can we go over once more what will be happening over the next few days? After all, this is how we'll be earning all that lovely money that Hendry Corp is paying out."*

Lou Gharr and Franklin Barr reentered the bunkhouse as if on cue.

Bailey had shakily resumed his seat - mopping at his florid face with a pristine white handkerchief. Benson had an extremely smug and very satisfied gloating expression as he watched him. Kimberly was reminded of the adage 'the cat who got the cream'.

But there was work to be done. She went over the schedule for the next three days. They had the precise route that the 1996 Texas University people had taken - the exact copy in fact left behind at the logging camp in case of emergencies. They had set off on their fateful hike almost twenty-odd years past, never to return. Hendry Corp had pulled some strings and had procured the original for them from the Canadian authorities. Kimberly Eastman had the map document scanned and blown up and had pinned it to the wall so all could see. The route was marked in red - overnight stops clearly marked. The total trip was just short of twenty-one miles. In terms of distance it didn't sound like much and didn't look far on the map. However, hiking across the rugged terrain would take them three days. Seventy-two hours of tough trekking to finally arrive back at the logging camp. Eastman pointed at the enlarged map with a laser pointer.

She spoke to the small group in tones that were deliberately calculated to get them geed up a little: *"From a purely filming point of view, what I need is good, exciting, thoughtful commentary, - let's make it vivid please, people! I don't just want viewers to be listening and watching images on their flat screens, munching popcorn. I want far, far more from you all. Dig deep on this one, folks! I want those guys on their couches to feel like they are with us. I want them to be walking along with us - sweating it out with us - tasting the adventure! Don't be afraid to say what you're feeling. Make it real - but more importantly - make it dramatic! Don't worry if you're going to look good on screen. Let Scott and myself sort that one out for you. We're experts at this - let us deal with that. I want you to concentrate on what it is you want to say."*

Despite her words, no one looked too enthusiastic. Unbidden, Barr slowly came to the front of the room to join her. This surprised Eastman somewhat. He glanced at her, not waiting for permission at the interruption and began to speak.

"Don't wanna say much to you folks. I don't know anything 'bout no TV stuff, but I do know these forests. And I know what's out there."

He hooked a chair with his foot, pulling it to him. Placing a foot on it, he leaned on his crooked leg. He then pulled out one of the biggest handguns that Eastman had ever seen. He had everyone's attention now.

Barr held up the brightly chromed semi-automatic pistol – it looked huge even in his big hand – he wanted everyone to get a good look. He certainly had everyone's attention.

"This gun is a Magnum Research Desert Eagle XIX 50AE, with a 6 Inch, brushed chrome fixed barrel." He dropped the gun's magazine from

the butt of the firearm into his other hand and placed the empty gun on the table in front of him before continuing. *"The magazine holds seven .50 caliber rounds."* He used his thumb to strip off the topmost exposed round and deftly caught the heavy bullet in his other hand, holding it up between thumb and forefinger to show them.

"These heavy rounds, folks, will pierce the engine block of a car at over 50 yards. But that ain't what it is used for. Don't get too many wild rampaging vehicles up here on the island. The forests can be beautiful. But they're also deadly. The brown bears up here are known as grizzlies. I'm pretty sure even city people have heard of 'em. These bad boys can weigh up to 850 pounds. They can run at 35mph and are known man eaters."

Eastman could smell the testosterone in the air after Barr had produced that hand cannon. The guys in the room were salivating at the sight of it. She ruefully realized that even she could certainly learn something about dramatics from this Haidan Indian hunter. She listened intently to what he was saying.

"Here's the deal. If we see one out there, we keep still and let it go on its way. Trust me when I say we don't want to antagonize it. A big grizzly, if it's riled up, can do a variety of damage - none of which you want to experience first hand."

Barr tossed the clip on the table. Quite unexpectedly and deliberately he took off his hunting jacket, letting it drop casually to the bunkhouse floor. He pulled his tee-shirt up and turned slowly around. The sight was shocking, eliciting gasps from several of the onlookers. Barr's broad back was a livid mass of deep, flesh torn scar tissue. Furrowed marks of several huge claws were starkly visible there - along with several gruesome long healed puncture wounds. Barr had obviously been savagely bitten. He let them all have a good look - then pulled his shirt back down and stooped to pick up his jacket from the dusty floor, brushing it off at the same time.

There was a stunned silence in the room. *Oh God,* thought Kimberly, *please let Rankin have got that!* She looked over at her friend and he anticipated her thoughts. He put his thumb up. He got it.

Barr went on: *"So you see folks, a grizzly ain't the thing we wanna be tangling with. They're normally quite shy creatures but can be a little testy if disturbed. Like I did by accident once years back when I was real young and real stupid. If one approaches you - stay still. If one attacks, you - just lie down, keep your hands under you and spread your legs wide so he can't turn you over easy. And play dead. It saved my life - might even save yours. Point is, don't go nowhere on your own out there. That's what I'm here for. If there's any risk to be taken, then I take it...OK?"* Everyone nodded in understanding. Even the normally glib Ed Benson had nothing to say on the subject. Seemingly satisfied, Barr continued, *"Now, if everyone will come with me outside, I'll show you a few tricks that might just save your ass in a pinch. And maybe some of you fellahs would like to try some shootin'?"*

He swaggered out of the bunkhouse, with the other men trotting after him like obedient, excited puppies. Olivia Hannah came up to Kimberly and linked arms with her.

"Kimberly, shall we go and watch the boys playing with their toys?" Eastman laughed. *"I guess we will, Olivia, I guess we will."*

***

The rest of the afternoon was spent with Barr and the 'boys' testing and firing the weapons that were the hunter's stock-in-trade. Barr was explaining what amongst his arsenal he would be taking and why. They were obviously having a great time and Kimberly was content to let them get on with it.

That was until one particularly annoying comment from Ed Benson riled her. He was saying something to the men along the lines that it was *'just as well they had all tried out a gun or two in case Barr was incapacitated. The girls might need some protection'.* She had been sitting on a stump a few yards away as she overheard it. Kimberly just couldn't let it pass. It simply wasn't in her.

She slowly walked over to the men that were gathered around Barr in a tight group, taking her time and listening. They were raptly studying the native hunter's SAS Voyager 62-inch Recurve hunting bow that he had deftly strung and held it out to them in his hands. The Haidan was carefully explaining what a 55lb draw weight meant in bow terms and was extolling the virtues of the steel-headed arrows to the men – the connection and reverence he felt when he hunted as his people had for countless generations - and was preparing to show them the weapon's power and his skill.

As she pushed her way in, Barr looked up, breaking off the demonstration. Ignoring the impressive bow, she said: *"Hey Barr, can I see that .50 caliber pistol of yours please?"*

Benson laughed. *"Careful you don't drop it on your toes, Kimberly. It's a bit heavy! Don't want to be carrying you before we even get into the woods!"*

She smiled demurely, sarcasm dripping from her, answering: *"Oh, I'll be really careful, I promise."*

Barr saw the look in Eastman's eye and instinctively knew that the woman was setting them all up and he happily played along. He un-holstered the big semi-automatic and handed it carefully to her. She turned it over in her hands a few times, feeling the weight and balance before addressing Ed Benson again - but all the time, concentrating on the weapon.

"You see Ed, it's like this." She expertly dropped the clip, checked its contents, then rapidly re-inserted it. *"I grew up on an Oklahoma farm with two brothers and a father. We were dirt poor and I had it hard. I grew up tough. I was firing shotguns and rifles before I was ten. By the time I was fifteen I could shoot the balls of a mosquito at 20 yards with almost any gun you can think of...and when I was twenty-six – well - I had a boyfriend who was an Army Ranger."*

She finally faced Benson, the gun safely pointed down at the floor.

"I was with him for nearly two years." She now looked around at the area they were standing in and picked out an old, water filled, rusting oil drum that was some thirty odd yards away. *"I tell you Ed, he really wasn't much good as a boyfriend. Really bad in bed, drank way too much...but as a special forces' combat and firearms drill instructor, well - I do have to say he certainly kicked proverbial ass. Oh - and I'd cover your ears right about now, if I were you."*

Eastman spun around so she was facing the drum – simultaneously pulling back the slide of the pistol, stripping a round from the clip directly into the chamber at the same time. Dropping into a combat shooting stance, holding the gun in an expert weaver hold and with a minimum of wasted effort, she rapidly and extremely efficiently emptied the entire magazine of seven rounds into the drum – the shots precisely grouped. Water sprayed high up into the air as the rusty cylinder shuddered under the impact of the heavy bullets that sliced right through it and ploughed heavily into an earth bank that was directly behind it. With the clip emptied, she quietly handed the gun back, butt first, to a grinning Barr. Kimberly turned on her heel and walked calmly away to find Hannah. Scott had naturally filmed the whole exchange.

The group of men watched her walk away and then hurried over to the drum to look. In stunned silence they saw that Kimberly Eastman had put the seven rounds into a tight area that was less than eight inches square.

Barr laughed out loud before commenting: *"Protect her? Yeah...right."*

***

It was the 23rd. The gear was packed into their rucksacks, the equipment was ready and so were they. Rankin focused the camera on Kimberly, and one handed counted her in; three, two...and she said: *"So, it begins."* She looked at her watch for dramatic effect. *"It is July the 23rd at precisely 10am at the Dinan Logging Camp on Graham Island, British Columbia. We are about to follow in the very footsteps of the 1996 university fieldtrip that mysteriously disappeared over 20 years ago. A trip that tragically claimed the lives of all twelve members of the party. What happened to them? Norton Bailey, author of the New York Times bestseller 'Myth & Super myth' feels certain that they inadvertently encountered the legendary mythical creature that the Haidan Indians call Gogit – perhaps better known to you and me as 'Bigfoot' or Sasquatch; and that encounter ultimately cost them their lives. What is the truth? Did that happen or is there another explanation that caused the disappearance of twelve people? Please watch and come with us now, as together we will follow their precise path and search for the truth in… 'Cryptid'!"*

Kimberly kept her deadly serious expression until Scott said: *"OK, Kim, you're out."*

The opening shot taken and with Barr leading the way, the group marched single file into the trees, watched by Lou Gharr until they had passed from view. Laughing and shaking his head in bewilderment at the spectacle, he muttered to himself *and good luck to you all'..*

Lou sauntered back into the bunkhouse for a beer - only glad he was waiting here at the logging camp and didn't have to go dragging his ass out into the forest.

He passed the rest of the day quietly - cooking himself a meal - catching up on a couple of reports and finally as dusk drew near, he got out his book and settled back on his bunk to have a good relaxing read. Something he rarely got the chance to do these days.

However, he must have dropped off because the twilight that had been coming on had now turned into blackest night. Luckily, he had left the main bunkhouse light on - otherwise he'd be stumbling around in the dark right about now trying to find the switch. He looked at his watch - almost 11pm. He smiled to himself, wondering what they were doing out there. Probably had eaten by now and were listening to some of Barr's outrageous tales of life in the forest. Come to think of it, he was hungry too.

He heaved himself up off the bunk, letting the open book slide off his chest and it fell onto the blankets. He made his way to the small kitchen to see what he could rustle up. As he walked in thinking about nothing in particular, a sudden shadow flashed across the kitchen window. It startled him. Just what in the hell was that?

He walked to the main bunkhouse door, opened it cautiously and peered out into the blackness. He could see very little beyond the corridor of dim light that was thrown out from the open door he was holding. They couldn't be back, surely? Had something gone wrong?

"Hey," he yelled out into the darkness. Complete quiet answered him - that was bizarre. The normally lively nighttime forest seemed blanketed in a heavy pall of silence.

Letting go of the door, he took a few tentative steps outside – again Lou called out into the dark. *"Hey? Who's out there?"* Then the stench hit him, causing an instant wave of nausea. *Oh my Christ*, he thought, his hand flying to his nose...*what was that rotten stink?*

That was one of the last things that Lou Gharr ever thought. Something flashed by him with incredible speed. As it did, the man instantly felt an odd tugging sensation at his stomach. He looked down to see an incomprehensible sight. His intestines were hanging from him in greasy loops that was accompanied by a welter of blood and excrement that spilled messily out onto the dirt floor.

Lou looked dazedly up to see the terrible sight that filled his vision. A cavernous wet maw filled with razor teeth - the instant before his face was torn off. Mercifully, the arteries and veins that supplied his brain were shredded apart with the incredible force of the attack. Death claimed him instantly. That was a mercy in itself - otherwise he would have had to listen - albeit briefly - to the creatures greedily devouring him in a feeding frenzy. It didn't take them long to finish off the remains of Lou Gharr. The grisly feast was concluded. The creatures' attention immediately switched to the forest; to the westerly path taken hours earlier by the rest.

As a single body, the group of titanic entities turned and bounded silently into the tree line, melting at once into the shadows.

The creatures still hungered. The hunt was on.

CHAPTER TEN

Graham Island, British Columbia

23rd July 2017

Barr took them gradually upwards following a rough, rutted trail comprising of a meandering series of twists and turns – a serpentine path that wound a tortuous route through thick undergrowth and towering western red and yellow cedars that made up this part of the dense forests.

Within a short space of time, none in the group other than their tall Haidan guide had any idea which direction they were heading - let alone where they were - in relation to the abandoned logging camp they had set out from.

Kimberly Eastman had intended to video a brief interview, while on the move, with Ed Benson regarding the native peoples of the Haida Gwaii, which is what the local Indians called the Queen Charlotte Islands. She had thought it a good idea to frame the first day's video footage with some local color, history and relevant mythology, but that plan had to be put on hold. The going was proving much tougher than Kimberly had anticipated so she decided to wait till they stopped for a break. That was if they ever would stop!

Barr was a living machine. He had the easy loping, flatfooted grace of a born woodsman. His steady pace ate up the distance on the rough trail, leaving the rest of the group breathless and struggling to keep up. If Barr was aware of the discomfort his pace was causing, he made no concession to it. The tempo continued unabated in the warm humid summer forests - so did the sweat - the accompanying salt soon attracted squadrons of flying insects that droned about their heads unmercifully. The repellent Deet sprays they had brought along seemed to be doing little to help - despite liberal applications. Myriads of the miniature tormentors still buzzed annoyingly around them all - except for Barr. For some reason they seemed to be leaving him well alone. After about three hours of this misery, Barr called a welcome halt for food and rest.

Eastman looked back down the slope at the path that they had traveled. The damp track looked like a ribbon of fire between the trees where the summer sun caught it. Barr was demonstrating his impressive woodcraft to the others as he quickly set up a small campfire to boil water and heat up provisions for their midday meal. Scott Rankin was filming the proceedings, so Eastman took the time to motion to Ed Benson; he broke away from the group who was milling around the Haidan and sauntered slowly over to her.

"Hey, Ed," she said, *"I'd like to do that native background piece we discussed earlier, that's if you can tear yourself away from Kit Carson over there?"*

He smiled at her, saying, *"Of course; anything for you, light of my life."*

She asked him to stay put and called Scotty to her as well - he ambled over, adjusting the camera's settings.

"Hey, how you holding up, kid?" Kimberly said quietly to him.

She had meant his drinking - but looking at him she realized that the rigors of the trip were taxing Rankin far more severely than his abstinence. The cameraman's red, sweating face showed her that he was plainly having a tough time of it.

However, he held his thumb up as if to say he was coping fine. Rather than dwell on the matter, she got straight to business, saying: *"I need you to set up for an interview with Ed Benson. Just pretty standard stuff; let's try and get the rest of the group in the background for some movement."*

Rankin nodded his understanding and positioned himself so Eastman and Benson were between the video camera and the rest of the group.

The cameraman quickly set the shot up and signaled he was ready whenever she was. Ed Benson stood patiently by the side of her and watched in bemused silence as Kimberly Eastman took out a small mirror from the top pocket of the hiking shirt she was wearing and flicked at her blonde hair, putting it into some sort of semblance that she was reasonably happy with. Then - much more to Benson's interest - Eastman undid a couple of shirt buttons, still looking in the mirror and adjusted it to make sure her impressive cleavage was displayed to its fullest possible advantage. She realized that the mythologist was staring at her boobs again. Kimberly politely coughed and gestured upwards with one finger - indicating to Ed that his eyes should be about a foot or so higher than the point that he was currently fixed upon.

Having reacquired his now slightly guilty attention, Eastman nodded to Rankin she was ready. With a couple of seconds grace, Scotty counted her silently in.

Unhesitatingly, Kimberly dove straight into it - staring and smiling directly to the camera lens. *"So, here we are, some three hours into the route followed by the vanished Texas University party of twenty years ago. I can tell you that it is tough going. Despite the physical conditioning we undertook preparing for this trek, we are all feeling the exertions of traveling through this wilderness of Graham Island at the height of the summer."*

Scott Rankin had to stop himself bursting out in cynical laughter at Kimberly's blatant lie about their 'physical conditioning'.

They had done jack shit in terms of prep for the hiking. However, he kept the shot focused as she ploughed on.

"I'm joined by Dr. Ed Benson, whom you may remember we met earlier; just to remind viewers he's the 'Cryptid' team's anthropologist and an acknowledged international expert in mythology." Kimberly now turned to Ed, before continuing.

"Can you explain to me Dr. Benson, and obviously to the folks at home, what significance - if any - is played by the fact that the Queen Charlotte Islands are the ancient home to a truly unique tribe of native Indians, the 'Haidan', in respect of the vanished party of Americans some twenty years past?"

Aware that the camera was now focused squarely on him, Benson drew himself up and gave his best profile for the benefit of the shot. He began to speak: *"Well, thanks for that great introduction Kimberly, and please,"* he said directing his remark straight to the camera, with a slight wink, *"call me Ed."*

Oh my God, thought Rankin as he kept the shot framed neatly on Ed Benson. *I thought that asshole Bailey was bad enough! What a friggin' ham.*

Benson continued: *"In my book, 'Mythology and Myth: A modern perspective' - still available in limited quantities from my website - I clearly make the correlation between many North American Indian tribes - their legends and mythologies - and the fact that many have similar threads running through them. It is fascinating that the isolated Haidan peoples with their unique language have many of the same common myths and legends readily found in many other indigenous peoples of North America."*

This wasn't really the answer or direction that Eastman had wanted to take it - but she pressed on - it might lead somewhere. If not, it could always be edited out later in the studio.

'Well Ed, I have to admit that I am slightly confused, as I'm sure the viewers at home are by what you've just said; but I do have to ask you what does this very interesting information have to do with the mysterious disappearance of those people in 1996?"

Ed looked squarely at the camera before answering in a grim and quiet tone.

"What I'm saying is that if even some of these common legends are true there is a possibility that the students and their professors stumbled accidently across what some believe are creatures that have consciously and deliberately hidden away from humanity for millennia. And that

'something' that may still abide within the darker recesses of this forested wilderness might have taken a deadly exception to being disturbed. The encounter - if it occurred - could have cost those people their lives."

Benson then slowly and dramatically turned away from the camera till he was facing a line of dense trees.

Shit, thought Kimberly, in genuine surprise, that was great! She indicated to Rankin to cut it there. Knowing the camera was now off them Ed Benson faced Eastman once more. *"So, was that what you wanted?"* he asked her.

"Outstanding, Ed...exceptional," she replied, *"but I didn't think you believed in these mythical 'creatures' of the forest."*

He grinned at her, replying; *"Hell Kimberly, you know I don't! But I do know that out there great American viewing public glued to the screen want to believe. So, let's play along - make a few bucks - give 'em what they want and everyone's happy."*

She laughed at him, replying, *"Yep, I can't argue with that."*

Ed sidled up to her, momentarily fingering the point of her shirt collar between his thumb and forefinger, obviously imagining rubbing some other part of her in the same intimate manner.

He said in a low tone: *"So, Kimberly, are you impressed enough with my performance to get to know me a little better over a glass of Châteaux de Benson later on tonight?"*

Kimberly had begun to take quite a liking to the oddly handsome mythologist over the past few days. She smiled demurely at him, saying: *"Well let's just say you scored yourself extra kudos points, Dr. Benson. And who knows what surprises the next few days will bring?"*

Benson grinned at her then turned away to join the others, having to content himself with that.

After an hour's lunch and a much-needed rest they packed up their stuff and headed out again. Eastman had managed to fit in a couple more interviews, firstly from Dr. David Sterling, the forensic scientist. He doubted that any large hominid creature existed here – at least not one that could have remained undiscovered for so long. He was also of the opinion that any trace of the missing party - any physical evidence - would have long since vanished during the intervening years due to the extreme weather on the islands - animal predation would have played a major part in disposing of any human remains.

Lastly, a brief interview was videoed with Olivia Hannah. She expressed the view - if in a somewhat restrained manner - that nothing in the natural world can ever be really ruled in or out of existence unless proved or disproved by empirical scientific data. They needed to look coldly at any evidence before making any firm conclusions. Both interviews were objective, giving a balance between healthy skepticism from the medical examiner – and a pragmatic approach from the cryptozoologist.

However, Kimberly was worried by Olivia Hannah's general attitude and composure. For some unknown reason, entering the forests proper had an increasingly detrimental effect on her. Olivia Hannah - normally quiet and introspective - was getting withdrawn - for the want of a better description in a state of anxious tension. The woman hardly spoke to anyone that whole day - had to be dragged into conversations or any group activities and tasks. It was apparent that the others had noticed the situation too. Kimberly determined to have a talk to Olivia later and get to the bottom of it. In the meantime, the hard slog of the trek continued. Kimberly Eastman was oblivious to the fact that Ed Benson was really getting to the bottom of something that was quite dear to his heart - literally.

Despite the overhang from the trees which kept the strong late summer sun at bay, the steadily winding uphill trail was hot, tiring, and sweaty. Ed Benson's own shirt felt wet and sticky against his damp skin, and the buzzing insects were a constant irritant. However, there were certain compensations. Walking directly behind Kimberly Eastman, he had observed - over a happy period of time - the fascinating journey of her clearly defined underwear beneath her tight shorts as they slowly worked their way up between her well-defined butt cheeks as she walked. She had occasionally reached behind, unconsciously clawing the migrating underwear back out; but as the walk dragged interminably on, she had now given up the effort and left them alone. He happily watched her magnificently swaying rear end. If things worked out the way he hoped, he might even get to sample some of those hidden delights himself. Kimberly Eastman, he reflected, despite being forty years old, really was an extremely hot piece of ass.

The sun was slowly settling down on the hidden western horizon now and the approaching sunset was beginning to flood the cloudless sky with subtle orange and purple hues. Mercifully, in a small clearing, Barr now called a halt to the day's torture. The group began wearily unpacking their camping gear and the Haidan silently busied himself with starting a night camping fire.

As the others were clumsily - and with an obvious inexperience - going about the business of putting up the tents, Scott Rankin moved amongst them and tried to shoot as much of the action as he could. Kimberly Eastman had cleverly orchestrated the conversations that went on between them and Rankin captured that on video as well. All in all, it had been a very productive days shooting with most of the first day's objectives fulfilled. There had been a good mix of the dramatic from Ed

Benson, the skeptical from David Sterling, and scientific speculation from Olivia Hannah. What she needed tonight was the day's overall perspective from Norton Bailey and maybe a few salty comments from Barr to round it up.

Eastman was thinking just along those lines, when she noticed something odd. Barr had set the fire and had been carefully tending it - but now he stood quite still to one side, staring out into the gathering darkness.

His whole posture and watchful demeanor gave rise to a feeling of tension. Then the hunter exploded into shocking action.

His frozen upright alert posture became a sudden crouch - his large hunting bow, fully strung, instantly appeared in his hands as if by some magical means known only to him and the weapon. In one smooth seamless motion, a shaft was nocked and poised, bow string taut at full stretch - the steel-tipped arrow ready to be released with deadly force into an unseen target.

He was scanning the fast-approaching gloom around them intently and slowly turned in this stooped posture and did a full 360 degrees turn.

The Indian now had the others' undivided attention; they had become silent in a communal unspoken fear. All efforts to erect tents had ceased as had any movement; they were watching the unknown drama unfold before their eyes. Scott Rankin, professional as ever, had his video camera squarely fixed on Barr and was filming the events as they transpired. A faint whiff of something truly putrid floated past heavily on the air. Kimberly's hand came up to her mouth and nose, almost by reflex at the foul stench. She wasn't the only one that did it. A few of the others mirrored her reaction, and a couple of disgusted gasps escaped also. The whole forest had appeared to become quiet and motionless – as if holding its breath waiting for some monumental and cataclysmic event to occur. As quickly as the uncanny moment had come, it was gone - like early morning mist touched by rays of harsh sunlight.

The dreaded event - whatever it was - had passed and everything returned to how it should be. The forest seemed to breathe again.

Barr straightened up and slowly released the tension on the bowstring. The arrow was plucked away from the bow by his experienced hands, and both bow and shaft disappeared as rapidly as they had appeared.

Kimberly beckoned Scott to come join her as she walked over to the tall Indian by the smoky light of the flickering campfire. The hunter had already put the fearsome bow back into the case where he had pulled it from unseen just moments before.

She waited till Rankin had got the right set up, then she spoke to Barr.

"Barr, can you tell us what just happened?" Kimberly asked with a mock breathlessness that was for the benefit of the camera. The rangy

Haidan finished securing the weapon into its case to his complete satisfaction and then slowly stood up to face her before replying. *"Thought that'd be obvious missy; there's something out there in the dark stalking us, now it's gone on its way."*

Kimberly pressed him, asking, *"Any idea what it was? Will it come back?"*

Barr looked at her blankly and shrugged slightly before replying in a non-committal way: *"Dunno, hard to say. Could have been a bear, I reckon. Might come back. Might not. But if it does,"* he picked up his bow case, fixing her eyes with his own, *" I'll be ready, you can be sure of that."* And that was all he'd say on the subject. He turned away from her and stalked back to the other side of the fire, the bow case held closely to him. Kimberly Eastman turned to face the camera.

"So, there you have it. It can be extremely dangerous here – as has been graphically illustrated by what you just saw. Luckily, we have the experience of Mr. Franklin Barr who is looking out for us. Barr, as he simply prefers to be called, is a native Haidan and has been hunting and trapping these island forests for most of his life."

Not wanting to lose the moment or impetus, Eastman looked around to see who she could catch a reaction from to this unexpected twilight encounter. It was then Kimberly noticed Olivia Hannah. She was standing stock still, staring out into the gloom of the densely packed trees. Kimberly offhandedly motioned Rankin to follow her. As Eastman got closer, it was obvious that things were very wrong with the cryptozoologist. Olivia Hannah stood in a bewildered daze, staring blankly out into space.

Kimberly placed her hand gently on Hannah's bony shoulder before asking: *"Olivia, are you OK, honey?"*

Eastman was genuinely concerned for the Dr. but still cynical enough to hope that Scott was capturing the woman's distress with the camera. Olivia suddenly realized that Eastman and Rankin were there with her. Benson and Bailey had strolled over too, apparently curious as to what was transpiring.

"What?" Hannah said, obviously fighting to recover self-control again, blinking furiously. *"What did you say, Kimberly dear? I'm sorry; I was miles away I think."*

Kimberly had left her hand resting on the taller woman's shoulder, replying in a tone of genuine concern: *"You were almost in a trance for a second there, Olivia. Are you alright?"*

Hannah, now fully back to herself, placed her own hand on top of Kimberly's, saying: *"I'm fine, thank you. It was just that awful stench, I think. It bothered me for some odd reason I can't explain. Did you smell it, Kimberly? Did anyone else?"* The small gathered group collectively murmured their assent.

Ed Benson threw out, *"I'm not much for the outdoors, but overheard Barr say it could have been a bear. Christ, does a bear really smell as bad as that? No wonder the things hibernate in a deep cave on their own. No one else could put up with the stink. Not even another bear!"* This remark brought forth a good deal of general laughter.

Norton Bailey cut in, *"Tell me, Dr. Hannah, if you can, as I'm a little curious. Why did this smell bother you so much? You seemed quite unsettled by it."*

Kimberly Eastman looked at Bailey then thoughtfully back at Hannah. There was an undefined, powerful undercurrent running between them.

It wasn't the first time she'd thought it either. Her instinct screamed at her these uncharted depths needed probing - there was something there between them; intriguing and unsaid.

Olivia Hannah hesitantly answered Bailey's question: *"I don't know, Norton. It was quite horrible. It left me personally bereft and for some unaccountable reason most terribly afraid."* She then hung her head down - all the energy and vitality in her tall frame had hemorrhaged away, leaving a dried-out husk. Norton nodded and, on the surface, appeared content with that answer - or rather the avoidance of it.

He left the subject alone; but the intense look he gave the distressed woman as he sauntered away belied that.

He had obviously wanted other comment and information from Olivia Hannah; but it was equally obvious to Eastman that the disturbed woman was not willing to say anything further at that moment. Kimberly shrewdly concluded that Norton Bailey knew more about the good Dr. than he was letting on. Whatever he knew, she was determined to know too.

The small group broke up now, each going their separate ways to finish up necessary camp tasks.

Kimberly made to erect the dome tent that she'd be using on this trip in the rapidly fading light. As she was trying to figure it out, she noticed with concern that Olivia was still standing forlornly in the same spot. And with even greater concern, from what she could observe, there were obvious signs that the tall woman had at some point lost control of her bladder.

***

The evening meal was a quiet affair. The group as a whole was generally fatigued and somewhat subdued by the day's exertions -

sprawled unevenly around the welcome flickering light of the campfire. Even Ed Benson's customary light and facetious banter couldn't lift the mood. Eventually he gave up trying and lapsed into silence.

With some relief, Kimberly saw that Olivia Hannah was a little more like her old self. She noted the cryptozoologist had changed her shorts. She let Rankin film away whilst she tried to engage some of the others in some relevant conversation. She tried Norton Bailey.

"Norton, would you like to give your thoughts about our first day's travel? Is this going pretty much as you expected?"

The author was perched close to the fire, gazing intently into the flames and had seemed utterly lost in his own thoughts. Eastman's inquiry brought him back.

He cleared his throat and smiled, realizing that the camera would now be fixed upon him. *"Pretty much, Ms. Eastman; but I do have a suspicion that we have been under observation for some considerable time now, just as the others were twenty years ago. I think that the earlier encounter that we almost had was a strong indication that we are being scrutinized by creatures seldom seen by modern man."*

Dr. David Sterling was sitting just outside the firelight's circle but was evidently listening and thought he needed to interject. He spoke out and Rankin let the camera pan to him on the adjacent side of the fire.

"Well Mr. Bailey, if that was what you call 'strong proof...'"

The stocky author interrupted him in mid-sentence.

"Excuse me, Dr. Sterling; I didn't say 'strong proof'. I said, 'a strong indication'. There is quite a semantic difference, you know."

The forensic scientist scoffed at him, shaking his head in derision. *"Come on, Mr. Bailey! Don't split hairs, man! You are trying to intimate to us here and everyone watching that what was in all probability a common-or-garden bear sniffing around for some food scraps, is one of the islands' mythical Gogits? A Sasquatch? Oh, please! Let's not insult people's intelligence either here or back at home who are watching this program."*

Sterling paused for a moment, gathering his thoughts for the briefest of moments. He then continued before anyone else could speak.

"Let's use a little critical reasoning, which some of us seem to be quite sadly deficient in. Think about it for a moment," he was addressing the whole group now, *"If there were some rampaging creature out here that was responsible for the deaths of twelve people - why then aren't people attacked more often on the islands? The cases widely publicized? If one or more of those creatures are stalking us, why weren't we assaulted straight away?"*

Uncharacteristically, Barr spoke up at this point. He stood up, facing the forensic scientist, his back to the campfire.

"See here, Dr. Sterling, you're an educated man." He rolled one of his cigarettes as he spoke. *"Seems to me you're a mite stupid too. Guess sense ain't common to everyone, is it?"*

Ed Benson laughed uproariously at this comment from the laconic Haidan hunter. Dr. Sterling just looked up at the Indian in chagrined silence. Barr went on. *"Also seems to me, Gogit or no Gogit, anything with a pinch of brains wouldn't reach right in and take on a group of things. Not till they knew what their strength was. That'd be mighty dumb."* He paused for a moment as he finished rolling the tobacco, licked the paper and flicked a match with his scarred thumb to light it. Taking a deep drag, he blew out a steady stream of blue smoke into the darkness before continuing.

"If you'd ever hunted flying geese, then you'd know the best way to catch most of 'em is to start at the back and work your way forward. Pick 'em off one at a time. You jump straight in - just shoot one at random - well that warns the others that you have some design on 'em contrary to their general good health - they'll scatter for sure. And the result is you'll end up with just the one...or maybe none. But there again, what the hell do I know?"

Barr shut up then and contemplated the end of his glowing roll-up.

Kimberly Eastman spoke next. *"Are you saying we're being hunted, Barr?"*

Barr just turned his head and grinned at her.

"Well, missy, I'm not city educated like you folks...Dr. Sterling reckons we ain't, so I guess I'll rest easy tonight knowing that. I'd get some sleep if I was you, folks. Gonna be a hard push come tomorrow." And with that cutting remark and last piece of sage advice, he strolled away from the group and out to his tent. That seemed to be a general signal for them all. The group broke up and went their separate ways for the night.

Kimberly crawled into her tent, and carefully lit the compact hanging propane lamp that brightly illuminated the small dark interior. Once inside, she gratefully began to pull off her clothes. Her shirt was dirty, and the bra underneath had been cutting into her flesh; the sweat had chafed under her breasts and across her shoulders. She happily shrugged both off and let them drop to the floor of the tent in a damp heap. These were followed by the tight hiking boots and then the damp socks. The shorts came next, then the cotton panties.

She hunted round for her flannel PJs. In the meantime, what she hadn't realized was that her undressing and redressing were clearly visible to other eyes due to the detailed shadows cast on her tent walls by the lit lamp.

Ed Benson had enjoyed the show from his vantage point at the side of his own tent. His penis began to inadvertently throb and stiffen as he watched the divine, heavy breasted, shadowy creature pull off the bra and remove the shorts and underwear. A vision of Kimberly Eastman bent over sprang unbidden into his mind; he imagined her huge ripe tits hanging invitingly down. In his mind she was reaching back and pulling apart her ass cheeks while he gripped her hips and he slid his....

Benson couldn't wait any longer. Nothing ventured, nothing gained, he reasoned. Quickly diving into his tent, he found the bottle of Australian Shiraz he had toted along in his pack. The corkscrew was located next. Sticking his head out of the tent flaps, he quickly scanned the camp to make sure that everyone else was tucked safely up. They were - he scuttled out of his tent and as quietly as he could quickly covered the few feet to Kimberly's small tent and scratched tentatively on the light nylon fabric.

"Yes," asked the woman's voice from inside, *"is that you Ed? I'm actually in bed now."*

He replied as quietly as he could, *"You too much in bed to have that drink I mentioned earlier?"*

Silence for a moment. A brief rustling then a zip was pulled softly up and Eastman's head, with her mass of tousled blond hair tied up, poked through her tent entrance. *"I'll have just one drink, OK Ed? And I do mean just the one - then sleep. I'm absolutely fried."*

"Sure, Kimberly," he assured her, *"A drink then off we go to sleep."*

She pulled the zip up further and scooted back to let him in.

The gas lamp was turned down within her tent - more of a glimmer than an actual light. But even at that, Benson could still make out the magnificent swell of Eastman's unfettered breasts. His penis twitched again, and he could feel it pushing against his jeans. Two plastic camping mugs were produced, and liberal amounts of the wine were poured into them. However, after a few minutes' conversation with her it became obvious to Ed Benson that although she was interested in him - and the time might well come on this trip where they would have sex - it wasn't going to be tonight. She obviously really was too tired. His wine nearly finished, he glanced down and spotted the heap of her discarded dirty clothes in the dimness. He could feel the build-up inside his scrotum. He needed relief after watching that perfect ass all day and imagining what he'd like to do to it. Benson couldn't resist it - he put down his now drained mug and leaned across to kiss her gently goodnight on her cheek. As he did so he deftly snagged Kimberly's worn panties from where they were sticking out of the pile and pushed them hurriedly into his back pocket.

Any port in a storm, he thought. He whispered goodnight to her and backed out of the tent. She whispered goodnight back and zipped up the tent. He stood up, the wine burning nicely in his stomach and the air was now chill despite the time of year. He breathed it in deeply and looked up at the scattered stars. They truly were magnificent; distant points of light, bright and cold, yet shining down on him with a wonderful energy that was all their own. The camp was silent now and in darkness; he was the only one still up. He needed to pee. Walking away from the brightly glowing embers that were the earlier camp blaze, he went to a convenient tree just outside the clearing perimeter.

He unzipped his jeans and pulled his penis out, happily relaxing his bladder, and a harsh heavy stream of steaming pee splattered and splashed against the rough bark. Benson finished and shook of the remnants.

His grip on his cock excited him. He looked back and could see no one moving about in the camp - as a precaution, he carefully edged a few feet deeper into the trees and faced outward so he could see if anyone was about.

Stroking his rapidly hardening member, he pulled Kimberly's panties from his jeans pocket and held the damp cotton up to his face. He would drop them by her tent flap entrance later; she'd think that they got dragged out by mistake when he left. The smell of her bodily excretions excited him beyond measure - he could hardly contain himself. Benson closed his eyes in ecstasy; he positioned the underwear so that the gusset was pressed hard against his nose and mouth. He breathed in sharply through his nose and mouth simultaneously and could almost taste Kimberly Eastman's pussy and ass. God, how he'd love to fuck her real hard and deep in that gorgeous butt...

Sadly, Ed Benson never got that last orgasm he was working so diligently towards. His pleasure was broken when he suddenly sensed something was very wrong. Ed opened his eyes. Ten short inches from his face, in the darkness, were starkly etched the nightmare features of a demon straight from the depths of hell itself. He staggered back a few paces in shock.

The creature was on all fours and even hunched down like that it was clearly gigantic in its proportions.

The cold eyes set deep in its face were luminous and huge - the head was a titanic hair-covered boulder; and now the cavernous mouth opened up - slack drooling lips peeled back to let out a low growling snicker - the gaping wet hole revealed two rows of terrible jagged razor-like teeth. The putrid stench that emanated from its maw was like death itself. Kimberly's panties, now quite forgotten, were dropped by nerveless fingers to the forest floor.

Shit, thought Benson with a measure of incredulity. *They're fucking real. That smug bastard Bailey was right all along.* And bizarrely, at that second, the chafing realization briefly caused Ed Benson greater distress than his imminent doom - almost. He had no time to scream, or even think about opening his mouth. Death was instantaneous. Scant seconds later, Benson's twisted corpse, its upper torso crushed, bloodied and mangled - practically stripped of its clothing - was dragged away into the deep blackness with a long-practiced stealth and in complete and utter silence. The raw dripping meat was taken into the dark secluded tangle of the trees, where others of its kind waited hungrily – yet patiently - for their share of the warm flesh.

CHAPTER ELEVEN

Graham Island, British Columbia

24th July 2017

The urgent unremitting whine of her small travel alarm clock joltingly woke Kimberly Eastman. Sharp tones dragged her away from a mindless state where work and problems didn't exist and back to hard reality. She reached blindly out and turned off the hateful noise that had selfishly awoken her.

Stretching, rubbing sticky eyes, she pulled her reluctant body to a position where she was sitting up in her sleeping bag, wincing at the pain the movement caused. It was cold out of the bag and her tired muscles ached - especially in the back of her legs and ass. Kimberly had no time to dwell on her discomforts. Scott Rankin was already outside her tent, adding to the misery, loudly urging her outside. She knew him well enough to realize that the tone in his voice meant that there were some major problems at hand. Mumbling a quick OK, Eastman began dragging out some fresh clothes from her pack; she dressed as hurriedly as she could in the confined space.

Kimberly was still feeling the dull ache in her abused muscles when she pulled herself out of her small tent and heaved herself stiffly upright with a stifled groan. Today, Eastman was feeling every one of her forty years – and she sincerely believed that a few more had been slyly added during the night. She looked at her watch. It was still exceedingly early. The sun was hardly up and there was a thin cold morning mist that crawled sluggishly on the ground - insidiously winding cloying tendrils between the surrounding trees. Looking round, it seemed like everyone was up in various states of dress. From their expressions, no one seemed happy.

It was Rankin that spoke to her now. *"Well, what you want,"* he asked her, *"the bad news or the really bad news?"*

She sighed inwardly. What she actually wanted was a mug of hot strong coffee - but she had an inkling that wasn't going to be forthcoming anytime soon. Wearily, she replied, *"Just tell me like it is, Scotty."*

So, he did. In a quiet monotone, Rankin told her: *"All my satellite up-link equipment has vanished. Stolen, I think. So has my satellite phone – and most of the cameras - all gone."*

She felt sleep deprived. The words didn't quite sink in. She looked blankly at him. *"What? What do you mean your up-link equipment has 'vanished'?"* Rankin looked at her intently, before replying.

"Exactly what I said, someone has taken the electronic equipment I need to upload our digital footage to the studio. Also, my satellite phone has disappeared. All I have left is my smaller digital video camera. That's about as succinctly as I can put it."

Oh shit. She had a nasty thought. Aches and pains temporarily forgotten, Kimberly Eastman turned and ducked back into her own tent. A brief search inside confirmed to her what she feared. She now saw something she had not noticed when she had first woken - the side of her own tent had been neatly slit open – giving just enough access for a thief to slip in and take stuff without risking waking her.

She came back out to face Rankin. She couldn't keep the despair out of her voice, although she did unsuccessfully try. *"Well, here's my bad news. My fucking satellite phone's gone too. It was right on the top of my pack and now it's missing. The side of the tent was sliced open. Just a thought, but I'd say you were right, and we've been royally robbed sometime in the night."*

Rankin nodded, before replying; *"I'd go further, Kim, and say we've been royally fucked. At least I still have my small HD video camera; I practically sleep with it. Whoever it was they didn't manage to get that, thank God. I mean, seriously - who the hell would rob us out here? We're miles from any damn where, we're the only people around."*

Kimberly stared back at him, saying; *"All things being equal, I'd say we're not the only people around though, are we?"* Hands on her hips, Kimberly Eastman stared silently at the ground for a few seconds, with unseeing eyes as she weighed the options available. Finally, she straightened up. *"OK, Scotty. Let's talk to Bailey. I'm sure he'll want to call everyone together and 'discuss' what we're going to do next."*

Rankin motioned urgently to Norton Bailey who ambled over to them. After a few minutes' hushed discussion between the three of them, the rest were called over. The group came together, gathering around Norton Bailey as the focal point.

Kimberly looked around and noticed the one conspicuous absence straight away. *"Where the hell is Ed?"* she asked to no one in particular, adding, *"We need everyone here."*

The assembled group just looked blankly at each other, until Hannah volunteered, *"I haven't actually seen him as yet this morning, Kimberly."*

The others murmured in agreement.

"Do me a favor, Barr?" Norton Bailey asked the hunter. *"Could you be so kind as to go along to Dr. Benson's tent and ask him if it isn't too much trouble for him, would he mind joining the rest of us? We'd certainly appreciate his presence."*

The barely disguised irritation in the author's tone was unmistakable.

Barr nodded and walked away to do as he was asked.

Bailey addressed them all again. *"In the meantime, ladies and gentlemen, while we wait for Dr. Benson to make an appearance, let me ensure that everyone is cognizant with current events. You may already have gathered that our TV crew were unfortunately robbed during the night of several thousand dollars' worth of equipment. The technical gear that they needed to film, along with the theft of their satellite phones, means we are now cut off from the outside world. As you know there is no cellular signal on the island. We were reliant on the satellite phones for communications."* Bailey paused to let them digest this information before continuing. *"Can I ask, has anyone else had anything taken?"*

There was a general murmured comment to the effect that no one else had, as far as they were aware. Norton Bailey nodded at this fresh information. He continued: *"However, the situation could be worse, I'm informed. Our position in terms of filming is not irrecoverable and all isn't completely lost. Even with the loss of most of Mr. Rankin's equipment, it doesn't stop him completing the filming as planned. He will be using his small HD camera for the remainder of the trip and will then be taking it back to the studio to be edited, instead of remotely uploading footage daily which was the original intention. It may put the program back a week, so I'm told, but that's about all, really."*

He paused again, before adding: *"There is one other glaring problem, as I'm sure you've realized. If we were to have an emergency, we could be in serious trouble. It is a point well worth considering. As a codicil, I should add that if Ms. Eastman or Mr. Rankin do not call in to the studios, help would be sent out to us by default. But in the circumstances, what we do next will affect all, it's only fair for the group to vote. The question I put before you all, is this. Do we continue, or head back to the logging camp? The majority vote has it."*

There was silence for a moment - Kimberly looked at Olivia Hannah; the cryptozoologist looked back and held Kimberly's gaze for the briefest of moments then broke off contact and looked down at the clearing floor, uncomfortable with the scrutiny that was given her. The others merely looked at each other. It was obvious from their body language what they wanted to do. The vote was a forgone conclusion.

"OK," Bailey said, *"all those in favor of going on? A show of hands please?"*

All hands were raised, although Kimberly noticed that Hannah's was more hesitant than the others, her arm slower to go up.

The Haidan returned to the group. He wasted no time with any preamble; he was his normally direct self, informing them: *"Benson's bag ain't been slept in. He ain't here. Don't look like he's been here all night, if you ask me."*

Shit, Kimberly thought again. *Shit, shit, shit!!* But her face outwardly remained calm and composed.

"OK," Bailey huffed in exasperation, *"this is getting quite ridiculous. Who saw Dr. Benson last?"*

Barr grinned mischievously, jumping straight in with, *"Reckon that'd be Miss Eastman. I spied him goin' into her tent late last night."* Kimberly felt herself reddening as the others' eyes fixed upon her.

She retorted, sharply, *"It's not what you think, Mr. Barr, not that it's any of your damned business..."* then after a pause added, *"...and if perhaps you had kept your eyes out as sharply as you did watching the comings and goings of my visitor, maybe we wouldn't have been robbed!"*

She could have left it at that, but the bitch inside her raged unchecked. *"Or maybe our equipment was just 'borrowed' by Raven, and he'll bring it all back when he feels like it?"*

Kimberly instantly felt bad for deriding Barr's tribal beliefs and was about to apologize but was given no real opportunity to do so.

Barr half-muttered something quietly, aggrieved by what she'd said, but didn't respond directly to her cutting remark or to the implied criticism. He merely turned and moved away from the group to tend to some of the necessary camp tasks. There was a lingering embarrassed silence for a few painful seconds that Norton Bailey broke, by saying; *"Has anyone actually seen Dr. Benson this morning?"*

No one apparently had. Bailey continued; *"So it appears to me that Dr. Benson didn't get back to his tent after he left Miss Eastman's. Considering that, I feel the need to look for him. I suggest we individually spread out for a few hundred yards in all directions and see if we can locate him."*

Barr, who had obviously still been listening, rejoined the gathering, shaking his head. *"I'm smellin' what you're steppin' in, Mr. Bailey, but it's a real bad idea trying to find someone that way. These forests ain't safe with the bears and such and wandering off out here - I tell ya' it's a sure way to get folks lost real quick and end up in a world of trouble."*

Kimberly spoke up. *"So, what do you suggest, Barr?"*

Their previous sharp exchange apparently forgotten with the current situation, Barr replied, *"We buddy up in teams of two. Then we head out, so and so,"* he indicated various directions with swift pointing motions.

"Everybody keeping in shouting distance of everyone else and we leave someone back here in case Dr. Benson turns up in the meanwhile. We look for one hour then rendezvous back here at camp. If we ain't found him by then, we head out in another direction. That way we can cover

ground more quickly, and not search the same area twice and, in that way, we don't lose nobody else."

Kimberly Eastman looked around the group. From their expressions, the Haidan's plan had made good sense - but as it turned out, the search was quite short lived. Within a few minutes of pairing up and starting out, Sterling, who had been searching with Olivia Hannah, shouted. They had found something.

The rest of them hurried back to find out what the couple had discovered.

Just a few yards outside the clearing of the camp perimeter, Sterling was crouched down in the mulch of the forest floor. The thick overhead canopy was excluding much of the early morning sunlight. Olivia Hannah was standing several feet away from him. The others hurried over - the forensic scientist stood up, and with his arms held out wide, he slowly backed out of the tangle of trees.

"Everyone stop!" Sterling shouted in a commanding tone. *"No one is to come any closer than this, please."*

Everyone had by now arrived at the scene. Breathlessly, his camera soaking it all in, Rankin asked, *"What is it Doc? What've you found?"* David Sterling turned to look at them all, his face grim.

He answered Rankin, but his words were clearly meant for all. *"I think we should prepare ourselves for the possibility that something quite awful might have happened to Dr. Benson."*

Norton Bailey, having arrived last, pushed himself to the front of the gathered group. In tones made shrill with an obvious nervous energy, the man asked, *"What do you mean, Dr. Sterling? What is it you have you found?"*

In reply, Sterling said, *"Take a look yourselves if you wish - but I caution you to go no further forward than I am. We are looking at a forensic scene here. I strongly suspect that Dr. Benson has been the victim of a predatory animal attack. Most probably a bear, I would assume. I feel certain that there will have to be an official investigation of sorts in these circumstances."*

Kimberly Eastman bridled at the suggestion something had happened to the likeable Ed Benson. This whole fucking debacle was turning into a nightmare! First these inexplicable thefts of their equipment, and now this!! Somewhat irrationally, she gave voice to her growing disbelief and frustration regarding the whole insane situation.

"Just what are you basing this assumption on exactly, Dr. Sterling?"

He regarded her coldly in a superior manner - her question was a personal affront to his professional capabilities. Finally, he said, *"Ms. Eastman, I was brought along to consult on this 'program' due to my*

114

twenty-seven years as a practicing medical examiner and forensic pathologist. Do me the courtesy to acknowledge that I have much experience in seeing and interpreting the scene of a possible fatality. It is my given profession!"

Somewhat abashed, she nodded to Sterling contritely. The doctor sniffed at her with some derision before gesturing for them to move in a little closer. Everyone crowded slowly into the spot where the forensic scientist was standing. Kimberly looked at them; except for Barr, it was clear that they were growing very uneasy with the way events were unexpectedly turning. Except Bailey, she thought, he seemed to be looking more excited than unsettled. She looked back at Sterling now - in full pathologist mode - as he interpreted what they were looking at through his experienced eyes.

"See there," he said pointing directly into the ground, *"caught up in that exposed tree root system at the base of that big cedar? Anyone recognize it?"* It was difficult to pick out at first, but their eyes slowly adjusted to the lower light levels beneath the tree's foliage. There was part of a brown hiking shoe jammed in there - part of the upper shoe that had become detached from the sole. It was almost as if the shoe had been twisted in there with some considerable force.

Scott Rankin, having the advantage of the zoom facility on his camera, said, *"I do...that's the type of boot that Ed was wearing. They had red laces. I remember them. Pretty sure it's one of his."* A palpable chill had entered the air despite the summer season as the cameraman spoke...and Kimberly Eastman shivered at his words.

Dr Sterling went on, in a completely cold detachment like he was lecturing to a group of medical students. *"It's difficult to visualize, unless you have a trained and experienced eye, but I think even a layperson can see the way that the surface earth in this portion is agitated compared with the surrounding area. Note the difference in coloration and textures."*

Kimberly Eastman could see what he meant. The rest of the forest floor looked virtually undisturbed, but the area he was indicating was clearly churned up - the texture different - a distinctly different color in parts that was apparent even in the dim light.

She glanced up, noting with guilty satisfaction that Rankin was filming busily away. Meanwhile, Sterling was still talking. *"...anyone identify this please? I think I recognize it, but I'd like someone else to do so as well if possible."* He pointed to a small heap of torn up dirty plaid shirt half buried in the loam, practically undistinguishable from its surroundings until he indicated its existence to the assembled group. He bent down near it. *"I can actually read the label in situ but don't want to disturb the evidence until we have made a record of it. It appears to be a green and black plaid Timberland shirt, size XL. Wasn't Dr. Benson wearing that color and type of top yesterday?"*

The question was addressed to Kimberly, as she was the last person to see him on the previous night. She answered, an increasing feeling of cold emptiness in the pit of her stomach. *"Well, I couldn't swear to it, but it certainly looks like the one he was wearing yesterday."*

Barr concurred, *"Yep, sure looks like Ed's shirt to me."*

Olivia Hannah was silent. She just mutely stood, soaking up the scene.

David Sterling, grunting slightly as he straightened up, backed out from the area to join the others. Regarding them all carefully, he said, *"I have some equipment and a limited supply of chemicals that could give some clearer answers. I think it may be in order to do some preliminary stuff. It won't interfere with the official investigation; it might even be of some help to them."*

Kimberly watched in numbed silence as Sterling looked quizzically at Norton Bailey - not that he was really waiting for permission from anyone - he was a professional and had already decided on a course of action and what his responsibilities were. Bailey simply nodded to the forensic examiner in what she assumed was kind of an unofficial rubber stamp agreement.

Sterling then walked back to the campsite, presumably to get the things he needed. No one knew what to say, really. This was obviously a terrible shock to all of them. Hardly a word was uttered as one by one they trooped after Dr. Sterling, back towards the clearing. Kimberly Eastman didn't follow. She stood alone, staring in a stunned silence into the cool greenness of trees and undergrowth. It was an innocuous seeming place; but one where it was very likely Ed Benson had been horribly killed - eaten by a wild animal. It made the complications of the theft of their equipment pale in comparison. She shuddered at the thought of the horror of what had been Ed Benson's last minutes.

She was still there contemplating it twenty minutes later when Sterling returned, accompanied by Scott Rankin. The pathologist was now dressed for business wearing an all in one paper suit with attached hood; his boots were covered by some kind of oversized socks made of the same white material. Latex gloves completed the ensemble. He was also holding a medium sized slightly battered aluminum tool-box type by the carrying handle.

Rankin was meticulously documenting his every move with the small HD video camera held in his steady hand. It appeared that no one else was in any kind of mood to investigate the grisly scene further. Eastman looked back, and she could clearly see Olivia Hannah sitting dejectedly by the remains of last night's campfire, poking disparately at the dead ashes with a stick. It also looked as though Barr and Norton Bailey were in some kind of animated and possibly heated discussion at the far side of the clearing, but they were too far away for her to hear their conversation. Kimberly turned her attention to Dr. Sterling, who laid his box of forensic equipment on the ground on a kind of small, folded plastic, painter's sheet. He had opened the aluminum box up and had extracted several small sealed bottles and flasks from within its innards.

Sterling was explaining as he went along, negating the need for Eastman or Rankin to ask what he was doing for the benefit of the camera. *"What I am going to be doing here is creating a small batch of Luminol. For the uninitiated, Luminol is a prepared chemical solution compound including nitrophthalic acid, hydrazine, and triethelyne glycol which is boiled down and then sodium dithionite is added...but this of course, means absolutely nothing to anyone unless you are a budding bio-chemist or a middle-aged forensic scientist such as I."*

As Sterling was talking, he had been carefully but quickly adding pre-prepared chemicals into a large clear flask with experienced hands. As the other two watched in silence, the Dr. then measured out a small quantity of clear liquid marked 'Hydrogen Peroxide' and added it to the powder in the flask. He then added another powder and vigorously mixed the contents with a plastic spill he had extracted from a sealed wrapper. The Dr. held the contents up, examining them, and then carefully poured this liquid into a spray bottle that had also been sealed in a plastic wrap.

He spoke again, *"And that is how we in the forensics field concoct the mixture called Luminol."* He held the now filled spray bottle up to the camera so Rankin could get a good clear shot of it. He continued to talk to the camera.

"Luminol, for those of you who don't watch CSI, is a combination of chemicals in a liquid solution that when it comes into contact with certain other substances gives off a liberated photon - one that is visible to the naked eye as a blue glow for approximately thirty seconds. To simplify things, amongst the various substances that react with Luminol is the iron content in blood. What Luminol does in effect is to demonstrate the presence of blood - amongst other things - where you might not be able to easily see it - such as outdoors or indeed indoors where an attempt has been made to clear it up."

He turned to Kimberly. *"Ms. Eastman, if you'd be so kind, I need to check if the Luminol I have prepared is viable. May I?"* Sterling held a small packet in his hand that he had taken from his box. It contained a very fine surgical blade.

Kimberly realized his intent at once, but asked anyway for the benefit of the camera; her presenter persona had assumed full control once again. *"You need to have a sample of my blood, Dr. Sterling? To test if your batch of Luminol is effective?"*

Sterling played along, catching on quickly. *"Yes please, if you'd be so kind, Ms. Eastman."* He extracted the blade from the packet, and carefully and thoroughly swabbed Eastman's thumb with an alcohol swab. A quick jab with the fine point of the shiny metal was all it took to produce the amount of blood Sterling needed which was dexterously sucked up with a small pipette. Placing the thin blood-filled pipe onto his box lid, Sterling then put a Band-Aid with a pad of gauze over the tiny puncture. *"There, wasn't too painful was it?"* he said. She shook her head but instantly realized Sterling had already dismissed her from his mind – the pathologist had turned away from her, busying himself with the blood sample.

His attitude demonstrated that he didn't care if obtaining the blood from Kimberly had been painful or not. For him, the science was the thing. However, she understood that kind of obsessive passion and professional dedication. They were qualities she readily recognized in herself. She spoke to the pathologist, drawing him back to Rankin's camera.

"So, Dr. Sterling, how will you test the Luminol?"

He turned back to her, replying, *"Quite easily really. Normally if I was spraying an outdoor crime scene, I would test several areas first to see what kind of results I could anticipate. Let me add that spraying a target area with this chemical compound will not affect any other testing that might be needed later. Although I do not think that that any other testing will be necessary in these given circumstances."* The man lifted up the blood-filled pipette to the camera.

"So, I take the blood sample..." he moved several feet away from the area where they had discovered the torn-up clothing, *"...and will distribute the sample both on the ground and foliage in this random manner."* And then he began to shake the blood around him in a shallow arc, directing it at the forest floor. *"Now,"* Sterling continued, *"I will use this sterile cloth I have here and will further randomize the dispersal pattern."*

Sterling got on his hands and knees and energetically rubbed around the ground with the cloth. Standing up again, slightly red faced from his exertions, he said, *"You'll note that the majority of Ms. Eastman's sample is now practically invisible to the naked eye; the blood for all intents and purposes has effectively vanished. Now, let's see if our Luminol will expose the blood for us."*

With gentle, meticulous sweeps, David Sterling washed the area with a fine mist he pumped from the bottle he held in his hand.

The light due to the tree canopy was forever dim. Beneath the thickly entwined branches was a world that excluded bright sunlight even in the summer months. Yet in that dimness, almost at once, a magical fairyland blue glow began to emanate softly from the forest floor wherever the Luminol touched it. It was quite amazing.

Rankin moved closer to film the reaction and Sterling grunted with satisfaction, before saying: *"Fairly conclusive evidence that the Luminol is working, I shall try it where the shirt and shoe were found now. Mr. Rankin, can you please ensure that this whole procedure is videoed. The Canadian authorities will want to review this for their own investigation, I have no doubt."* Sterling moved back to the area that the clothing still lay and gently began spraying the area. If anything, the effect was even more spectacular in a totally macabre sense. Sweep after sweep of the bottle revealed further patches of blue luminescence. The glow was suddenly all in front of them, from the ground and even apparently leading into the trees.

However, Kimberly Eastman could see that Dr Sterling was clearly mystified at what the Luminol was revealing. He stepped gingerly and with some difficulty between the patches of revealed blood until he was at the base of the tree where the shoe was discovered. He sprayed against the trunk - the tell-tale blue radiance was instantly revealed. The pathologist was obviously examining the pattern that was being displayed - and was scratching his head in consternation. He sprayed higher, reaching up as far as his arm would allow. Wherever the Luminol touched, the ghostly light appeared. He stood back, obviously in deep thought - examining the tree from another angle. Sterling then moved and tried examining it from another. He then stepped back and rejoined Eastman and Rankin.

Turning to the cameraman, he asked, *"How tall would you say Ed Benson was, Mr. Rankin; six feet perhaps?"*

"I'd say a shade more," replied Scott. Sterling scratched his head again, looking back at the area he had sprayed and at the odd glow that was now fading away. He turned back to the other two.

"This is a little perplexing." Before Kimberly Eastman could ask the obvious, Sterling held up his hand to stop her. *"I need to talk to Barr and demonstrate what I'm going to tell you. Don't worry, it will all make sense when I do; or at least I hope so,"* he added with an air of mystery.

The three of them walked quickly back to the camp. Olivia Hannah was now in her tent, but Barr and Bailey were still in the midst of their still quite animated discussion at the far edge of the clearing. They stopped however, rather abruptly Eastman thought, as soon as Dr. Sterling called them over to join them.

Sterling informed them that the Luminol had revealed the presence of blood…quite a large quantity of it. Turning his attention to their Haidan guide, Dr. Sterling said, *"Barr, I'd like to ask your opinion on something if I can; to draw on your expertise and knowledge of the local wildlife."*

"Sure thing, doc," the guide replied. *"What you wanna know?"*

"What would normally occur Barr, if someone was attacked by a bear, speaking in strictly general terms that is?"

Barr considered Sterling's question for a moment before replying. *"Well, doc, nothing good, I can say that much with certainty. The bear either runs you down if you try getting away or rolls you over if you don't. When you're pinned, it starts in on you. After the bear's finished you gonna be a mess, all things considered."*

Sterling looked at him for a second, obviously thinking something through before replying. *"Hmmm…yes Barr, thank you. That pretty much confirms everything I have ever read on the subject regarding bear attacks and predation. Now I need to ask you something else."*

Kimberly could sense that something was coming - a gut instinct that one of those TV moments that only came along once in a blue moon was about to occur. She waited with bated breath, casting a surreptitious sideways glance to make sure that Rankin was getting it. Of course, he was.

The pathologist continued, *"Then we have somewhat of a mystery, Barr; you might be able to help solve it. How, in your opinion, would a bear lift or throw a six-foot man far enough up a tree to get blood spatter patterns at eight feet - or possibly higher? That is what the Luminol testing has shown up. Blood distributed up to a considerable height on the outer bark of the tree. The same tree that we found Dr. Benson's shoe under."*

Barr and indeed the others looked at Sterling in some puzzlement. The native Indian, however, answered Sterling quickly enough.

"Truth is, doc, it can't. At least not that I've ever seen. A bear don't throw you up in the air like a ball. It knocks you flat. Then it tears you up. I reckon the blood got up that high from the injuries…you know from the torn blood vessels, arteries maybes? That'd spray quite a distance, wouldn't it?"

The pathologist shook his head. *"Not possible, Barr. Let me demonstrate if I can…would you mind?"* The Dr. indicated that he wanted Barr to lie down, which he did. *"You were attacked by a bear yourself, weren't you? I've seen your scarring and they are textbook illustrations of defensive injuries in those kinds of predatory attacks on humans. Your arms were extensively lacerated and punctured, weren't they?"*

Sterling mimicked the position and posture of a bear standing over the prone Barr.

"You see everyone, as the animal attacks..." he pantomimed a vicious if somewhat exaggerated slow motion swipe at the hunter *"...the first thing that inevitably comes into contact with the bear's claws and teeth are the arms of the victim as they are lifted up in defense."* Sterling stretched out his hand, helping Barr back to his feet.

The Dr. continued to explain. *"After that initial attack, the victim invariably enters a fetal protected position, covering the vital areas of the head and neck with the arms and hands. This is where and how the back and side lacerations occur as you have all seen on Barr's torso. Arterial blood under normal pressure could not have found its way so high up from this position."* Dr Sterling paused for a second, then: *"There is an outside, marginal possibility that Dr. Benson could have been attacked - got away momentarily - and climbed the tree to attempt an escape; this is a highly improbable scenario. I have closely examined the tree. There is nothing to gain purchase on. No branches or protuberances. I have examined the bark in that area - there are no signs that the tree was scuffed by his boots as he tried to climb it."*

Norton Bailey, who had been silent up to this point, content in a most uncustomary fashion to simply listen, was at once excited. He jumped straight in with, *"So what you are saying in essence, Dr. Sterling, is that you have no plausible explanation as to how Benson's blood was discovered so high up on the tree?"*

Sterling reluctantly nodded his assent, replying, *"Yes, Mr. Bailey. That is what I'm saying, in essence."*

Bailey stepped forward, placing a meaty hand on the older man's arm. *"Then, sir, I have an alternate explanation. One that more readily fits the facts - Ed Benson has become yet another victim of the creatures that abide in these forests. He was attacked by a hominid so large and powerful that it was able to lift or throw him several fe..."* Bailey never finished his sentence.

Unnoticed, Olivia Hannah had joined them. She walked into the center of the group, almost as if she was sleepwalking. The look on her face brought down a silence and fixed everyone's attention on her. Hannah lifted her head up then looked blankly into the darkened canopy of gently swaying trees that surrounded the clearing - the wind was rising, Kimberly Eastman noticed for the first time. She watched in rapt attention as Olivia Hannah clapped her hands to her ears before dragging them slowly forward to cover her nose and mouth with loose fingers - she sank to her knees murmuring, quietly and unintelligibly at first, then louder and distinct – the words became a fugue - tumbling out - overlapping, tripping over each other in their haste to leave her slack mouth. Finally, the phrase became clear - ending in a repeated shriek: *"They're here. They're here. They're here."*

The men looked on, unsure what to do; Rankin trained his camera on the distraught cryptozoologist – more from habit and professional training than anything else. Perhaps if he had consciously thought about it, he would have turned the camera off. Kimberly Eastman moved forward to offer the other woman some comfort and to help her up. Then the world suddenly spiraled into madness and horror.

As Kimberly reached down to Olivia Hannah, a blur of motion shot past her. Before she realized what was happening, she had been knocked heavily to one side as if she'd been hit with a car and Eastman found herself on the floor with the breath knocked out of her. A scream cut through her haze and she pushed her head and shoulders up off the ground to see an incredible sight. She could scarcely believe what her eyes were telling her. A huge shaggy creature - at least nine feet in height - stood just beyond where they had all stood seconds before. People had been scattered like bowling pins thrown flat to the ground as if a lightning bolt had impacted violently in their midst. Only Olivia Hannah hadn't moved. She was still on her knees, position unchanged. The only difference was that while the woman's head was still down, her hands were again clasped tight over her ears, trying simultaneously to block out the sight and sound of the hideous nightmare standing just aside from her. Kimberly dazedly looked around her, tearing her eyes away from the monster with difficulty.

Rankin was about fifteen feet to her left, attempting to struggle to his feet - camera trained squarely if somewhat shakily on the giant shape in front of them. Norton Bailey was down on the floor close to the cameraman, unmoving, his face planted in the dirt. She couldn't see Barr so she thought that he might be behind her.

It was Sterling however who was in the most precarious position - practically at the titan's feet. Kimberly looked on, wide-eyed and helpless. Dr. Sterling stared up into the demon's face. Whatever horror the forensic scientist saw in the creature's eyes terrified him beyond human endurance. He screamed out in terror and anguish in a way Kimberly thought was not possible. And if the scream sickened her, what happened next revolted her beyond any nausea. Sterling's hands were raised - waving in supplication – desperately begging for his life – an existence that was about to be extinguished. The gigantic being reached down - almost casually with one enormous hand – the huge appendage completely encompassing David Sterling's head. A casual effort lifted the screaming man high off the floor.

Eastman watched in a transfixed horror as the pathologist's legs jerked and twitched spasmodically as if trying to run or defensively kick out at the creature in front of him. The massive powerful fingers inexorably closed on the skull with a sickening sound like thin wooden strawberry crates being stepped on. Sterling's head instantly imploded under the vast pressure. Grey brain matter mixed with scarlet fluid, hair, and bone shards in a fusion of violent death. The pathologist's body flopped loosely to the floor, collapsing into a heap now devoid of any semblance of a head.

At that, Kimberly vomited noisily onto the ground. One of David Sterling's eyes had popped from its orbit socket and had rolled messily to within a few inches of her. It stared up at Eastman - partially covered in dirt, the dark pupil was dilated and fixed - yet it looked at her with an accusing stare.

She heaved again.

The creature now stooped down and gathered Sterling's corpse under its hair-matted arm. It made as if to make off with it, obviously unafraid of the rest of them and contemptuous of any defense that these poor pallid things could offer it. As it ambled away scorning as unnecessary its earlier turn of frightening speed, it stopped by Olivia Hannah. Enigmatically it bent down to her, still clutching its prize, and seemed to study her face for a moment, its head tilting from side to side in obvious curiosity. That pause was its undoing.

Kimberly felt more than heard a low powerful thrum and a pressure wave that passed closely by her right cheek. The monster stared down to its left side, suddenly realizing that something there was amiss. A shaft of obsidian black had suddenly sprouted from its hair-covered ribs. Then a second one magically appeared higher up in its torso. Dropping Sterling's remains in a messy, blood leaking bundle, it pawed at the two stumps that were protruding from its massive body - obviously it was unsure as to what to do with these odd things that must be burning deeply in its soft organs. Then a third arrow slammed into it.

By now the giant hominid was beginning to get an inkling that it was in real trouble. It straightened up, raising its dome shaped head - huge dark saucer eyes peering around looking for where the stinging torment had originated from.

Kimberly Eastman looked back, seeing that Barr was there, bow in hand, nocking a fourth steel-tipped hunting shaft that would follow its brothers into the evil beast's stinking flesh and end its foul existence. She felt exulted at the prospect. This thing had murdered Ed Benson, David Sterling and God knows how many more. As Barr drew back the bowstring to let another arrow slam into the target, the monster must have finally realized that it was Barr that was causing the pain it was experiencing - it sprang forward, its superhuman speed surging to its defense. A fraction of a second before it did, the Haidan must have sensed its intent and threw himself flat, his bow carelessly falling with him and out of his reach. The monster, now on all fours, had covered the distance between them in a bounding blur. However, as Barr had dropped, it miscalculated the gap that separated them, perhaps because of the injuries that had been inflicted on it - and flew straight over Barr to come to a sprawling stop some yards beyond, taking out the Haidan's tent at the same time. It struggled groggily to its massive feet entangled in the tent, the nylon material slowing it up and distracting it, the piercing wounds caused by Barr's arrows contributing to its anger and distress.

Kimberly noted with alarm that as Barr had gone down the barbed arrow that had been poised to fly into the murderous creature that confronted them had fallen from the bow and had ended up skewering Barr's right forearm as he went down. The wound was bleeding profusely.

He looked back and realized he had very little time before the monster had extracted itself and was upon him. He looked desperately at Kimberly as he reached under his jacket and hauled out the huge .50 caliber Desert Eagle. It was obvious he couldn't use it effectively due to his injury - but he knew that she could. Kimberly's skill with a gun was probably their only chance of survival. She knew what he wanted her to do and nodded in grim determination.

Time seemed to slow down. Barr tossed the heavy gun to her and it traveled in a slow, lazy parabola. The titanic being had extricated itself from the clinging remnants of the tent and was moving towards Barr with a deliberate and murderous hate.

It was less than a few feet away from the downed Haidan when she caught the heavy semi-automatic with both hands, and rolled to her knees, pulling back the slide on the pistol to strip a heavy round from the magazine and into the chamber. Fragments came back to her now - memories of things drilled into her by an expert – lessons that would now save not only her life but the others' too. Aim for the center mass. She did. Relax, don't tense up. She did. Breathe out as you squeeze the trigger. She did.

It all came together as the immense demon from some unimagined hell reared up over the Haidan Indian, intent on ending his life.

She sighted coolly and squeezed the trigger. The gun roared in fury and kicked back and up in her hands with a bright muzzle flash – and a hollow pointed projectile struck the creature squarely in the chest, exiting in a welter of blood and lung tissue from its back. Incredibly, despite all its injuries it still didn't drop, but stood there swaying as if moving to a primitive music produced by the surrounding forest that only it could hear. Kimberly got to her feet.

She advanced quickly in a crouched combat stance until she was only a few feet from its huge form. With no real conscious thought, she squeezed the trigger once more. The big gun roared again, kicking back. This time the heavy round hit the monster in its massive throat. Without a sound it sank slowly to the floor on its knees, before crashing over to its side like a gigantic felled oak tree. It was finally dead.

Kimberly dropped the firearm to the floor and pulled Barr to his feet. He looked back at the dead creature and then turned to Eastman, saying, *"You did real good Ms. Eastman, real good."*

She didn't answer him. She didn't feel like she'd done 'good' - she just felt sick to her stomach. If anything even resembling food was still down in there, Kimberly felt sure that it would be making an appearance around now.

Turning from Barr she walked back to Scott Rankin who was still filming away.

"Did you manage to get it all, Scott?"

Unsmiling he replied shakily, *"Did I mana...Kim, this is our ticket to the absolute top of the world. We can call our own tune after this! It was absolutely in-fucking-credible!"*

She smiled at him but there was no humor in it. *"I take it that's a 'yes' then?"* Rankin merely tapped and rubbed the side of the small camcorder in great satisfaction, like it was Aladdin's lamp.

Bailey was now attempting to rouse himself from the floor, shaking his head in an attempt to clear it of the fog of semi-consciousness. Walking over, Kimberly helped him get groggily to his feet. He was teetering around a little, slightly unsteady and sporting a bruise and a swelling the size of a pigeon's egg over his left eyebrow - but apart from that he seemed OK. Barr had taken the remains of the tent that had temporarily come to their aid and had used it to cover up the cadaver of poor David Sterling.

The immense corpse of the dead creature was left where it had fallen. She looked at the grotesque scene for a moment. She could feel the tears welling up. Eastman wanted to cry for Sterling - for Benson - for all the others; but most of all for herself. Angrily., she pushed the sorrow back down inside herself again; there would be time for tears later, but not now.

She moved now to the pathetic form of Olivia, who was still on her knees - hands pushed firmly over her ears – her eyes tightly shut. Kimberly sat down beside her and pulled the trembling woman into her own lap. She stroked her hair and cooed mindlessly in soothing tones - Hannah relaxed a little. Her hands slowly came away from her ears and the cryptozoologist wrapped her arms around Eastman. She then sobbed quietly away, and Kimberly let her. Eventually Olivia's head came up and she let go of

Eastman, taking a second or two to rub at her eyes with the back of her hand and wipe her nose in a most unladylike fashion on her sleeve.

Having regained her composure somewhat, she finally spoke: *"Do you remember back in LA that I told you when I got to know you better, that you could call me something else?"*

Kimberly Eastman stroked her hair, replying, *"I remember, Olivia."*

Olivia Hannah smiled at her, her face wet with tear streaks, saying, *"Well firstly thank you so much. I can't think of anyone else I'd rather spend my last few hours with."*

Kimberly Eastman grinned at the disheveled woman at her side, putting her arm protectively around her shoulder and pulling her close, saying, *"Olivia, we killed the creature and I don't think we're going to die just yet. We have a long walk back to the logging camp is all. I'm sure we can manage that, can't we?"* This seemed to galvanize Olivia Hannah – she wrenched herself away with a surprising strength and held Kimberly's head in both of her hands and pulled her face towards her own, fixing her eyes with an intense gaze.

"Oh no – poor, poor Kimberly - do you honestly think that they'll let us kill one of their own and do nothing?" She let go of Eastman's face and stood shakily up, facing the darkening rim of the forest that surrounded them.

Kimberly looked up at the sky. Storm clouds were fast approaching. When the storm came it would get dark. *"Can't you hear them, Kimberly?"* said Olivia. *"They're coming to take us now. They're angry. It's time to feed and they'll be hungry."* And then sniggering in a horrifying childish manner Olivia Hannah let go of Kimberly's face and began to walk away. Kimberly merely stared at her retreating back in stunned silence. After only a few paces, the cryptozoologist stopped and turned back to face Kimberly - almost as an afterthought, saying, *"Oh yes, Kimberly. I nearly forgot. You can call me what all my good friends call me now."* Kimberly stood up. There was a low keening moan emanating from somewhere in the distance, yet echoing from everywhere simultaneously. It had an eerie, discordant quality to it - a sound that sent ice water through her bowels. She looked around, slowly taking the measure of it - and then made her way to Scott Rankin, huddling up to him for some measure of security - however false it was.

They were somewhere out there in the darkening tangle of trees - although obviously some distance away. Hannah had been motionless, listening to the weird cacophony herself but now had started to walk away again toward the tree line, giggling as she went, saying in a strong Texas accent: *"Call me Bobbie. Y'all can call me Bobbie."* And from deep in the forest the sounds abruptly ceased - the creatures were on the move. They were coming to wipe them out.

CHAPTER TWELVE

Graham Island, British Columbia

24th July 2017

As a small child and later as a teenager, Kimberly Eastman had learned to hate thunderstorms to the core of her being.

Not because of the crashing sounds and unleashed fury that the storm would bring - or the possible twister – it was that if the weather was bad, her father would be in the house; and if they were in the home together only one result ever followed. She'd be cornered by her father in some quiet spot then…She shuddered at the pitiful memory. However, the approaching storm's first flickering bright light high above, accompanied with the low resonance of vibrating thunder that echoed through the trees, was far better than the unnatural wail from the multitude of demonic creatures that were surely closing in on them. She silently thanked the storm for that small mercy.

The caterwauling had stopped. Kimberly Eastman used that lull to tap into a hidden reserve deep within her. A wonderful source of unexpected calm and deliberate energy. She moved away from Scott Rankin, who was equally transfixed by the nightmarish events that threatened to engulf them in a wave of violent destruction. A brutal fight for survival was upon them all; and something inside Kimberly had awoken. A fierce determination they would not meet the same fate as others had in the past - recent or distant. Yet even with this she looked around at the others with an odd feeling of disconnect - of being separated from them and what was happening - as if she had become one of Scott Rankin's cameras - observing events but not being a part of it. She pushed that feeling away. She knew she couldn't employ this learned strategy - the one that had allowed her to manage shock, distress and trauma without becoming a total basket case - to deal with the shit that visited her frequently in life. That coping mechanism wasn't going to work. Becoming coldly detached from this terrible situation wasn't going to help her.

Kimberly was very much part of this thing and it would take all of them working together to live through what was to come.

Barr caught her attention first. The injured Haidan was cradling his damaged arm against his chest - blood slowly soaking into his shirt sleeve and front - the arrow still protruding where it had pierced through his forearm. His right hand appeared clawed and frozen…but despite this horrific injury he was standing upright; the hunter's eyes were incredibly fierce and watchful. Amazingly he was not cowed into submission by the terrible things they had all just witnessed. And on top of that he had produced his large, wickedly sharp-Bowie type knife that was now clutched determinedly in his good left hand. It was obvious that when these monsters attacked, they would have to earn their meal - the Haidan wouldn't go down without a fight.

There was something about the man. Despite his grizzled exterior and rough manner, Barr had a rare quality of honor and decency about him that she had to admire. A sudden unexpected wave of pride washed over her as she looked upon him. Kimberly's eyes misted briefly, and she had to swallow hard.

Quickly she moved her attention from Barr to Norton Bailey. His story was much different. The stocky author paced around in a ridiculous circle while inanely mumbling to himself - bargaining with some unseen presence…throwing his hands up one second then holding his hands to his head the next. It looked like the frantic man was about to start tearing out his hair. His normally calm round face was unusually animated - its complexion had assumed an unhealthy grey hue. A pitiful figure really.

Kimberly ignored him for the moment and looked around for Olivia Hannah. She had moved back from the edge of the clearing and was sitting cross-legged on the blood-soaked ground – extremely close to the hulking corpse of the creature. At first glance it looked as if the cryptozoologist's burning scientific curiosity had reasserted itself despite their terrible predicament and Hannah was examining the remains of the cryptid. Eastman, on closer observation, realized that the tall woman was doing no such thing. Inexplicably, Hannah was stroking its filthy hair-matted remains, singing to it in the pitifully childish manner she had adopted earlier. It was now evident Olivia Hannah had completely retreated into herself. She was blocking out the present grim reality - substituting it for a more palatable fantasy of her own creation. She would be of no use, Eastman thought.

Scotty was doing ok. He was busying himself with his precious camera; almost grooming it. Kimberly turned her attention away from the big cameraman and ignored Norton and Hannah for the time being.

She went over to Barr and pointed to his injured arm, saying lamely, *"That looks really painful; does it hurt?"*

At her words, Barr took his sharply focused attention from their surroundings, blinking at her in some confusion for a second, then looked down at the arrow that had impaled his forearm - the blood still oozing out of it - as if seeing his injury for the first time.

His head snapped back up to her and he answered, *"Oh you mean this little toothpick that's clean through me? No, Ma'am it's just a tribal ornament we all wear.... of all the stupid ques... 'Course it damn well hur..."*

She put her hands up in apology, interrupting his tirade before he could get properly started, interjecting, *"Sorry Barr, you're right - stupid question - it must be hurting awfully."*

Rankin had now joined her. They were all silent for a few seconds. The cameraman looked at them both for a moment before directing himself at the Indian, saying: *"Think we ought to get it out of you, Barr? You might be able to move better without it; I'm guessing."* Barr nodded grimly in agreement. Rankin went on, *"So how do we do this? How do we remove it without causing further damage to your arm?"*

Barr looked at it, saying: *"Well, damage has already been done I reckon. Some of my tendon is cut clean through. I can't use some of my fingers. Artery isn't damaged though. I'd have bled out by now if it were."*

To demonstrate the tendon damage, he flexed his arm. Three of his fingers didn't move at all, they just remained clawed and useless.

Barr continued: *"What I'm gonna need to do is cut the head and the flights of the shaft and then draw it out fast. You need to have some wadding and a bandage ready to put on the hole that's gonna be there quick smart when it comes out. I reckon it'll bleed some."*

Without further debate, Kimberly trotted quickly back to her tent for the first-aid kit she had been carrying, glad to have a task to perform; but still looking around her all the time and straining her ears for signs of the creatures that were waiting menacingly in the forest, out of sight. No appearance was evident; at least not yet. She grabbed the small first-aid kit from her rucksack and then hurried back to help Rankin with Barr. Kimberly saw as she ran that Olivia Hannah was still occupying her place by the creature's corpse, a vacant expression replacing the once bright intelligence that had been. Norton Bailey had stopped his histrionics however and had evidently crawled into his tent for reasons of his own.

In the meanwhile, thankfully for Kimberly, Barr had already asked Rankin to hold onto the shank of the arrow, keeping it as still as possible, while he had used the big Bowie knife to score an encircling deep groove around the head end of the shaft. As Kimberly arrived, Barr advised her to get out the supplies from the first-aid kit she would need to patch the wound up. Kimberly laid the kit on the floor and opened the box up. She then grabbed what she thought she would need.

Seemingly satisfied at what she had prepared, Barr waited no longer. He spoke a sharp, hurried few words to Scott: *"Let's get this right brother...smooth and quick the way I told ya...ready?"* Rankin nodded, gripping just below the feathered end of the arrow tightly, his knuckles white with the effort. With the briefest of nods back to him, the Haidan's powerful fingers effortlessly snapped the arrowhead from the shaft. Barr took a deep breath then nodded to Scott. In one smooth movement Rankin drew the shaft straight out. Barr yelped quietly, almost under his breath. There was an instant small spurt of rich blood as the slickly wet shaft was withdrawn but Eastman was ready with a wad of gauze and cotton wool pads. She quickly placed it hard over the wound and a bandage was tightly wrapped dexterously round it.

Barr's face now had a dangerous livid color to it - a fine sheen of sweat covered his face - but he was breathing deeply and regularly; he nodded his thanks to them both. At least he was still on his feet, Kimberly Eastman thought gratefully.

It was Rankin that voiced what his friend was thinking. *"We need to get the fuck out of Dodge folks. We need to make a run for it...now!"*

Barr, gripping his huge blade tightly, his face a mask of obvious pain, scoffed at the cameraman. *"How far you think we're gonna get through the forest with those things chasing us down, huh? Don't know if you've noticed buddy but the good lady doctor ain't exactly with us now...and as for Bailey..."* He paused for a second, mulling something over and was obviously about to say what he was thinking - then thought better of it *"...well, boy, you've seen how fast they are."*

Rankin was beginning to get angry. Fueled by obvious fear and desperation, he snapped back at Barr: *"So what do you suggest we fucking do then, oh great hunter? Just wait around till that one's buddies decide to show up to finish off what he started? Christ, I can't believe this is happening! They're real! They're fucking real and two of us are dead and..."*

Kimberly Eastman could feel her own fear beginning to get a grip on her with Scott's rising voice, so she butted in, cutting him off: *"And...we certainly won't survive if we start fighting amongst ourselves and giving in to panic, will we?"* Her words had the desired effect, and Rankin shut himself down, adding that she was right, and he was sorry.

Then events took a bizarre turn. Bailey reappeared from his tent, rucksack on his back and walked over to join them. In a totally unexpected move, he came up to Barr and with no warning, his pudgy hands shot quickly out – reaching up, the shorter man grasped the injured hunter round his throat.

The author began to scream at Barr in total hysteria: *"Barr, you bastard sonofabitch, fucking asshole...you've killed us...killed me...you said I'd be safe...you lying sack of shit..."*

Both Eastman and Rankin stepped back in shock and alarm. It took the Indian a few seconds to react as the two men staggered together, locked in combat - the smaller man fighting with surprising strength and ferocity.

Kimberly Eastman saw the struggle was an uneven match and obviously one sided; even in his blood loss weakened state, Barr was certainly more than a match for Bailey in both raw power and technique. Pushing the distraught smaller man from him, the Haidan brought his uninjured left arm up in a short yet powerful swinging arc. Barr's elbow connected with a crunching force into Bailey's prominent nose. Blood gushed for the second time in the last few minutes - but now it was from the author. His hands flew up to his broken nose and he swayed for a second on wobbly legs before they gave way. Bailey sat down heavily in a crumpled heap, all thoughts of attacking Barr gone.

Kimberly Eastman was incensed and crossed the few short steps to where Norton sat on the ground nursing his bloodied nose and face. She could not hold it in and voiced her anger and frustration at Bailey in no uncertain terms.

"What the hell is wrong with you, Bailey? Aren't we in enough damned trouble already without you wanting to create another shit-storm of your own?"

The seated man looked up at her - face pale, eyes swollen and watery - the epitome of misery and self-pity. She sighed. Going to the first-aid box, Kimberly pulled out another wad of gauze, went back to Bailey, squatted down, and without further comment handed it to him. She then stood, moving away from the crumpled heap that was Norton Bailey. Somewhat calmed, she spoke to Barr. Rankin said nothing but she noted that his video camera seemed to be in action again.

Ignoring the camera, Kimberly bluntly asked Barr what that little fracas between them had all been about. The hunter avoided Kimberly's inquisitive eyes, still alertly scanning the trees around them. The storm was getting nearer now, the thunder and lightning increasing in power, frequency, and intensity. The first few fat drops of heavy rain had begun to fall. She asked him again. She wasn't going to drop it. Sighing in resignation, he finally turned to her, saying; *"You might say that we've had kind of a misunderstanding. I think Mr. Bailey sees things one way and I see them another."*

The author was now back on his feet, face blotchy and angry, still wiping the blood from his face and delicately dabbing at his rapidly swelling nose and tearing eyes. For a second Kimberly thought the small man would unwisely risk flying at Barr again in his rage but that moment seemed to pass as instantly as it came.

Finally, the author spluttered out: *"You sir, are a liar. You said you knew. You have taken a great deal of my money. You gave me certain assurances before you agreed to undertake this expedition...you told me that...gah!!"*

Bailey stopped himself from saying anything else. Despite the danger they were in, this was getting intriguing, thought Kimberly. She had a feeling that things were not as they had initially seemed - and now it looked like some unspoken truth might come out.

"Enough of this bullshit! Would either of you care to enlighten the rest of us?" she yelled.

Barr looked at the floor and then back out towards the storm front approaching from the west. Bailey merely stood in silence and held the wadding to his broken nose in an attempt to stem the trickle of blood that still ran from it.

Rankin now spoke up. *"Well, one of you bastards needs to tell us what the hell is going on! You're not just playing with your lives; you're playing with ours too."* Barr now locked eyes with Bailey and they held the stare between them for several long seconds. The tension was tangible. It was as if Bailey was daring the Indian to tell the others what he knew but if he did, the outcomes would be dire for both. Finally, Barr broke eye contact - not because he was cowed by Norton Bailey's surly looks or the author's implied silent threat of a bad outcome - but because the Haidan had come to a decision. He had decided to tell the others what he knew.

"Seems to me like we all need to come clean; ain't that so, Mr. Bailey?" Norton merely growled at Barr, muttering an incomprehensible phrase through the blood-soaked gauze he was holding tightly to his face.

The Indian ignored Bailey and continued speaking, looking around at the storm darkening landscape. The straight-line winds were now picking up in intensity. The increasingly powerful gusts were beginning to make the tops of the high cedars sway around in a lazy motion. Barr's volume increased so he could make his words heard over the storm: *"I'm guessing we might not get out of this, and there are things that need to be said regarding my long association with him..."*

His good arm shot out at Bailey, an accusing finger pointed out straight and true. It was almost as if he had physically thrown something at the other man, because the stocky author seemed to visibly wince at Barr's gesture. *"Let's see, I first met this nice fellah, Mr. Norton Bailey back in '02 I guess. I was down in Skidegate - that's a biggish town for hereabouts. I was hanging round the ferry terminal waiting for a party of mine to come in from Moresby Island. As it turned out the folks I was waitin' on was late, but I spies me this fellah Bailey coming in off the boat. We got to talkin' and I found out he was here to see the Tribal Council 'bout our legends an' such…that's right ain't it, Mr. Norton Bailey? Yeah, he's a real scholar!"*

Barr started to laugh raucously; his own comment apparently amused him greatly.

The author pulled the bundled-up crusted gauze away from his face, shouting out at Barr: *"I'm warning you Barr! Stop this now!!"*

Barr grunted back, *"Yeah, yeah, Mr. Bailey…whatever you say."*

The Haidan then turned his back on him and addressed Kimberly and Scott directly - and of course, Scott was videoing it all.

"So, we went into the one bar that Skidegate has for a drink, and I realize that what Mr. Bailey is doing here is just chasing a hair covered rainbow. I knows all them old stories about the Gogit, 'cus my Grandpa told me about 'em when I was just a kid…but hot damn, not one of us younger ones believe any of that moose shit now. It just makes a good story for the tourists an' such."

Bailey, Kimberly noticed, had now taken off his backpack and was rummaging inside it, apparently ignoring Barr and his story altogether. Barr was still talking. *"But that's when he showed me the picture of them folks from '96, the ones that all disappeared. Well I didn't know it at the time, back when I was a younger fellah, but I recognized the picture of the girl when he showed it to me. An' I told him she wasn't dead, or at least she wasn't back then. It was me that found her out in the valley in the river."* Barr smiled at the recollection. *"Yep, I told him I'd pulled a gal from the river deader than alive, half drowned. And it was her, no doubt. Well, he got real excited at this and asked me what other details I could recollect about the whole thing. So, I told him what I remembered…then I kinda got carried away, I guess."*

"Carried away," Kimberly Eastman repeated, *"what do you mean by that?"* She was so captivated she had almost forgotten what was waiting for them out in the trees - almost.

Barr smiled ruefully at the obvious embarrassing recollection. The rain was coming down a little heavier now and the sound of the thunder rolled in from the west with a muted grumbling roar, ever closer. Barr scratched his head with his good hand. *"Well…err…I told him that I'd actually seen the things…even been attacked by it deep in the woods one time…showed him my scars and such, spun him a yarn about how I'd survived and got away. I said if anyone else ever asked me about the scars I had picked up I told them it was a big grizzly that attacked me. But now he knew the truth. I know I shouldn't have done it I guess, but I could smell the money…greed made me sort of reckless and such."* Eastman could understand the Haidan's motivation. She'd seen firsthand how the native people lived on the island. It was obvious to her that money on the Queen

Charlotte Islands was always an issue - or rather the lack of it. Poverty was poverty, no matter what part of the world or how idyllic the surroundings. She comprehended that as she'd come from it herself.

Bailey was still digging through his rucksack like a raccoon hunting after food in a stream; and he was still pointedly ignoring what the tall Indian had to say. Either he didn't care or he'd decided to just brazen it out when the time came. *"So, Mr. Bailey here is now hooked. He wants me to take him out into the forest to show him where I'd found the girl and what happened to her afterwards, but I put him off that idea with a few half-truths and such...told him that the salmon were migrating and the bears in these parts get kinda antsy and territorial that time of the year."* From the way he said it, Barr seemed to think he'd somehow redeemed himself with the next part of the tale, or so Kimberly thought.

"The salmon...bears' main food ...well it was till the factory salmon started giving migrating wild salmon sea-lice as they swam past the pens. They get sea-lice on 'em and that's all she wrote, kills 'em off quick. I tell him it's not safe to go wandering out unprepared. Then he wants to know about the girl and was stuck to me like flies on a turd for three days, goin 'over and over the story. I told him how I took her to our cabin way out in the woods an' grandpa an' me had nursed after her for weeks till she was all better. Then, one day we came back in the morning, she'd gone, vanished. Took some of grandpa's money from under the floorboards I recall. I told Mr. Bailey everything I knew. He couldn't ask grandpa as he was dead three years past. But the interrogations from him were worth it, 'cus he gave me lots of money and the promise of more to come. We kinda kept in touch over the years, by letter and such, he'd send me a few bucks, it was a 'retainer' he called it."

Barr sniggered at that but went on, *"And I got the feeling from him that he was getting close to something that really excited him. He hinted at it and kept askin' me if I'd be willin' to take out a party into the forests...and I said 'hell yeah'...if the money was right. He told me that money would be no object, and as long as I scratched his back, then he'd scratch mine...shit, I had no idea what he meant at the time...but I sure as hell know now."*

He shot a vehement look at Bailey who had now apparently finished with the exploration of the contents of his rucksack, and was sitting in silence on the damp ground, staring back at Barr with an equally venomous look.

"Wanna know where your equipment is, Mr. Rankin? Where both yours and Ms. Eastman's satellite phones went missing to?"

Bailey growled from the floor, *"It's the last time I'm going to tell you Barr, shut the fuck up."* The Indian must really be getting to Bailey, thought Eastman. That was only the second time she'd ever heard him curse.

Barr however merely laughed derisively at the smaller man again, pointing now in the general direction of the huge creature's carcass, but more in particular at Olivia Hannah. Barr said, *"Ask him about Doc Hannah there...ask him what..."* Then he seemed to think twice about what he was about to say and shut down. Olivia had now stopped her muted ramblings, finally taking in what was going on.

The willowy woman got up, walking over to the rest of them. *"Tell me, Barr,"* she said quietly, her voice quite hoarse from her singing, *"What were you going to say? Were you going to say something about me?"* The Indian looked at her with pity in his eyes, laying a gentle hand on her thin shoulder.

"I was gonna say, 'ask how poor crazy Doc Hannah there lost her job at the university'. That was what I was about to say."

"How did I lose my university tenure, Barr...can you tell me please?" Hannah's voice was trembling - raw with emotion.

Before the hunter could answer her, Bailey suddenly became the point of everyone's attention. He strode forward and from somewhere he had produced a large semi-automatic handgun – and it was pointed directly and unwaveringly at Barr. The weapon looked impossibly huge in his small hands - but the very fact that he was holding it seemed to make the short man instantly bigger.

Norton Bailey knew well the power that a gun, money, fame, or position loans a person. As he froze everyone with the threat of the firearm, with a voice that oozed with his fear and extreme anxiety, he said: *"Barr, I asked you to shut up. Now I'm telling you. You open your mouth again and I'll put a bullet through it. Think I won't do it? Say something else and see."* Barr stepped forward - the other man took a hesitant half step backwards. Kimberly saw that, although the gun was beginning to shake in Bailey's hand, his finger was slowly tightening on the trigger. She put a restraining arm out across the Haidan's stomach that stopped him moving towards Bailey, saying; *"I think Norton's quite serious, Barr."*

Norton relaxed marginally at these words and the fact the woman had stopped Barr coming towards him. His finger relaxed on the trigger.

The thunder rumbled harshly and then the rain started hammering down with a vengeance, beginning to soak them all. *"That's better,"* said the author. He wiped a sleeve across his forehead, wincing slightly, the rain running through his hair and down his face. Rivulets of the water mixed with his sweat - they were washing tracks through the crusting blood that had started to dry on his skin. *"Now why don't we see if we can get out of here alive, shall we?"*

Rankin had slowly and deliberately dropped the arm which was holding the camera down to his side, so as not to antagonize Bailey or make him any more jumpy than he already was.

He said. *"That's a damn good idea Norton - what do you suggest?"* Lightning flashed brightly and the thunder rumbled again.

Bailey's voice was much calmer now. *"What I suggest, Mr. Rankin is that we go now - as quickly as we can - back towards the track that leads to the Dinan Logging Camp. Mr. Barr is going to show us the way. In the meantime, we set up a diversion that these creatures will follow. While they are occupied with our little subterfuge, we will make good our escape."*

The rain was lashing down now, rapidly turning the loamy clearing floor into a quagmire. Bailey gestured with the pistol, *"Let's go, Barr, whilst we still can."* But before they could even move, Olivia Hannah pathetically sidled up. She pawed at Norton Bailey's arm in a hesitant manner as if afraid he would shatter if she held onto him too firmly.

The cryptozoologist spoke to him in a quiet tone that was barely audible over the rain's thundering hiss and ever rising wind of the storm. Kimberly was standing quite close to them, but had to strain to hear the woman's words. *"Tell me Norton, what Barr was saying about how I lost my tenure...my students..."*

Bailey shrugged her off impatiently, yelling: *"You stupid bitch! Who cares about your fucking students or stinking job? Do you want to die here? Move your skinny ass!"* And he began to shove her along using his weight to propel her light frame forward. But Hannah was nothing if not tenacious. She dug her feet in, leaning into the heavier man, unwilling to let the matter drop, even in these awful circumstances. She went on at him with a single-minded determination. *"Tell me, Norton; you must tell me..."*

He let go of the gun with one hand, gripping her soaked shirt with the other, shaking her fiercely. The front of the shirt started to rip but she would still not let it drop. If she was the terrier, then he was the bear. *"Tell me Norton, damn it!"* Her voice was becoming shriller. Bailey pulled the taller woman into him, till their dripping faces were only inches apart.

"OK you silly, stupid woman. If you really must know, it was me. I arranged it..." Olivia stopped struggling with him, going dead weight in his hand, forcing him to release her. She fell with a splashing thump to the muddy floor. With a distraught expression she looked up at him – hair, wet sopping strands - wormy tails that fell across her forehead almost concealing her eyes. With a forlorn voice, she asked: *"But why, Norton, why? Those students were my whole life. I loved my job...why would you do that to me? What have I ever done to you, to be so deserving of such a*

terrible treatment?" Bailey laughed down at the distressed woman at his feet, in complete contempt of her.

Kimberly Eastman could feel her anger rising as she stood in mute witness. She could see her dead father so clearly in Bailey at that moment - not only him but many other men she had grown to hate throughout her life. She felt her fists balling up in rage.

Norton stopped laughing and spoke to the downed figure, his voice dripping with sarcasm - the sadist in him having full rein. *"Well, being as you've asked so nicely, Dr. Hannah, then I'll tell you. I got you dismissed because I had to have you in a position where you needed money desperately. I wanted you to be here with us at this time."*

Eastman could hold her tongue no longer, despite the gun that Bailey was holding. *"Bailey, stop being such an asshole - needlessly torturing the poor woman."* And heedless of the firearm or the pounding rain, she knelt down next to Olivia to give her comfort, shielding her from the rotten bastard. For some reason this scene seemed to delight the stocky author even further, propelling him to new heights of amusement.

"Oh, come on, both of you! Haven't any of you guessed? I needed Olivia Hannah to be here with us. She was the lone survivor from 1996. It took me years to track her down; made more difficult being as she didn't remember herself what happened."

Olivia's head had been buried in Kimberly's shoulder; now she looked up at her tormenter – the architect of her present misery - eyes frightened. Bailey leaned down to the two huddled women, waving the gun around in an almost demented manner, seemingly to punctuate his words. *"You blocked it out over the years didn't you, Dr. Hannah? You sneaked back to America from here and reinvented yourself...but things are changing since you've come back here to the Island. You're remembering again."*

It was too much for the poor tormented woman and she snapped. With a primal scream of rage, she appeared to levitate from the sludgy ground and launched herself like a wildcat at Bailey's face - hands outstretched and claw-like racking his soft facial tissue with her long hard nails. They bit deep into his flesh, causing long bloodied furrows. Screaming, he fell back, desperate to protect his eyes. Bailey's hands reached up to his face – as he did the gun was raised too - Barr saw a chance and took it.

The Indian launched himself at his adversary, Bowie knife raised to stab down into Bailey's torso but Barr hadn't factored in the slippery ground slick with rain and blood. The Haidan lunged, intent on burying the blade deep in Norton Bailey's heart - his boot sole skidded sideways in the mud sending him crashing down on the floor, three feet short of his target. Barr tried to struggle up out of the mud but was hampered by his injured arm. The author had no such physical limitations. Staggering back, Bailey brought the muzzle down and fired down at his would-be attacker.

The gun went off with a loud crack and a sparking muzzle flash that made Kimberly, who was still on the floor, jump in her skin.

Olivia Hannah reacted totally differently. Unbridled in her aggression she went for Bailey again and this time he was forced to try to grab her wrists to protect himself – an action that proved practically impossible; not only was her skin wet and difficult to grasp but he was trying to hold onto the large semi-automatic at the same time. Kimberly stared wildly down at Barr who was writhing on the floor. He was gripping his right shin in agony; blood flowed heavily, covering his pants and mixing frothily into the mud that was rapidly turning crimson around him. Glancing around from him she saw that Rankin had now crept behind the struggling forms of Bailey and Dr. Hannah. Without further hesitation she launched her own attack at the man holding the gun. Rankin had grabbed the arm holding the pistol and pushed it up so even if it went off it would do no real harm. Kimberly entered the fray concluding that it was Norton Bailey that needed rescuing from Olivia.

The once seemingly mild cryptozoologist had her teeth locked firmly into his cheek - biting with such force the man screamed out in agony. Under this brutal attack all thought of the gun was gone now from the author's mind. Bailey released it so he could use both hands to try to pry the ferocious, screaming, vengeful banshee's jaws from his face. Rankin now had the gun and was pointing it at Bailey. Kimberly meanwhile had to fight to get Olivia Hannah to release her grip on her victim - eventually she succeeded.

By this time though, Norton's face was a torn, bitten mess, with several deep lacerations and bites. *"Bastard...I'll kill him...let....me...go..."* screamed Hannah as Kimberly Eastman's arms wrapped tightly around her from behind, pulling her slowly away from Bailey. The man was cringing more from the threat of Olivia viciously attacking again than the gun Scott Rankin had trained on him. After a few futile seconds of thrashing around, and calmed somewhat, Hannah stopped struggling and held up her hands in surrender to Eastman.

Taking a deep breath, Kimberly cautiously released the taller woman. *"Jesus holy Christ,"* breathed Rankin heavily, *"we won't need those things to kill us; we're doing a pretty good job on our own! Looks like Barr's still with us."* He indicated down to where the Haidan had already wrapped some sort of rough and ready bandage around his shin and was now standing up, using a long stick he had found as a makeshift crutch.

He hobbled over to them, grinning. *"Old Barr is still here folks...just got me in the leg."* He cocked his head over to the woods behind them. *"I think they're gathering - scared of the guns for sure, but they're coming soon, you can bet on it."*

He then glanced at the pathetic sight that was Norton Bailey and hobbled close to him, then leaned down to him so his lips were next to the author's bloodied ear. The icy words were meant to be private but Eastman, who was now the closest, heard them and they sent a chill down her spine:

"Mister, you're gonna wish that this good lady here had killed you. Or the creatures had killed you. Or a truck had hit you...anything rather than what I'm fixing to do with you if we get out of this mess. You're a dead man, Bailey. And I swear - you're gonna take a long painful time in getting there." Then he limped back. Norton's face was chalky white under the mask of smeared blood, cuts and contusions.

Barr spoke again, but this time his words were meant for everyone.

"I was fixin' to dig out your satellite phones where Bailey had me hide 'em so we could call for help - truth is they're gone from where I set 'em down. That's what we were arguin' 'bout this mornin'. I don't think this piece of shit," he pointed at Bailey, *"moved 'em again. I think it was them things out in the woods. I think they took 'em."*

Rankin shook his head in puzzlement, saying; *"I don't understand why Bailey had you hide the phones and camera equipment, Barr. What the fuck could he gain from that?"*

Kimberly Eastman laughed bitterly. *"Haven't you worked it out, Scott? Bailey did. It's the fear factor. I did a piece for a TV station on prey and predators years ago - I learned a lot. The more scared we are the greater amount of adrenalin our bodies produce and the higher the likelihood they will attack us. These isolated creatures evolved as hunters. They are attracted by chemicals and pheromones our bodies release if we are afraid and excited. Removing important equipment that we rely on manufactures a stress situation. It artificially boosts our adrenal levels - chumming the water for sharks. He was chemically guaranteeing that one of them would make an appearance - even if it cost us one of our lives. That about right, Bailey?"* The bloodied author glared at her. Kimberly continued.

"What he didn't know was that Ed Benson had already been killed in the night – that rattled him. So he decided he needed to get the phones back to summon help...guess what...they were already gone."

Norton just looked sullener. She had obviously hit home.

Barr interjected; *"Yeah - now I'm thinkin' 'bout it, I reckon I know why we don't see 'em. It's 'cus us folks that live here on the islands kinda blend in. We don't smell like prey to 'em - they just leave us be. Keep out of sight of us like, mainly sticking to the forests at night."*

He looked up into the rainy leaden sky as if considering the matter further, then added; *"But I'm thinkin' that with the wild salmon stocks goin' down, which is what most of the big critters up here rely on for food, well I hope I'm wrong...but I think we might be seein' more of 'em."*

Eastman grimly nodded her head in agreement. She then turned to Olivia Hannah, asking her in a quiet tone of urgency – and for the first time deliberately calling her by her old name; *"Is it true, Bobbie? The part about you? Were you here? How you survived might give us a clue to staying alive."*

Hannah looked at her, brushing her dripping hair from her eyes before replying in a dull quiet voice, *"I don't know, Kimberly. I was here, I'm sure of that. I get flashes now and then, but I can't offer anything more useful than that...I just can't remember it. It was another life for me, another time."* Kimberly patted Olivia on the shoulder in friendly understanding - there was no help to be had from her - no sense in pushing for information she simply couldn't give. Olivia Hannah – or Bobbie as she had been twenty years past - had been terribly traumatized by the events of two decades past. She did not want to remember the details. Well, that was something Eastman understood. The fleeting horrible image of her leering alcoholic father flashed unbidden into her mind, cold groping insistent hands, and his whisky sour breath. She pushed it back down deep inside herself, shutting it away. However, there was one positive that they could take from this - that was Olivia Hannah was standing here with them; living proof that an encounter with these things was survivable. The trick was how?

Rankin broke through her thoughts with an insistent; *"We've got to go Kim, now!"* He was right.

She addressed Barr; *"OK, which way to the trail? How far is the mining camp from here?"*

"Well," the hunter answered, *"you're gonna have to head that way,"* he pointed to the east, *" 'bout two miles. Then you'll see the trail. Just head south on that for about six or so miles, there's a few twists and turns but eventually you'll come into the camp."*

"Right then," said Kimberly, a new note of determination entering her voice due to the challenge that was before them. *"What weapons do we have? Let's tally up."*

Barr had Rankin retrieve the .50 caliber Desert Eagle from where Eastman had dropped it earlier. He had a total of 15 rounds of ammunition in his pack not including what was left in the magazine. They also had Bailey's confiscated Glock .40 which had 9 rounds remaining.

The bow was retrieved out of the mud – however the drawstring was badly frayed, looking to be in danger of snapping if pulled back. Barr said it was unsalvageable. They had Barr's vicious looking Bowie knife and a Lagana tactical tomahawk - a brutal looking piece of hardware; one end of the blade was a razor edge, the other a nasty looking spike. Rankin just looked at Barr when he produced it.

"What the fuck do you use that for?" the cameraman asked him in incredulity.

Barr shrugged. *"Dunno really, always liked 'em...perhaps it's just the Indian in me."* Then he started to chuckle at his own bad joke. Scott just shook his head.

Bailey was in the process of pulling on his large rucksack. Barr limped over to him and pulled it away, throwing it to Eastman. *"Let's look in here shall we, Mr. Bailey? See what you might be holding out on us."* Kimberly rummaged inside and couldn't believe what was in there. There were two metallic objects at the bottom weighing roughly about a pound each. Both were spherical in appearance, olive green in color and had light alloy handles attached to the top of them. Then in bright yellow stenciled letters round the body of the ball shaped case were the words:

'M67 FRAGMENTATION HAND GRENADE'.

"God Almighty," breathed Kimberly. *"You might be a total maniac, Bailey, and I don't know how the hell you got these here, but I'm damned glad you did."*

Kimberly looked up and noted that Barr had a sheepish expression on his face. She knew how Bailey had gotten them here but wisely didn't ask any questions. Both Rankin and Hannah looked at what Eastman was holding in total disbelief.

Olivia asked, *"Can you use those, dear?"* Kimberly gave her a cold nod as a reply, dropping them back into the rucksack and hurriedly pulled it onto her back. *"Oh, it's that old boyfriend of yours again, isn't it? I suppose you can, then."*

Barr and Eastman made sure the guns were loaded. She kept the Magnum and offered the Glock to either Scott or Olivia, whichever one of them felt most comfortable with it. Olivia instantly shook her head in adamant refusal and put up her hands. Kimberly thrust the semi-automatic into Rankin's hands.

"Know how to use it?" she asked. *"There's no safety, so be careful. Hardly any recoil - just point and squeeze the trigger."*

Rankin nodded, saying, *"Those things are so fucking big Stevie Wonder could shoot at one of them and not miss."*

Satisfied at their armaments and defenses, such as they were, Eastman said, *"OK - let's go find that trail and good luck to us all."*

Barr shook his head sadly. *"Sorry Ms. Eastman, but I reckon I won't be coming along."* They all stared at the tall Haidan in disbelief - even Bailey couldn't quite believe it judging from his bewildered expression.

"Come on, Barr," yelled Kimberly, straining to be heard over the howling wind and rain. *"We're in this together. We all go, or we all stay."*

Barr grinned at her. *"Ma'am, I have a crippled right arm and a shattered right shin. Just exactly how much distance you think I'm gonna cover like this?"*

She cursed out loud. *"Shit Barr - we'll make a litter...we'll carry your sorry ass out."* He had a rueful smile as he awkwardly twisted round to observe the storm and the western tree line. He hobbled back round to face to her.

"Any minute now those bastards are gonna come tearing outta them trees. How far you think we'll get with you folks carrying me? Talk sense, girl! Least this way I can give that diversion that Mr. goddamned Bailey was proposin'. It'll give you the chance to maybe get away. Go on, go now, run damnit...I hear 'em!"

The hunter turned to look at the trees. Something fearsome was in there, they all knew. It was ready to close in on them with its incredible speed. With ripping hands and tearing teeth. Unseen titanic hulks that slunk toward them that were as yet still concealed in the dark snarl of trees. Kimberly still stubbornly refused for a moment, thinking desperately of some way - any way at all - they could all go. But even as her mind trotted round in circles she knew in her heart that Barr was right. He turned back to her one final time.

"Go, Kimberly. Live. Have a long and happy life."

She moved quickly to him, gave him a quicksilver kiss on his cheek, then was away at a dead run. The others asked no questions but just followed along in her wake. In seconds the four of them were swallowed up into the trees.

Barr then faced the opposite tree line, bracing himself as well as he was able, pulling out the knife in one hand and holding the tomahawk awkwardly in his partially crippled other hand, winding its leather thong tightly around his wrist to keep it there.

He prepared to sell his life dearly. Terrible huge shapes began to cautiously ooze from the shadows of the trees, slinking out into the rain, fanning out. They were careful now, afraid of the things that they knew could hurt them - but knowing that there was only one of the pallid small creatures waiting - only one. And they could also smell the tantalizing fresh blood and far fresher acrid fear which spurred them on. Spreading out further, they began to close in - to converge hungrily towards the lone figure that stood patiently waiting for them, shouting out his words above the storm.

"This ain't no free lunch today, boys. This is one time you gonna work for it. You're gonna work for your meat real hard."

They slowly closed in around him.

CHAPTER THIRTEEN

Graham Island, British Columbia

24th July 2017

The storm was now almost at its zenith.

Despite the thickness of the entwined overhead canopy, the force of the driving rain still managed to find a way through the dense greenery. It lashed down, soaking the gasping, fleeing group even more than they already were - if that was at all possible. Flashes of brilliant lightning arced ferociously high above the forest within the dark pendulous clouds. Fortunately, that discharged energy was randomly giving of an occasional illumination to the gloom laden forests below.

It was difficult to see their way ahead as they stumbled through the sodden forest floor in their frantic haste. The flickering storm occasionally lit patches around them, lighting their way with a weird strobe like effect. They had been dog trotting for only about thirty minutes but were tiring rapidly. Kimberly Eastman was clutching the large firearm to her sodden chest as she lurched along with the others; half blinded by the rain running down her face, half deafened by the roar of the wind and thunder.

The other three were all in equally poor shape. She could hear their panting, ragged breaths and occasional muted curses as they pushed themselves forward for their lives. The four of them were not only fighting the harsh weather conditions and the impossible tangle of closely woven trees but their own stark fears also. Imagination breeds its own terror. They saw a creature lurking behind every tree, one crouched and waiting to pounce in every shadow. Kimberly gritted her teeth and plunged on, heedless of branches that cruelly whipped her face and arms or exposed roots and forest debris that littered the ground, threatening to send her sprawling into the mud at any second.

She felt the cold if slippery security of the heavy gun; it was cocked, and she was ready to bring it up and fire instantly if needed. She gripped it tighter for further comfort. Eastman half-expected one of the fearsome titans to suddenly rear up somewhere in front of them at any moment, though as yet she had heard no sign of pursuit. Olivia Hannah staggered up to her side, forcing her uncomfortably into a slower pace. The cryptozoologist draped her arm over Kimberly's shoulders, pulling their staggering bodies close to each other. She gasped out a sentence, but a crash of loud thunder made Eastman miss the first few words.

"Wind and rain...our allies. So is the thunder and lightning..." another crash of thunder meant further missed words, *"...examined them, noticed that they are adapted primarily for nocturnal hunting. Pupils are huge to make most of...available light."*

Worryingly for Kimberly, they slowed even more as Hannah struggled to get her breath back and tried to talk to her again.

"Nasal slits too...have heightened sense of smell, like a...canine...rain will dull that...lightning will be advantage for us...wind, thunder...all of it helps us not them...probably would have a hard time tracking us...waiting for storm to pass..."

Eastman gasped back into the taller woman's ear. *"We...just need...to keep...keep moving. The greater the distance...between us and those...fuckers, the better I'll like it!"* Olivia wearily nodded her agreement and the two separated again, continuing their weaving, breathless flight towards the logging path that lay tantalizingly somewhere in the dark in front of them.

The trees miraculously thinned out. There was a gentle downward slope making the going somewhat easier. With the trees being so less densely packed together it was also perceptibly lighter, but with less overhead coverage the rain was finding an easier passage down to them and was pounding now with an increased force.

Despite the streaming torrents of rain, Eastman hoped that they would now make better time if the terrain remained like this. She tried to work it out roughly how far they had come - probably about a mile and a half – they had at least the same distance to cover again before they even got to the track; the one that would lead them to the relative safety of the logging camp. At least that was what Barr had told her. Poor Barr - he must be dead. Kimberly felt tears welling up but pushed the emotion away. No crying - not now. Hopefully there would be time for that later. If any of them had a later. Kimberly tried to shut out all thoughts and concentrated on keeping moving. She had thought herself reasonably fit but realized that she had deluded herself. Her leg muscles were trembling with fatigue and her lungs felt like they were on fire.

The slope was increasing downward now, and she had to slow herself on the treacherously wet muddy floor to negotiate a particular clump of gnarled cedars without sliding headfirst into them.

Holding onto one of the trees, she glanced around and took the time to see how the others were holding up. Norton Bailey had surprised her. Despite being on the heavy side he seemed to be faring better than the others. He was breathing hard to be sure, and was mud-streaked from the flying wet earth that had splattered his clothing and chubby face as he had run. But other than that, he still seemed reasonably fresh. Olivia Hannah however was in slightly worse shape than the stocky author. She was older than Bailey and her willowy frame made her fragile and weak; ill equipped to this kind of rigorous exercise. She was keeping up though, her fear giving her that much needed spur. But Scott was another story altogether. He was quite a way behind. In other circumstances, if she had watched him lumbering along to catch up, he would have cut a comedic figure. But there was nothing remotely funny about this situation. Rankin was red faced, gasping for air; his substantial bulk and layers of fat jiggled and rolled across him as he came down the slope at a far slower pace than the others; dangerously slower. As Kimberly watched her friend coming down towards her, she snatched a few seconds of rest, trying to catch her own breath. Olivia Hannah staggered over to her. Bailey glanced contemptuously at the two women and then kept heading down the slippery slope regardless of the others. He was obviously just intent on trying to save his own skin. *No real surprise there,* she thought bitterly.

Were they complete cretins? thought Bailey.

Kimberly Eastman, he observed, had stopped on the slope by a group of trees and that crazy bitch Hannah had too. He sped away from the women, moving as quickly as he could. They were waiting for that fat slob Rankin who was still further up the hill he noted, staggering towards them. *Stupid fucking assholes,* thought Bailey. If they wanted to stay behind and die, then let them. While the hominids were busy with them it would exponentially increase his chances of getting away. He was doubly glad of all the hours he had spent with the weights in his gym. He'd installed it and all the exercise machines and benches initially as a vanity, a 'must have' accessory in his smart New England home, along with the hot tub and indoor pool. But Bailey had become addicted to it all.

He looked fat but in fact was quite muscular under those layers of extra flesh. He imagined himself as a powerful sumo at times.

He kept jogging down the hill, avoiding the various outcroppings of trees and other indiscriminate foliage that sprouted up in patches around the terrain like a discouraged lawn. At this rate he'd be at the path in no time and fuck all of them. They could take their chances. Served them right anyway. Ungrateful bastards, messing up his carefully laid plans like that! He hoped they all got what was coming to them, especially that fucking Indian, Barr. *I hope he suffered a lot before he died; like I hope that bitch Eastman does too. All of them, suffer and die. Suffer and die.*

Fifteen minutes later, the man was at the rutted logger's trail. The deep truck tracks that comprised it were filled with muddy water from the torrential rainstorm. *Now, let's think. Which way had Barr said...south wasn't it? Now which way was south? Was it left or right?* Bailey honestly didn't know. He had no idea and couldn't work it out. He knew the sun set in the west, and the cardinal points of the compass but when one couldn't actually see the sun due to an overcast rainy sky, then how do you tell? He had no idea. Wasn't there something about moss growing only on the north side of a tree? Time was running out; he needed to get moving. In desperation he studied the nearest tree to him. It seemed like there was moss or lichen all over the damned thing. Bailey moved to another on the far side of the trail, obliviously splashing through the water filled tracks and squelching mud only to observe that the green flecks on it were fairly uniform across its rough exterior also. *Which fucking way? Calm down, Norton*, he thought. *Use logic!* Well the Dinan logging camp was in the valley close to the lake. Water always runs downhill so the right way must obviously be to head whichever way was heading down.

He stood in the middle of the swampy trail, looking left and right. It appeared that as the track headed off to the right there was a slight drop. That was it then, he had to head off to the right! Confident he had made the right choice, he headed off on the side of the track as fast as he could. Norton Bailey was traveling north.

***

Back in LA at Hendry Corp, Bruno Harts' mild concern for the group had progressed into a worry that was rat gnawing at his insides. Despite numerous attempts from their end, there had been no communication from Eastman, Rankin or the rest for several hours; something was obviously badly wrong. In frustration, he stepped from his office and went down the corridor to Hendry Corp's plush workplace.

The door was open and one glance at the face of the company owner told Harts that the man looked like he felt but probably for different reasons, thought Bruno, somewhat cynically. Richardson Hendry ceased pacing upon noticing Bruno Harts' entrance. The TV executive could smell the desperation in Hendry's office; the kind that comes with paralyzing thoughts of huge impending lawsuits.

Hendry asked, *"Bruno, give me some good news. Has there been word from them?"*

Bruno shook his head. Hendry studied Harts' face for a second, reading in it the same thoughts he was having himself. That simple connection galvanized the older man. Hendry decisively moved across the office's plush carpet to his desk and picked up his phone. Enough was enough; it was time to call for help.

***

Olivia put her hand on the dripping rough tree bark close to Kimberly Eastman's shoulder - head hung down - panting heavily and painfully.

She spoke haltingly and somewhat disjointedly, but Kimberly got the sense of it. *"I thought so...I was right...not coming after us yet...if they were...be here by now...hard for them to track us in storm...soon as it ends or gets less though...need to keep going..."*

Kimberly nodded to her in a silent agreement, forcing herself away from the welcoming support of the tree and pulling Olivia up with her at the same time.

Scott was with them now. He looked about all in. His facial skin was mottled and wet, the wetness a greasy combination of rain and sweat. His hair was plastered in a molded black cap flattened to his head. Kimberly looked at his eyes, dismayed to see the disconsolate look she found there. The dull expression of resigned inevitable defeat.

"Come on, Scotty," she gasped at him, trying to lift him. *"We can beat this. We'll be safe soon enough. Think about the networks airing the footage and then us writing our own ticket, you know? Just like you had it planned out!"*

He shot back a forced dispirited grin, muttering, *"It's a sure thing, isn't it? Boy, are we gonna hit the big time with this, or what!"* He patted the small HD camera he held in his hand. The words however were hollow; the look of utter hopelessness did not leave Rankin's eyes for a second. He knew himself that he couldn't go on much longer. Rankin was beaten and he knew it. Desperately trying to encourage him, Eastman gripped the sopping wet sleeve of his shirt and pulled him along after her; within a very few yards though he was trailing behind again; moments later the gap between them widened further. Ten minutes of them negotiating the tree strewn, rain saturated slope, Scott Rankin was quite a way behind - now the storm was almost over.

The lightning was decreasing in intensity and duration. The rain had slackened to a steadily persistent downpour instead of the stinging deluge of minutes earlier. Eastman and Hannah who had been keeping pace with each other exchanged worried glances. They collectively had the unspoken thought. All too soon the creatures would be in pursuit, if indeed they weren't already. There was little either of them could do. Rankin was just too big for them to drag or carry. If they had to keep stopping for him to keep up, their own chances of survival diminished exponentially. Kimberly Eastman also knew that she and Scotty had been friends for years. She could no more leave him behind than he would leave her if the situation was ever reversed.

She motioned Olivia Hannah to go on and turned round to wait for him by a small stand of trees. As she stopped, so did the other woman. Angrily, Eastman waved Hannah on, shouting out: *"Go! There's no sense both of us waiting! We have the guns...Just keep moving...the track is close now. Go...go!!"*

Olivia Hannah hesitated briefly, concern written on her face. With the briefest of backward glances, she started moving again down the slope.

Rankin finally caught up to Eastman, but he was in a terrible state. The cameraman's lips had a distinct blue tinge to them, and he was fighting for breath; his whole body trembled with his exertions. He had come to the end of the road. She knew it and he knew it. He couldn't physically go further. She patted him understandingly on the shoulder and then put her arm around him in comfort.

"Rest now, Scotty. Sit down. Get your breath, kid. We'll keep them off between us."

He pushed her roughly away, gasping, *"Hell no. Fuck you Kim! I'm not having your death on my conscience...if I die and then you died because of me, I'd never forgive myself."* He laughed at the absurdity of what he'd said. They both did - briefly. The rain was easing. Kimberly looked up at a sky that was breaking out into brighter patches of less dense clouds. She took a nervous look far up the slope where the tree line thickened. Her hand instinctively tightened on the gun butt. Scott reached out, pulling her to him, crushing his friend up against him for a second. His lips brushed her tangled hair - just as quickly he pushed her away to his arm's length.

"Kim, I never actually told you this, but...well, thanks. Thanks for all the times you've put up with my crazy shit. Thanks for all the times you've been there for me. You've been a better buddy to me than I ever deserved." Not able to look her in the face, Rankin pushed the camera into her empty hand. He then pulled out the Glock .40 from the waistband of his jeans. He studied it for a moment, turning it over in his hands, as if seeing it for the first time, then slowly and deliberately pulled back the slide and released it. He spoke to her without looking at her directly, studying the gun, embarrassed to face her. *"Tell them, will you? At least my little girl will always know that her dad wasn't always a big fat no-hoper drunk and in the end he didn't go out like one either."*

Kimberly could hardly bear it. But a glance up the slope told a story. Huge unearthly shapes were moving cautiously down toward them, wary of the weapons their prey carried, but still possessed of a deliberate and murderous purpose. The nightmare would soon be upon them. Damn it, Kimberly told herself fiercely, if Scotty was going to stand and make a fight of it, then she would too. She took a step back, keeping a wary eye on the advancing monsters - dropping the clip quickly to double check, slamming it back home again.

Rankin looked furiously back at her with genuine anger that she'd never seen in him before. *"What the hell are you doing, you stupid bitch? I told you to go! Fucking run! I need you alive to tell my kid and Maria that I was straight at the end and I was really trying. Tell them my death meant something and I wasn't drunk...And tell them I loved them."*

Kimberly wavered, uncertain what to do. He took a step toward her and backhanded her across the face. Not hard but it hurt more than any blow she'd had in her life. *"Go!!"* he yelled. He then turned and raised the gun to face his death.

Her face stinging, she looked at him one last time, then turned and raced down the wet slope, limbs flailing madly, running as she never had before. She caught up to Olivia minutes later. The first spaced out shots began in the distance. They continued for quite a little while. And still Kimberly Eastman would not allow herself the luxury of tears even at the thought of Scotty facing those evil creatures alone without her.

Finally, just as they arrived gasping raggedly for air at the track that Barr had told them would be there, Rankin's gun fell ominously quiet. The last shot echoed through the trees and faded into silence. Kimberly Eastman desperately hoped that she would hear another. No further shots followed. In some lonely and secret place in her mind – a hidden refuge - Kimberly said a silent goodbye to her friend, Scott Rankin.

Both women stood at the edge of the track to gather themselves up for one last supreme effort that would hopefully carry them those last few miles to the sanctuary they so desperately wanted to be waiting for them at the logging camp. They looked at each other. They were bedraggled specimens – filthy, wet and stinking. Their faces and arms bore a multitude of similar cuts, bruises and scratches – jointly accumulated on their mad fight for survival.

"Which way should we go?" Olivia Hannah asked Kimberly.

With a sigh, bent almost double trying to recover her breath, the other woman indicated left with the gun she still clutched. *"Are you sure? Is that definitely the right way?"*

Eastman wearily nodded, pulling out a tiny compass she had taken from the camp earlier that day and had kept in her pocket. Having caught her breath a little she said, *"I'm certain...that way's south and a few miles further is the logging camp where we started out from."*

Hannah looked sadly at Eastman. She came up and brushed Kimberly's wet hair back from her forehead. She was close to her, and said in a hushed tone, *"We aren't going to make it, are we?"*

Kimberly pulled back - the very suggestion instantly bridling her - she retorted sharply back, *"Two brave men gave their lives so we can make it...so that's what we are going to do. We are going down this path...we aren't going to stop until we are safe...do you understand me? If anything gets in our way or tries to stop us, I'm going to use Barr's gun. I'm going to kill it stone fucking dead!"* It was only then Eastman realized that she was gripping the other woman's thin shoulder in a vice-like grip - had been shaking her - yelling hysterically to make her point. Poor Olivia had cowered in the face of the other woman's fury.

Embarrassed at her outburst, Kimberly now caressed the same thin, boney shoulder she had grabbed with such violence. *"Oh God, I'm sorry Bobbie, let's just go, eh?"* And with that they both hurried away.

***

The sounds of distant gunfire stopped Norton Bailey dead in his tracks.

He strained to hear what was going on. The forest had an odd effect on the sound; distorting it, making it difficult to judge from which direction the shots were coming from. However, after hearing three shots in rapid succession he judged it must be coming from somewhere above him over his left shoulder. The author listened intently. Silence again. By the time the last shot had faded into silence, Bailey was already on the move, unwittingly still hurrying in the completely wrong direction.

Scant minutes later, Norton Bailey discovered his horrifying mistake. A lightning fast blur shot across his path, so quick that he didn't quite believe what he had seen. Gut instinct however slowed his pace to a hesitant crawl then finally to a grinding halt. Something fell with a large splash at his feet.

In a kind of blind rapture, he looked slowly down. There, grotesquely bobbing in the filthy water of the tire track was Scott Rankin's head - the features frozen in an awful expression of violent and sudden death - lips pulled horribly back from smashed teeth giving the suggestion the decapitated head wanted to speak even after death. Mesmerized by the horrific sight, Bailey barely noted that it was getting dark.

A shadow fell across him, blocking the light. He knew what was standing there before him but he couldn't look up. He wanted to cry, vomit and shit all at the same time. But his eyes betrayed his body and looked up into the face of his impending death. He barely got out a whimper as the gigantic creature in front of him picked him up by his throat and started to squeeze, sniggering horribly with its gaping red wet maw.

The last thing that Norton Bailey heard was the terrible thundering beat of his heart as it pulsed inside his head; the pressure increased on his neck crushing his throat and larynx flat and splintering his vertebrae into shards. Then the darkness came to greet him.

He was terribly afraid of that and his mind whimpered again because the last thought of Norton Bailey was that blackness would surely bear him away to a hell of his own creation.

⚔ ⚔ ⚔

Incredibly the women had managed almost three miles when the creatures' attack finally fell upon them.

There was a bend in the track with the steep tree covered slope to their right and an even steeper drop to their left. A tree filled ravine of sorts lay below. *A perfect place to ambush us,* Kimberly thought to herself. Unfortunately, that realization came a fraction of a second too late to avoid it. With a loud crack that sounded like the very gates of hell slamming shut, a massive tree, thirty plus feet tall, crashed down onto the track in front of them, barring their path. Eastman had just enough time to spin round to see one of the giants bounding up the track towards them on all fours.

Taking a quick aim, she fired. The powerful gun kicked hard into the palm of her hand. The heavy bullet hit the monster high in its shoulder, spinning it around and knocking it to one side in a sprawling, writhing heap at the very edge of the drop off. Eastman realized her error. These things had learnt to be afraid of firearms - they knew that they could be hurt or even killed by them. So, they had devised a strategy to combat it; the oldest one known - diversion.

Kimberly spun round with that realization to face the real attack that she knew would be coming over the obstruction in front of them. It was too late to shoot; she had badly underestimated the raw intelligence these things possessed. They weren't animals. They were organized, thinking beings. The next thing she knew she was tumbling through the air; something had smashed hard into her. Kimberly thought she felt a rib crack under the brutal impact; she was rolling over and over, the world became a crazy kaleidoscope of spinning sky, ground, and trees. Finally, she stopped rolling along the ground and groggily looked around her. By some miracle she was still alive and had not released her tenacious hold on the deadly .50 caliber.

Through a tear blurred vision she saw that she had been knocked far down the rutted, muddied track several yards away from where she had been standing when she had shot the first creature. Her short ribs on her left-hand side hurt like fire and she had an idea that one or two were broken.

Three of the horrors were standing by the felled tree; Hannah was cowered at their feet but hadn't been attacked yet. However, a fourth one, the one she had shot, had now regained its feet and was slowly moving towards her; vicious shark-like teeth bared in a leering grimace of pain and anger; its one huge arm hanging down limply at its side, shoulder shattered by the heavy round. Kimberly didn't hesitate. She raised the gun and fired at it again. This time the bullet struck it in its lower face - part of its jaw was torn away by the impact. It gave out a gurgling scream, its one functional hand and arm flying to the injury that was now bleeding profusely. All thought of attack had now gone from its mind. Kimberly got painfully to her feet, covered in the wet mud and feeling a terrible pain in her side. The hair-covered titan began to stagger backwards towards its fellows. As it did so, it tripped over on some unseen obstruction and fell heavily back onto the rutted track, mud and water splashing up as it hit the ground - too weak to rise.

Eastman stumbled forward, teeth clenched with her own agony - drawing level with the fallen giant - and shot it in the face at close range.

It convulsed - then died instantly - part of its skull was blown out, brain tissue splashed out onto the soaked ground. *That was for Barr*, she thought savagely to herself.

The other three creatures did not seem to know what to do. Kimberly felt sure they wanted to attack and were hopping and milling around trying to summon up courage enough to move forward – but their fear of the shining object in her hand was preventing them. Olivia Hannah was still on the floor at their feet. *"Stay down!"* Kimberly Eastman screamed at her. She then took careful aim at the largest center one. But she never got the shot off. Something bowled her and swept the feet from under her. Eastman had been knocked to the boundary of the track where it dropped into the deep ravine. She had been blindsided by an unseen smaller creature – one that must have leaped at her from the cover of the wooded slope. Fortunately, it had struck her uninjured side - not causing further damage but it still hurt terribly. Barely seven feet, she thought, as she sized it warily up from her position on the floor, she realized it was a young inexperienced one - it hadn't moved straight in to kill her after knocking her down. It had backed off, taking its time, crouching to spring again, reveling in its power and accomplishment. She fired at it even as it leaped. The bullet hit it in the chest, straight into its heart and lungs, dropping it instantly but its impetus carried its lifeless corpse into her, slamming into Kimberly hard again, throwing her and it backwards - straight over the edge.

Kimberly Eastman got one fleeting look at Olivia's face as their eyes briefly met - then she was gone. Olivia watched in horror as her last hope was thrown to her death. With a wailing cry she was scooped up by one of the hairy monstrosities and carried speedily away. Now finally she remembered - she knew where they were heading. *Oh God,* she remembered! And if Olivia Hannah had a gun at that moment, she would have used it on herself.

As Kimberly fell, she had the presence of mind to roll into a ball and hit the fast-approaching slope like that.

This terrible danger they had been thrust into had made her sharper than she'd been in a long time; more alive in the face of death than she had for years. It was almost exhilarating. Luck dealt her a good hand. The creature she had killed was tumbling into the ravine with her. Death had made it loose limbed and floppy - somehow it had got underneath her. Its corpse hit the slope first, and Kimberly slammed into it with enough force to knock the breath from her body, sending a further zipping lightning bolt of agony through her abused ribs. As painful as it was, it still broke her initial fall.

She bounced off the creature's corpse, and rolled a little down the loamy slope which gradually slowed her, finally coming to rest against the bole of a huge cedar that was snaking up, strong and tall from the bottom of the ravine fifty odd feet below. The lifeless creature was not so lucky – although it was far beyond caring. The remains totally missed the same huge cedar that had saved her and went crashing down in a flurry of wet leaves to be lost in the tree filled depths.

Kimberly, with her back against the supporting bark, groaned in pain, examining herself as thoroughly as she could. Her ribs hurt like fire. She felt gingerly along and around them – carefully probing - she was now certain that none of them were broken as she'd thought they might be. More importantly there were no signs of internal bleeding. Kimberly looked around for the gun - she had become separated from it as she was thrown over the edge. It was too much to ask for it to still be conveniently around. It was. There was no sign of it. Sighing, she still had the comfort of the backpack that contained two M-67 grenades she had 'liberated' from Norton Bailey and perhaps most importantly the camera; the precious item that held the evidence of their encounter. Remarkably it had stayed in her shirt where she had placed it.

A sudden fleeting image of a grinning Scott Rankin came to her then. Kimberly pushed it away. She sat back against her savior tree and rested for a moment, listening intently for any sound that those things were climbing down after her. They weren't - probably just glad to be rid of her.

Now what, she thought? *Do I try to make it back to the logging camp and get help? That would be the logical and smart thing to do. After all, if Bailey makes it back - knowing that bastard he probably will - he sure as hell wouldn't be sending out any search and rescue units for them.*

Kimberly Eastman suddenly didn't feel particularly logical or smart. There was a burning need in her gut; or perhaps it was just that she had her own personal demons that needed to be exorcised. Her vile, drunken incestuous father. Those calculating bastards that had used her when she was nineteen in front of the camera, promising so much and in the end delivering only shame and regret. All those men that had abused and used her over the years as she had climbed the weary ladder of her profession. There were way too many Norton fucking Baileys in this world and not enough good men like Ed Norton, Scott Rankin, or Franklin Barr. She thought of the expression Olivia Hannah had on her face when she went over the edge. That awful look of utter despair that no one would or could ever help her. That exact same look that had been on Kimberly's own face so often in her own past. Coldly she stood up, wincing at the pain that lived in her ribs.

She started the tough climb back up into the light. Today, she decided, things were going to be different. If Olivia Hannah was alive, help was coming. Kimberly set her teeth together in raw defiance and attacked the upward slope.

***

It was the same as before; a grisly déjà vu for Olivia Hannah.

She was being carried away, slung over the huge hairy stinking back of one of the creatures. Soon, they'd be descending the slick dark tunnel into the depths of the cavern lair. It would only be a matter of time before she was viciously raped by one of them or eaten by the group – or probably both. Her mind wanted to shut this horror away - to retreat into itself - to escape. Hannah was determined not to give these abominations the satisfaction of sending her down into gibbering madness. Olivia needed a clear head, because she was not going to allow these things to rape her again. When opportunity presented itself, she must end her life in any way that she could manage it; even if the only way was to provoke them into killing her. It was a sin, yes. But a far greater sin would be to allow these demons of hell to violate her again.

All too soon they arrived at the familiar cavern entrance. And down they trooped into hell once again.

***

Kimberly Eastman had now scrabbled to the top of the ravine – keeping low and concealed, she peered out onto the track.

Other than the fallen tree, there was no sign that these things had ever been there or that a desperate fight had taken place. They certainly cleaned up after themselves. Satisfied that none of the monsters were around, she hauled herself painfully over the lip and lay panting and sore on the wet mud of the track. Shit! She couldn't believe it! There, right in front of her, half buried in the mud was Barr's .50 hand cannon! She pulled it out of the muck and examined the gun carefully. It looked OK as far as she could tell. Hurriedly ripping off the bottom of her shirt, she used the cloth to clean the Desert Eagle as best as she could. The shirt was already filthy and bloodstained to boot, but it sufficed to remove the majority of the mud from the weapon. The state the gun was in would have probably give some gunnery sergeant or gunsmith a fatal attack of apoplexy. Kimberly didn't care how it looked - as long as it still functioned.

She pulled the pack off her back, which again caused her considerable discomfort. Then Kimberly put the small video camera inside the rucksack to keep it safe.

After doing that she then removed spare .50 caliber hollow point rounds from one of the pack's side pouches and replenished the gun's magazine. She then carefully took the M67 grenades out from the bottom of the pack and hooked them into her jeans belt. The last couple of .50 caliber shells she had left she jammed into her ass pocket. She checked that the camera was secure inside the rucksack, and then put it back on again.

Satisfied with her preparations, it was now time to go and get her friend.

***

Olivia Hannah was in the huge, fantastical, fungus lit cavern once more that served these gigantic hominids as home. She was dumped unceremoniously into a 'nest' as she had been last time and then left alone. This time though there was a startling difference - the nest had a previous occupant. The crippled Franklin Barr was already laying in it. She could scarcely believe what her eyes told her.

She began to cry. *"Oh Barr, we thought you were dead,"* she sobbed. *"Poor Mr. Rankin and Kimberly are gone…I think the creatures killed them…but I saw Kimberly kill at least two of those abominations with your gun before they got her …oh Barr…poor Kimberly."*

Barr was in obvious pain, but pushed himself up as best as he could. He ruffled the woman's hair, saying, *"Well Doc - sure nice to see you too. Wish it was in better circumstances though. Thought I was done for after I buried my knife in one of them thing's chest and my tomahawk in another one's eye; but the damn things just knocked me down an' carried me off. I couldn't fight back, not having weapons and such - so I went along kinda quiet and peaceful like. But to be truthful my leg is so badly busted up I didn't think I could get away even if I'd wanted."* He looked at her intently now, saying, *"I gotta tell ya the truth as I see it, no point lying to ya, ma'am. I figure we are here and still alive for only one reason..."*

Olivia shuddered but answered him in a low tone. *"I know Barr; I was here before. I've seen it. They like their food fresh."*

He nodded grimly.

"Barr," she said in the same low tone, *"I need to ask you a favor. Please don't let them..."*

The Haidan put his hand gently to her mouth, interrupting her before she could finish saying the obvious. *"Don't you worry 'bout that... They won't take you alive and you won't suffer, I promise you that much."*

That seemed to give Olivia a measure of comfort because with that she rolled over to him and sank her head onto his chest, and quietly sobbed till she fell asleep.

***

Kimberly walked in the general direction she had thought the creatures might be heading with Olivia. By chance she spotted them from a distance as they were lacking their customary stealth because of the burdens they hefted with them.

Of the three, the last in the group was carrying Olivia - another carried the hulking corpse of the one Kimberly had downed.

At the distance she observed them Kimberly couldn't tell if Olivia Hannah was dead or alive; but occasional movement suggested some resistance to being carried - whilst the corpse of the dead creature just sagged loosely across the huge shoulders of the equally large being carrying it. Eastman had to believe in her heart that Olivia was still alive - else what was the point?

She dropped low and watched carefully as the group of giants made their way slowly up a far slope and headed for what looked like a low cliff, the base almost completely concealed in the trees. Finally, they disappeared, and they were lost from sight. She waited patiently, watching, observing, but they didn't re-appear. With great care, Kimberly worked her way to the slope – then made her way slowly upwards - taking her time and using every piece of natural cover to remain unseen. At the top of the rise from the tree line, Kimberly could clearly see the cliff now. From this vantage point it was obvious to her where the monstrous slinking pack had vanished. There was an offset cave entrance in the cliff - just left of center. As far as she could see none of the creatures were in evidence; surprisingly not even one of them had been left behind to guard the entrance to what must surely be their domain. She waited for a few minutes in nervous anticipation - senses on full alert - but all was quiet. Kimberly crept from the trees, gun at the ready, making her way cautiously to the black entrance in the cliff surface. Eastman peered in. It was as dark as the proverbial tomb inside; all was deathly quiet. A stench hung in the dank air; the rotten odor of something dead and long unburied. She stepped quietly in and the dark swallowed her completely.

***

Barr was shaking Olivia awake. She had almost forgotten where she was for a moment; but the misery of their dire situation flooded back into her instantly. *"What is it Barr, what's ha..."* He silenced her.

It was all Olivia Hannah could do to restrain herself from yelling out in surprise. There in front of her was a welcome, wonderful face; one she thought she'd never see again this side of heaven. Kimberly Eastman!

Olivia's head was bursting with questions; words wanted to spill out in a torrent but there wasn't time for that.

She was simply ecstatic that Kimberly was alive and had come back for her as she promised. Kimberly Eastman put her head silently against Olivia's in greeting. That simple human gesture filled Hannah with a warmth beyond description.

From the sounds that reverberated around the huge cavern, Olivia knew the titanic creatures that lay stretched out in the darkness were asleep. But that could change in an instant she knew from experience - they could be roused from that sleep by any sound or movement that was out of the ordinary. Olivia, without being asked, quietly straightened herself up and helped Kimberly to pull Barr upright in the nest that they had lay on. He was still favoring his good leg - despite his injuries he made no sounds of pain as they heaved him upright. Supporting Barr between them, Kimberly Eastman began to lead them towards the steep channel that she had groped her way down - until she had discovered the lit portion of the passageway that led into this vast cavern. That passage was the way back into the light. They had covered less than ten paces when their luck - which had held so well - finally ran out. As they moved awkwardly forward, Barr tripped on a loose piece of rock - the resulting twisting movement caused him searing pain in his injured leg; a sudden agony so intense that even the stoic Indian could not help but to cry out. A half-stifled groan of pain – soft - but it was enough to rouse the cavern's terrible inhabitants. Almost at once, a fearsome shape loomed up directly in their path, blocking their way out.

Kimberly pointed the semi-automatic up and pulled the trigger.

The gun roared - the noise in the huge cave was deafening; reverberating round the walls, the sounds increased exponentially. The creatures didn't like it. They howled in their fear and anger at this unwelcome thing in their home. This shrieking made matters worse - confusing and disorientating them further.

But this new circumstance gave the three humans a slight edge. Eastman attempted to drag Barr along but another creature popped up to take the place of the one she had just fired at. The supply of ammunition was limited. There were certainly more of these things than she had bullets for.

"This way, quick!" yelled Olivia. *"I know a way out, but we have to hurry before they stop us!"* She started off for the center of the cave, supporting Barr on her wispy frame as best she could - leaving Kimberly free to shoot the menacing things down that were all around them in the ghostly green light.

Kimberly could clearly hear running water as they neared the middle of the creatures' lair. The light wasn't good this far in the cavern.

Eastman could feel her skin crawling and tingling as she sensed rather than felt the unclean presence of the gigantic hellish vermin as they closed in. Before long the creatures would rush them - she instinctively knew it. In desperation, Eastman fired blindly around her in a short arc. Three shots in three directions; at least one hit something from the howl of pain that resulted.

Olivia was yelling something about getting into the water - Kimberly felt the warm stinking putrid breath of one of the monsters almost in her face. She jerked the gun up and squeezed the trigger twice in quick succession at the unseen demon - but only got one shot. The clip was empty, and she had no time to put any remaining bullets in the emptied magazine. She hurled the useless gun into the darkness, in the direction she thought one of the hideous monsters might be.

This is the end - with all hope gone and as a final act of defiance, Kimberly Eastman dully pulled the grenades off her belt and pulled out one pin and then the other. She threw one up as far as she could; releasing the lever. Something was yanking her backwards. Was it one of the creatures? Was this death?

Fuck it, she thought. As she went down, Kimberly dropped the second grenade to the floor. The fuse was 10 seconds. She heard Barr curse and Olivia scream; then she was in an icy, fast flowing water, being pulled under into a powerful current. All Kimberly could do was to seal her mouth to the water. Then amidst this roiling black liquid, confusion came a diffused bang and a percussion wave that hurt her ears terribly. That was followed almost instantaneously by a massive pressure wave that seemed to roll her around and tear at her - propelling Kimberly's unresisting body forward with greater energy than the strong current already possessed. She was turned over and over - colliding with rocks and other unseen obstructions. Then all was blackness and silence.

Kimberly Eastman came to herself choking and feeling sick. Barr had her on her front and was pumping cold river water out of her lungs. She didn't know how, but she was still alive. Rolling over on the muddy riverbank, she held out her hands weakly in protest.

"OK, OK...I'm OK now, thanks." Eastman slowly sat up, feeling queasy but glad to be around.

Her elation at being alive was short lived.

Close to them, lying on the bank was Olivia Hannah. Poor Bobbie. She hadn't made it, with no real wounds on her body that Kimberly could discern, she was certain the older woman had drowned. The icy water had been too much for her and it had taken her life.

Barr had respectfully arranged her arms and legs and closed her eyes. *"I tell ya Kimberly, I spoke to Olivia before you showed up. She certainly preferred this, a clean death, to what those big hairy fuckers had in mind for her, trust me. She was one happy lady when you showed up. You might not think you saved her seein' her like this; but trust me girl, you did."* Kimberly Eastman was just too numb to think. Something suddenly occurred to her. She frantically felt all around her torso. Her shirt was now in tatters and the rucksack was gone, and if that was gone then so was the camera, lost forever somewhere at the bottom of the raging underground river. Disappointment didn't really cover what she felt at its loss.

She asked Barr in forlorn hope, *"My pack? Did you see it or take it off me?"*

Barr sadly shook his head, guessing her thoughts, asking, *"The camera was in it?"*

All she could do was nod. The tall Haidan went on; *"Sorry - I reckon it's good 'n gone."* Barr patted her arm in a cold commiseration. *"But on the plus side none of the creatures followed us out either. Before I pulled you and the Doc into the water, the roof was coming in. Grenades must have triggered a cave in. It was all collapsing in on itself, millions of tons*

161

of rock I reckon. Whatever was in there is buried along with it I guess; permanent like." He spat on the floor.

Kimberly was cold and was starting to shiver, despite the early summer evening. Barr noticed and pulled her closer to him, warming her as best as he could. A few minutes later came the welcome sound of a helicopter. It was the search and rescue team that Hendry Corp had sent out. They both watched in grateful silence as it floated in over the trees towards them.

Kimberly Eastman buried her head in Barr's chest again. She thought of the coldly scientific David Sterling, the irrepressible Ed Benson, and the sad, bewildered and tormented Olivia Hannah who was now finally at rest. But most of all she thought of the gallant Scott Rankin to whom she owed a debt she could never repay - her life. It was time, Kimberly Eastman decided; and she finally let her tears flow out.

CHAPTER FOURTEEN

Graham Island, British Columbia

23rd Sept 2022

The young couple in the brand new hiking gear looked around them in complete bewilderment. The huge trees that had minutes ago seemed so friendly and welcoming had now taken on a different aspect.

The couple was now feeling disquiet; an odd sensation - one that they somehow vaguely feared.

"Maxie," yelled out the woman at the top of her lungs. *"Maxi-mill-ian."*

No answer was forthcoming. The forest remained ominously silent.

The woman turned on the man with what was something less than quiet annoyance, growling.

"Where the hell has that kid and stupid damned dog disappeared off to now, for fuck's sake! They were on the path with us here two friggin' minutes ago, just right behind us!" The man sighed, a pained expression on his face.

He replied, *"Let's just go off and look for them, shall we, instead of standing here and shouting? They aren't far away, I'm sure of that... Max is just playing a stupid game. Hiding or something, you know what the kid is like."*

But the woman wouldn't be fobbed off easily.

"But Adrian, the stories about those things..."

He merely looked at her with a raised eyebrow, shaking his head before replying, *"Seriously – does anyone actually believes in that horse shit? It's an urban legend. C'mon Linda...just quit it - it's a myth!"*

And something - indescribably inhuman, huge, unmoving, and silent - watched them from deep within the trees.

And waited.

CHECK OUT OTHER GREAT BIGFOOT NOVELS

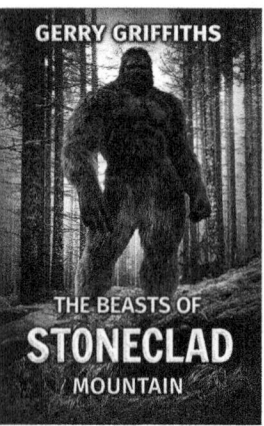

THE BEASTS OF STONECLAD MOUNTAIN
by Gerry Griffiths

Clay Morgan is overjoyed when he is offered a place to live in a remote wilderness at the base of a notorious mountain. Locals say there are Bigfoot living high up in the dense mountainous forest. Clay is skeptic at first and thinks it's nothing more than tall tales.

But soon Clay becomes a believer when giant creatures invade his new home and snatch his baby boy, Casey.

Now, Clay and his wife, Mia, must rescue their son with the help of Clay's uncle and his dog, a journey up the foreboding mountain that will take them into an unimaginable world...straight into hell!

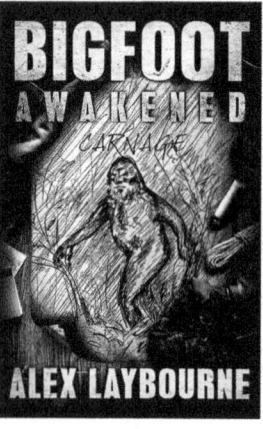

BIGFOOT AWAKENED
by Alex Laybourne

A weekend away with friends was supposed to be fun. One last chance for Jamie to blow off some steam before she leaves for college, but when the group make a wrong turn, fun is the last thing they find.

From the moment they pass through a small rural town they are being hunted by whatever abominations live in the woods.

Yet, as the beasts attack and the truth is revealed, they learn that despite everything, man still remains the most terrifying evil of them all.

CHECK OUT OTHER GREAT CRYPTID NOVELS

SWAMP MONSTER MASSACRE
by Hunter Shea

The swamp belongs to them. Humans are only prey. Deep in the overgrown swamps of Florida, where humans rarely dare to enter, lives a race of creatures long thought to be only the stuff of legend. They walk upright but are stronger, taller and more brutal than any man. And when a small boat of tourists, held captive by a fleeing criminal, accidentally kills one of the swamp dwellers' young, the creatures are filled with a terrifyingly human emotion—a merciless lust for vengeance that will paint the trees red with blood.

TERROR MOUNTAIN
by Gerry Griffiths

When Marcus Pike inherits his grandfather's farm and moves his family out to the country, he has no idea there's an unholy terror running rampant about the mountainous farming community. Sheriff Avery Anderson has seen the heinous carnage and the mutilated bodies. He's also seen the giant footprints left in the snow—Bigfoot tracks. Meanwhile, Cole Wagner, and his wife, Kate, are prospecting their gold claim farther up the valley, unaware of the impending dangers lurking in the woods as an early winter storm sets in. Soon the snowy countryside will run red with blood on TERROR MOUNTAIN.

CHECK OUT OTHER GREAT CRYPTID NOVELS

RETURN TO DYATLOV PASS
by J.H. Moncrieff

In 1959, nine Russian students set off on a skiing expedition in the Ural Mountains. Their mutilated bodies were discovered weeks later. Their bizarre and unexplained deaths are one of the most enduring true mysteries of our time. Nearly sixty years later, podcast host Nat McPherson ventures into the same mountains with her team, determined to finally solve the mystery of the Dyatlov Pass incident. Her plans are thwarted on the first night, when two trackers from her group are brutally slaughtered. The team's guide, a superstitious man from a neighboring village, blames the killings on yetis, but no one believes him. As members of Nat's team die one by one, she must figure out if there's a murderer in their midst—or something even worse—before history repeats itself and her group becomes another casualty of the infamous Dead Mountain.

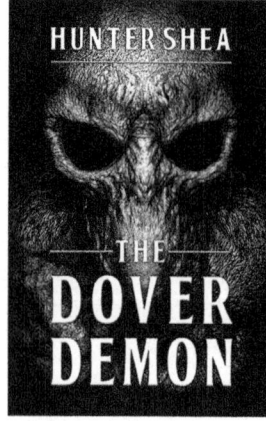

DOVER DEMON
by Hunter Shea

The Dover Demon is real...and it has returned. In 1977, Sam Brogna and his friends came upon a terrifying, alien creature on a deserted country road. What they witnessed was so bizarre, so chilling, they swore their silence. But their lives were changed forever. Decades later, the town of Dover has been hit by a massive blizzard. Sam's son, Nicky, is drawn to search for the infamous cryptid, only to disappear into the bowels of a secret underground lair. The Dover Demon is far deadlier than anyone could have believed. And there are many of them. Can Sam and his reunited friends rescue Nicky and battle a race of creatures so powerful, so sinister, that history itself has been shaped by their secretive presence?

Made in the USA
Monee, IL
20 January 2021